Beware
Beware

ALSO BY STEPH CHA

Follow Her Home

Beware Beware

A Juniper Song Mystery

STEPH CHA

MINOTAUR BOOKS

A THOMAS DUNNE BOOK
New York

A THOMAS DUNNE BOOK FOR MINOTAUR BOOKS.
An imprint of St. Martin's Publishing Group.

BEWARE BEWARE. Copyright © 2014 by Stephanie Cha. All rights reserved. Printed in the United States of America. For information, address St. Martin's Press, 175 Fifth Avenue, New York, N.Y. 10010.

www.thomasdunnebooks.com
www.minotaurbooks.com

Library of Congress Cataloging-in-Publication Data

Cha, Steph.
  Beware, beware: a Juniper Song mystery / Steph Cha—First edition.
     pages cm
  ISBN 978-1-250-04901-8 (hardcover)
  ISBN 978-1-4668-5015-6 (e-book)
  1. Women private investigators—Fiction. 2. Screenwriters—Crimes against—Fiction 3. Los Angeles (Calif.)—Fiction. I. Title.
  PS3603.H27B49 2014
  813'.6—dc23

                            2014014366

Minotaur books may be purchased for educational, business, or promotional use. For information on bulk purchases, please contact Macmillan Corporate and Premium Sales Department at 1-800-221-7945, extension 5442, or write special-markets@macmillan.com.

First Edition: August 2014

10 9 8 7 6 5 4 3 2 1

To Matt

Acknowledgments

❖

Thanks to my agent, Ethan Bassoff, for your indispensable insight, diligence, and encouragement. I expect any children you may have fathered in the last year will grow up loved and happy.

Thanks to my editor, Anne Brewer, for taking me through draft after draft of this novel. Your hard work has been one of my greatest assets over the last few years.

Thanks, too, to Karyn Marcus, Justin Vellela, Shailyn Tavella, and the rest of the people at St. Martin's Press who have helped me along the way.

Thanks to Katie McClain and Andrew Renzi, for letting me borrow a thing or two. You guys are the best. (And congratulations on your impending marriage, which will be awesome.)

Thanks to Tristan Clark, Heidi Onion, and belatedly, the Jorges Camacho, Jr. and Sr., for helping an amateur out with some research.

Thanks to my parents, my brothers Andrew and Peter, and to the rest of my family for all your love and support.

Thanks to my husband, Matt Barbabella, for marrying me between drafts of yet another novel full of dead men.

No thanks to Duke Charbabella, who is a basset hound, but I do love him very much.

Beware
Beware

One

❧

The weekend hovered in full view an hour away, like an island in silhouette gaining color with its steady approach. There was a time when this meant something to me, when the school bell or the desktop clock said it was time to go home, time, at least, for happy hour.

I sat on the floor with my bare foot flexed under the desk. It was a slow day in the office, and my toenails were about as long and dirty as I'd seen them, and they'd been long and dirty before. There was no sense keeping them pretty from November to March, with my flip-flops put away. It was February now, and my nails chafed against the insides of my shoes. They were starting to hurt.

A thick rind flew off a big toe with a crisp, clacking sound. It ricocheted off the back of my desk, the panel of cheap wood that hid me from view should a client barge in. As I reached to pick up the crescent, footsteps shuffled behind me and a sneaker pushed into my lower back. I turned my head and looked up at Chaz Lindley, who stood arms crossed and scowling.

"Song, if Art sees you like this I'm the one who's got to suffer. You know that, right?"

A week ago, I'd walked into Chaz's office and caught him with his shirt up, tweezing nipple hairs with a binder clip. I'd shuffled out the way I'd come in, and neither of us had brought up the incident. I felt the easy comeback on my tongue, and let it go unsaid. Chaz was my boss.

I met private investigator Charles Lindley under strange circumstances. He got me out of a couple good tangles, and when I was in the clear, he recruited me. I'd always liked the idea of PI work. I spent a lot of lonely years dreaming of Philip Marlowe instead of living my own life. When I crossed paths with Chaz, I was in the thick of my first real case, which I hadn't asked for in the least. I wasn't half bad at the work, but it ended disastrously anyway. It scoured me clean of any romantic feelings for the job, but when Chaz offered to hire me, I was grateful. The fact was, I had nothing better to do, and we both knew it.

I joined Lindley & Flores as a gofer, with the idea that I'd get my own license once I racked up the work experience. He ran his practice out of a small office in Koreatown with a forty-five-year-old ex-cop named Arturo Flores. Chaz said they could use a scrappy errand girl with nothing to lose. His exact words.

So far I'd done grunt work in the office and three straightforward assignments on cheating spouses. Two pissed-off husbands and one pissed-off wife paid good money to learn things they already knew. It was low-glamour stuff, but I knew that going in. I spent a lot of time in the office, bored out of my mind and always uncomfortably hot. I helmed the receptionist desk, and when Chaz wanted to look good for a client, I played the quiet, efficient office lady as best I could in blue jeans, but mostly I just sat around. Arturo had been out all morning, and it was just me and Chaz passing time. I knew better than to clip my toenails with Arturo around. He was a serious man with a line for a mouth. He thought I was a bit of a joker, who Chaz had hired out of pity. He was probably right.

I started to get up off the floor when Chaz plunked down in my chair. "You can finish," he said. "But then I have some actual work for you."

I stood up and slipped my feet into my shoes. "What's up?"

"I got you a client." He smiled, broad and goofy, showing his big teeth. "Girl needs someone to check up on her boyfriend. You up for it?"

Quitting time was around the bend, and I jumped at the chance to postpone it. The week had been slow and I had nothing in the way of weekend plans. "Sure. Cheaters are kind of my specialty."

"Yours and everyone else's." He pushed a Post-It onto my desk with a phone number scribbled in his incongruously elegant hand. "Name's Daphne Freamon. Give her a call. I think she needs a woman's ear."

With three divorces under my belt, I was starting to feel a little comfort in the job. Each assignment was quick, simple, and dirty in a way that didn't compromise me. I cleared them, and with each clearance I increased the distance between me and my past mistakes. I wasn't delusional enough to think this was good work that might buy my atonement, but it helped to put whatever skills I had to someone else's bad use.

My new client had a 917 area code. I dialed, and she answered after three rings.

"Hello?" She sounded quiet and expectant, like she was speaking into a darkened room—she'd been waiting for my call.

"Hi, Miss Freamon? This is Juniper Song, with Lindley & Flores. How are you today?"

"Call me Daphne, Miss Song." She had the kind of distinctive voice that I knew I could recognize out of context months, maybe years later. It was timid thin-wired high-pitched but a little raspy. I wondered if she was a smoker.

"Sure, Daphne. Call me Song. It's what people call me. What can I do for you today?"

"Well," she said. "Listen, Song—Mr. Lindley says you're twenty-seven, unmarried. Is that right?"

I smirked. "Yeah, that's right. What else did he say about me?"

"Oh, no, nothing much. It's just—we're the same age. I talked to Mr. Lindley for a bit, but I think he thought I'd rather talk to you."

"Would you rather talk to him?" The idea didn't offend me. Despite his groin-scratching solicitous dad-ness, Chaz was the pro to my peewee league. I'd go straight to him if I wanted shit done.

"No, no, this is much better," she said. "Song, do you have a boyfriend?"

"Nope."

"Well, I called you guys because I'm worried about mine. We're long distance. I live in New York and he's in L.A. He got this gig ghostwriting for Joe Tilley about six months back and moved out there for a while. Do you know Joe Tilley?"

The name sounded familiar, but it was generic enough. "I might. Who is he?"

"He's an actor. A pretty big one. He used to be a bit of a heartthrob in his twenties, but he's turned his career into something pretty serious over the last decade. He was nominated for an Oscar a couple years ago and a lot of people think he was robbed. You'd probably recognize him if you saw him. Late forties, lot of muscle. He kissed pop stars on-screen in the nineties. These days he plays mysterious men with obsessions and dark pasts."

I typed the name into Google and the face clicked into place. "Oh, this guy. I know this guy. Nice. He's a pretty big deal."

"Jamie—that's my boyfriend, Jamie Landon—Jamie says Joe's been keeping him busy writing this screenplay, but I don't really know what else he's been up to. He disappears for days at a time, won't answer my phone calls, and I'm afraid he's getting into trouble again."

"What kind of trouble?"

There was a lip-biting pause. "He has a coke habit. *Had* a coke habit. It's supposed to be past tense, but I'm skeptical. I'd say the odds are good that he's holed up on a coke binge, who knows who with."

"Has he done that before?"

"Yes." She hesitated for a second, unsure of how much to share. "He's been in rehab twice. I gave him an ultimatum. Told him it's over between us if he falls off the wagon."

"You must be pretty serious about it to call me."

"You have to understand. Jamie thinks of himself as this nice guy, but as soon as he can blame asshole behavior on anything else, he becomes an asshole. Drugs are an easy scapegoat. It isn't so much that he blames the coke to my face—it's that he can tell himself it isn't him, so he cuts himself tons of slack when he's high or between highs. I wouldn't even have to know about it."

"Oh," I said, and waited for her to continue.

"I'm a painter. My painting—it's one of the most precious

things in the world to me; it's my life. I had an exhibit a few months ago, a really important one. He knew about it for months, bought plane tickets and everything. I was stressed out and emotionally restless to begin with, and then he disappeared, never got on the plane. I couldn't reach him for days. You know that feeling? When you want so badly to reach somebody, and you just can't get them to hear you?"

I nodded into the phone, mumbled recognition. I knew.

"My mind always goes to the darkest places. I almost called the police because I was so convinced that he couldn't do this to me, that he would sooner be dead in a ditch than stand me up on that day. But I thought, how embarrassed will I be if he is, in fact, holed up doing blow, betraying me for a stupid high." She sighed, one raspy drawn-out note. "So I told myself if I found out he was getting high again, it'd be over. I've given him about eight second chances, so I decided to throw some money at it this time around, hire someone and see if maybe that would make this breakup stick."

She paused for a while, so I said, "Sure." It came out more callous than I felt.

"Sorry. I've been going on and on."

"No, not at all," I said quickly. "Can I ask why you've put up with him until now?"

"Good question." She laughed, a bitter, cornered laugh. "When he's good, he's really good, you know? He's sweet and he's got this puppy-dog charm. Sometimes I look at him and I just want to take care of him, do you know what I mean?"

"I do," I said. "Okay. When is the last time you heard from him?"

"It's been three days now, and I've been calling." Her voice thinned to a gasp, and I listened to her held breath for half a minute, afraid that it would dissolve into tears. "I'm really worried, Song."

"Okay Daphne, so what is it you want me to do for you? You want me to check on him?"

"Yes. Please."

"Today?"

"Starting today."

That caught me off guard. "You want a tail on him, then."

"Yes. I guess that's it."

"Can I ask why?"

"What do you mean?" She sounded defensive.

"No, it's just—I thought you just wanted to know if he was alive or coked up or whatever. I could find that out for you in an afternoon."

One thing I learned quick about PI work was that the over-whelming majority of it was overwhelmingly boring. Chaz and Arturo didn't deal in big mysteries, didn't come across too much of anything that wasn't straightforward. The job was almost rou-tine, and after all the upsets of the previous year, I kind of liked its plainness. All the same, my heartbeat responded to Daphne's meaningful silence.

"There's more," I ventured.

"There might be more. I'm not really sure."

"Okay, well, that's why you called us, isn't it? But this will work a lot better if I have a vague idea of what to look for." I rubbed at the hinge in my jaw and kept my voice level. "What are you wor-ried about, Daphne?"

"I'm worried," she said. "I'm worried that he's using, but I'm also worried that he isn't *just* using."

"You want to know if he's selling?"

There was a rustle on the other end of the line, a wordless shake or nod. "Yes," she said a few seconds later.

"Do you have any reason to think he is?"

"Other than that it would be so in character for him to start doing something stupid for easy money?" She chuckled, a little trickle of sadness. "I don't have anything solid. He mentioned once that he had a friend who was slinging, and it stuck with me. If he's really back to using all the time, I know that's how dealers get started."

"Okay," I said. "I'll follow him around for a few days. Where can I find him?"

"His place is in West Hollywood, but his roommates say he hasn't been home either. I'd start at the Roosevelt Hotel in Hollywood. That's where he told them he was going to party, apparently. He didn't bother to tell me, and that was on Wednesday."

"Okay, let me get his address anyway."

She gave me an address near Santa Monica and Crescent Heights, on Havenhurst Drive. "Just find him for me, please. I need to know what he's been up to."

"I'll report to you tonight. What time do you go to bed?"

"Call anytime. I'll pick up."

The Roosevelt was an old, historic hotel on the loudest stretch of Hollywood Boulevard. Marilyn Monroe called it home for two years, and in 1929, it provided the venue for the first Academy Awards. It fit right into the glitzy story of tourist Hollywood.

I had little use for this part of town, a dingy neighborhood dressed up with buzzing neon lights and the dull trodden stars of the Walk of Fame. Grown men dressed as Spider-Man and

SpongeBob SquarePants showed up day after day and suffered startling heat during most of the year to make lousy livelihoods posing for photographs in front of the Chinese Theater. They might have looked lively to a passing bus of tourists, but I saw them whenever I drove by, and I knew the sight was a picture of desolation, of crushed dreams dressed in grimy fourth-hand garments.

I circled the hotel for a good ten minutes before giving up on street parking. I pulled into the valet station and made a note to expense the fee. It was guaranteed to be costly.

It was five in the afternoon and the lobby buzzed with people. It was a nice space with a Rat Pack vibe, with heavy drapes and tall floor lamps built to look like wrought-iron torches. Small pillars met small arches, and a Spanish-looking fountain grew waterless from the center of a burgundy tiled floor. A man in a gray pinstriped suit paced with a cell phone clamped to his ear; a young couple held each other's knees on a long, low sofa upholstered in tufted tobacco leather. I never figured out who stayed at the hotel. I'd been inside a few times to eat and drink, and the place seemed constantly busy, spilling at each entrance with skinny blond women and men in shiny shirts, every night of the week. The clientele fit a type, but it wasn't native Hollywood. Maybe Jamie Landon would give me the answer.

I took a seat on an armchair and opened a book, my heart jumping more than I liked. Stakeouts were boring, but they kept me skittish. I always brought a book that I could never quite enjoy. I looked up after every paragraph with whatever stealth I could manage. It was like fishing—I hated almost all of it, but there was a small joy in reeling in the fish.

I studied the picture Daphne sent me on my phone. Jamie Landon, twenty-nine years old. He had a good-looking face, as far as I could tell, that looked vaguely familiar. The shadow of some celebrity, or a cluster of white male schoolmates who shared his features. He was supposed to be five-foot ten, around a hundred and fifty pounds. He favored plaid shirts and hoodies, slim designer jeans. He could be easy to spot or impossible.

After a quiet half hour, I walked across the floor to the cocktail bar. I ordered a bloody mary and carried it back into the lobby, where I repositioned myself on one of the sofas in reach of a coffee table.

I was halfway through my second drink when Jamie Landon hurried out of an elevator, eyes washing over the ground ahead of him as if he were wielding an invisible vacuum cleaner. He was easy to spot, as it turned out, though his jittery walk was at least half the picture. The other half was pleasant enough. His hair was a mess, but a good-looking mess, bedhead, thick and brown with the kind of beachy, loose curl I could never quite coax into my sheet-straight hair. I knew he was almost thirty, but he looked impossibly young.

Behind him was a middle-aged man in a tight graphic T-shirt and faded blue jeans with artful tears at the knees. He wore sunglasses and a tweedy fedora, but it took me only a couple seconds to recognize him as Joe Tilley.

I swallowed my drink and made a quick exit to the valet stand while the two men settled up at the front desk. I was still waiting for my car when they came out the door after me.

There were about a dozen people within view of the front entrance to the hotel, and a strange hush came over them all when Joe Tilley appeared. No one looked at him with anything amounting to pointed interest, but there wasn't a person with eyes who didn't know he was there. The man had star power— that was clear enough.

I ventured a closer look. Despite the stupid hat, he was a pretty sight. His face was almost generically good-looking, well angled and masculine with a strong, broad jaw. He was shorter than he looked on-screen, about five-foot-nine on the generous end. His T-shirt had a paper-thin, overwashed look, and it stretched translucent against his chest, showing the meaty outline of his pecs, the textured points of his nipples. I wondered if he was shooting a movie, or if he worked out every day of the year.

Jamie stood in front of him, somehow shrinking himself in the foreground as he handed the valet his ticket. My car came first.

I tipped the valet and sat in the driver's seat playing with my phone while Jamie waited for his car.

The car that crept into my rearview mirror was a yellow Ferrari, waxed to eye-searing brilliance, by my estimate not more than a day or two old. Jamie got behind the wheel, but I guessed the movie star was the legal owner.

I left the lot before I imprinted my Corolla's plates on their short-term memory and idled down the block for the thirty seconds it took for them to drive out.

In my time with Chaz, I'd gotten a fairly good grasp on the art of tailing. My car was gray and forgettable, and I could follow any unsuspecting driver across the city without getting obvious. Flashy sports cars just made my job a little easier.

It helped, too, that Jamie drove slowly. I guessed driving a celebrity's two-hundred-thousand-dollar vehicle made one a little cautious. He avoided lane changes and signaled at every turn. I followed them out of Hollywood on Sunset, then up north toward Griffith Park and into the Los Feliz Hills, where the streets became smaller and strictly residential. The houses flanking both sides of the drive grew big and splendid, structures of alarming taste and beauty tucked into the hill like luxe pocket squares. I followed the Ferrari at a safe distance for as long as I could manage, then started to lose it in spurts as it climbed the hill. Just as I was about to give up and wait at the bottom, the car turned into a grand driveway.

This belonged to a magnificent house, a Spanish-style mansion with a look of perfect preserved grandeur. It was a corrupt clergyman's house, or a real estate king's, or an A-list actor's. The actual structure was a good quarter mile in from the street, obscured from most angles by a thick wall of brambly hedges manicured to a well-managed chaos. The better to block out cameras, I supposed.

I passed the house after a quick disciplined gawk and parked uphill facing back down. Five minutes later, a dusty silver BMW nosed its way out of the driveway. Jamie drove, alone, looking exhausted.

I laughed out loud, tickled by a sudden jab of recognition— Jamie looked familiar because I'd met him once before.

It was a parking encounter a few months earlier, one of those silly interactions that happens every second in Los Angeles. I'd had a depressing day, one of many in a row, and Lori insisted on going out to dinner at a popular restaurant in Los Feliz. I searched for fifteen minutes before finding an empty spot. I signaled, finally triumphant, and a second later a silver BMW swooped in to take it. When the driver got out, I rolled down my window and said something impolite. He looked at me, and his eyes went wide. "Oh, shit, don't tell me," he said. "I ate your lunch right out of the fridge."

My anger deflated. "As long as you know what you did," I said.

He offered to move, and when I waved him off, he insisted.

"I'm offering to vacate a parking spot. How often does that happen in this city?"

Before I could decline more sincerely, he hopped in his car and drove away. That was all there was to it, but I remembered it clearly. It was a rare sparkle of decency that left a deep impression—an episode of mundane anger transformed in an instant to one of flushed pleasure.

I was sorry when he left. I wouldn't have minded getting his name. Now I knew—that was Jamie Landon, and I wasn't exactly repaying his kindness.

I followed him back onto Sunset, the direct path from Los Feliz to his apartment in West Hollywood. The slow ooze of Friday traffic let me keep a loose, steady tail until we reached our destination.

The neighborhood was not quite as royal as the one we'd come from, but it was pleasant, respectable, and I guessed the rent was moderately high. The building was old but well maintained, a one-story complex that might once have been a giant single-family home, parceled into a handful of units. The exterior walls were a bile-colored stucco, broken up by a few square windows. Jamie parked his car on the street, a lucky break for his tail.

The clock in my car said 8:50 P.M. I called Daphne.

"Well, he was at the Roosevelt," I said.

"Did you see anything?"

"Joe Tilley was with him. Jamie dropped him off at his house. I guess he'd left his car there. They're close, huh?"

"Joe likes Jamie. Their work is pretty intimate and they hang out often, from what I understand. I don't know anything about them hanging out in a hotel together, though."

"Joe Tilley—is he a family man?"

"He has a son and two daughters. None of his kids live with him, though."

"Wife?"

"Number three. Willow Hemingway. Actress. C-list." She spoke like she was directing me to an unattractive item in a mail-order catalog.

"She's at home?"

"As far as I know."

I stretched the fingers of my free hand on the steering wheel, let the knuckles crack in percussive succession. "So he's leaving her at home overnight to hang out with Jamie. Does he have a history of drug abuse?"

"Might be his most famous relationship." She drew in air through her teeth. "I guess they could be doing drugs together."

"I'll keep watching him."

I pulled out my laptop, found some unguarded wireless, and did a little background research. Internet stalking was the first and handiest tool for any private detective, and I made good use of it before and after I got the job. I wondered sometimes in an idle way if private detectives weren't already going obsolete. Information was our primary ware, and it was plain enough that the Internet was bad news for all middlemen.

I ran a search for Joe Tilley, figuring he'd be the easiest player to look up. I skimmed his long, detailed Wikipedia entry and scrolled through the column of his life's work on IMDb. Everything Daphne had told me was publicly available, as was a surfeit of boring factoids made newsworthy by his fame.

Jamie Landon had an IMDb page, too. Sparse, with a small

headshot and a few writer credits in shorts and small produc-
tions. Nothing else really came up. No one cared where he ate
his breakfast.

I lingered on his picture and wondered if I should tell Daphne
about the coincidence of our prior encounter. It was a funny
story, but it was almost too trivial to mention. I decided against
it without much thought—I only remembered him because I'd
found him attractive, and there was no need for her to know
that.

I looked up Daphne next, more out of interest than anything
else. I googled "daphne freamon artist" and the first result was a
feature review in a prominent New York magazine. I whistled—
Daphne Freamon appeared to be somebody. The review was
fairly involved, and it included photographs of both Daphne and
her paintings.

Daphne was black, as it turned out, and my brain experienced
a brief delay as it processed that minor revelation. I'd heard an
uninflected accent, a nonethnic name, and pictured, without thinking, a white girl. I may have grown up Korean in Los Angeles,
but my brain couldn't quite shed those middle-American default
settings. She hadn't mentioned her race, but why would she have,
anyway? It hadn't occurred to me to mention mine. I felt a scorch
of shame at my own surprise.

She was also very pretty, but that part didn't surprise me at
all. I had a lot of Raymond Chandler in my PI training.

The review was laudatory, though it struck me as somewhat
tone-deaf. The critic was a white dude, and I couldn't help but
cringe at his lingering praise for the "lusty," "voluptuous" "sensu-
ality" of her work. I had a high school kid's appreciation and understanding of art, but even I could see there was more to Daphne's
paintings than sexual heat. I found several of them all over the

Internet, and spent a good fifteen minutes taking in her portfolio. The paintings were striking, haunting, bloody and visceral in bright splashes of color, and they made me feel uneasy. That probably meant she had talent. Good for her.

Daphne was my age, and for a second, I wondered what I had done with my life. To my relief, I felt admiration rather than jealousy, a sort of creeping desire to be her friend.

I googled myself—nothing at all. All things considered, a blessed result.

Daphne heard from Jamie an hour later, and she sent me home for the night. It was just after ten o'clock, and Lori was home, unusual for a Friday.

She greeted me at the door, a habit of hers that put me in mind of a little dog. Lori would be something small and energetic, a Maltese or a Yorkshire terrier.

"Are you home for the night?" I asked. She was in her pajamas, a blue-and-white pinstriped two-piece set with girly scalloped cotton shorts. She had a few of these matching sets, and she rotated them weekly sometimes. She saw little sense in washing her pajamas between wears.

Lori and I had been rooming together for about six months, in a two-bedroom apartment in Echo Park overlooking the lake. The ad on Craigslist touted the lakeside location, the jogging path, the calming views. We were savvy enough to visit before committing a thing, and we found that the lake had been drained and fenced off months before. We wrangled down the rent and moved in. Half a year later, the lake was still a yawning dirt ditch, with no apparent signs of a return to glory.

She nodded. "Have you eaten?"

It had been a long time since I'd had a roommate, but I was getting used to it. Lori was messy but surprisingly thoughtful. Within the first month, we figured out our arrangement. Common areas were never cleaned unless I cleaned them, but Lori cooked all her meals for two. She was a good cook—she'd learned from her mother, and she could whip up a good Korean meal in minutes. I'd spent so many years dining like a bachelor—on Hot Pockets and yogurt and a lot of milk and cereal—I hadn't realized how much I'd missed home cooking.

My stomach growled on cue. I hadn't eaten since lunch. Lori nodded and heated up a bowl of kimchi fried rice while I took off my shoes. She placed it on our dining table and sat down next to me while I ate.

"Thanks," I said. "No plans tonight?"

She shook her head. "I thought I'd hang out with you."

"Don't let me get in the way of your weekend. You see me every day."

She shrugged, and I saw in the way her eyes watched her nose that she had something on her mind.

"What is it?" I asked.

She hesitated, bit her lip with her one crooked tooth, and gave me a dolorous, expectant look before sighing. "It's nothing."

Lori was not quite a friend in the usual sense—she was flighty and giggly and twenty-three, the kind of girl I never got along with even when I was her age. But she was, I had to admit, something more important, a hybrid of little sister, daughter, and mother, slapped together out of mutual convenience and desperation. Less than a year earlier, her mother, Yujin, had been arrested for murder—a murder that I witnessed, and that had happened at least in part because I was there. It was a vision of hell that I'll never forget, but it was much worse for Lori. Yujin was arrested on the scene, and Lori only saw her in prison these days. Yujin may have been one twisted mother, but she was the only parent Lori had.

I made the decision to latch Lori's life to mine. It wasn't a hard decision, and it wasn't one made entirely from guilt. When Lori and I met, I was virtually alone, my father and sister dead, my mother living with family in Texas. I'd had a couple close friends to sustain my social needs—I lost them both within days of meeting Lori. The trouble followed from her to me, but I knew it wasn't her fault. I forgave what there was to forgive, as she forgave my involvement in the calamities that fell on her side.

The truth was, we were both stranded, and we drifted together as naturally as a couple of ions. With her mother gone, Lori couldn't stand living in her house by herself, and I started staying in Yujin's bedroom. When it became clear that the house would have to be sold to cover legal costs, we signed a lease together and made things official.

She called me *unni* like my little sister had when she was alive, and though I hardly knew her before we moved in together, she inspired the same range of emotions as real family. Among these, annoyance bubbled up the most often, followed closely by affection.

"If you want to talk, we can talk, but don't make me fish for it," I said.

"It's just . . . boy stuff."

"Are things not going well with Isaac?"

Isaac was Lori's latest suitor, and they'd been hanging out with some regularity for the past few weeks. He was the first guy she seemed to like at all since last summer, by her admission, an unusual hiatus. It was understandable, of course—Lori attracted deadly men, and they'd brought her enough grief to send any woman running to the nearest nunnery. I was relieved when she started dating Isaac. He was a nice Korean boy, who wore polo shirts and went to church, who feared me a little, though not enough to keep him out of my home.

"No, everything's fine with Isaac," she said. "For now, anyway."

"For now?"

"No, don't worry. It has nothing to do with Isaac."

"There's someone else already, then?"

That got a laugh out of her, and the tension in her face seemed to soften. "Not exactly. It's just—there's this guy who works with my *samchun*."

Taejin Chung was Yujin's younger brother, Lori's uncle. He was Lori's only family in Los Angeles, at least outside of prison. He was divorced, with no children, and he and Lori were close. I'd only met him once. My picture of him was certainly colored by what I knew, but he struck me as a quiet, lonely man waiting for his life to spool out. He ran a body shop in Koreatown called T & J Collision Center, the initials scooped from his name to provide a thin illusion of all-American blandness. He worked with a small handful of employees, and he seemed to spend most of his time there. He even lived in a small loft above his office. Yujin had used this shop as a hiding place for the byproducts of her misdeeds. In a town like Los Angeles, cars were big give-aways when something went amiss. If a person was meant to disappear, a car had to disappear with her. When Yujin was arrested, the cops found two missing cars in Taejin's garage—proxies for dead bodies, one of which was supposed to be mine. As far as anyone knew, Taejin was completely unaware of his sister's crimes. I believed in his innocence, but I had little reason to want him in my life.

"One of Taejin's minions?"

She shook her head. "I think he's an investor or something. He loaned *samchun* some money."

"What's he have to do with you?"

"Well I met him today, at the shop."

"Ah, okay." I laughed, getting it. "He liked you. What's this guy's deal?"

"His name is Winfred. He's probably thirtyish. Korean guy. Tall. Muscular."

"A dreamboat, huh?"

She blushed. "No, he isn't my type."

"You don't like him better than Isaac, then?"

"*Unni,*" she said, turning redder. She lowered her voice to a whisper. "I think I like Isaac *a lot.*"

"What's the problem then?"

"When I was talking to Winfred, *samchun* was looking at us funny, like, watching us. I told him later that Winfred asked for my number, and he turned kind of pale."

"So he doesn't like him. You're basically his daughter, you know."

"I know, and at first I thought that was it. But then he told me to be nice to him."

"To Winfred?"

She nodded, and something heavy sank deep in my gut.

"Well be nice to him, then. It's easy enough to be nice."

She nodded again.

"And if you're supposed to be much nicer, come talk to me. *Unni's* got your back."

TWO

✤

Lori and I spent the night in our pajamas, talking and watching TV. She told me more about Isaac, and I made us ice cream sundaes—my sole contribution to our culinary life. All in all, it was an above-average Friday night. My social life had never been vibrant, but these days, its embers barely glowed.

When I woke up the next morning, I was ready to delve back into my new job. I worked the whole weekend, and Monday morning I reported to the office to share my findings with Chaz and Arturo. I didn't have much, but I walked in as excited as I was nervous.

At 9:30, Chaz sent an e-mail to me and Arturo requesting our presence at a debrief meeting in his office at 10:00 A.M., "to touch base on Ms. Song's assignment." I heard him giggle when he hit Send, and both Arturo and I submitted verbal RSVPs without leaving our desks.

We gathered right at 10:00, and Chaz let me sit behind his

desk while he and Arturo took the client chairs. I made sure they both had coffee when they sat down.

"So," Arturo started, "Chaz tells me he gave you your own client." He eyed me over the rim of his paper cup. He wore his skepticism like a name tag.

Arturo—or Art, as Chaz, and only Chaz, called him—intimidated me. He was one of the few people I'd ever known who had that particular effect. There was nothing physically imposing about him—he was five foot seven or eight, with a bit of a paunch, and, oddly, the sculpted calves of a furniture mover. He wore his straight black hair in a crew cut, and his face, brown-skinned and handsome, was clean shaven. His features were stern but not scary. He was younger than Chaz, but he was the one with gravitas, the straight man of the duo. If they were my workplace parents, then Chaz was my dad and Arturo, my father. I was afraid of disappointing them both.

"I hope that's okay," I said. "Chaz thinks I can handle it."

"Don't worry, Song. We already talked it out, and Art's on board." Chaz winked. "What have you got? Regale us."

I filled them in on Daphne and her request, and then I told them everything I'd learned about Jamie, both first- and second-hand. They listened dutifully while I ran through what I knew.

Jamie was a Boston native who'd moved to New York for college with all of his optimism intact. He'd graduated from NYU with a mule's load of student loans and bigger dreams than ever. Since the age of fifteen, he'd worked as a dog walker, a babysitter, a library clerk, a waiter, a bartender, a bookstore cashier, a substitute teacher, and now a ghostwriter, but his aspirations were for Hollywood glory. These brought him to Los Angeles, where he lived with two roommates, old friends trying to crack different parts of the same Hollywood game. One of them owned a basset hound, but Jamie was the one who walked her.

He was an upbeat, charismatic guy, and very well liked—Daphne told me as much, and I could see it, too. He had an inordinate amount of human contact. After six months in Los Angeles, he saw more friends in a day than I saw in a month. Over the weekend, I'd followed him to and from two boozy brunches, two sit-down dinners, downtown cocktails, and one house party.

So far, though, I had found nothing incriminating. He had no record of any sort, unless you counted a school reprimand during his sophomore year of college. His proceedings in Los Angeles seemed cheerfully harmless. Daphne wanted me to keep at it.

"So long story short, you had a boring weekend," said Chaz.

I shrugged. "It wasn't so bad. I got to drive around town a lot. Got some reading done." I found myself wishing I had more to report, something big and exciting to get my bosses' attention. "But is there something else I should be doing? Should I be getting in there a bit more or what?"

"I wouldn't worry about it," said Arturo, looking unworried and unimpressed. "Sounds like this guy just came off a bender, so he might behave himself for a bit. Just keep following him if that's what the client wants."

"Thanks," I said. "How about—well I was wondering, can I get a GPS tracker? Stick it on his car and monitor where he's going? That would save me some legwork, I guess."

Chaz laughed, and I felt my cheeks prickle with embarrassment. I knew Chaz and Arturo used trackers once in a while, but I'd gotten the idea from television.

"Your legwork is cheap, Song. Equipment is not. This is a recession," Chaz said, still chuckling. It was a phrase I'd heard him use many times before, and I had no doubt he'd kept it in steady rotation since 2008.

"And besides," chimed in Arturo, "you're still new to this. You shouldn't rely on technology to do your detective work. Not until you've nailed down the basics."

I nodded. "Okay, fair enough. Just had to ask."

"Is that it, then?" Arturo placed his hands on the arms of his chair.

"Sure. Think so."

"Then get back out there," said Arturo. He stood up and left with a halfhearted salute.

I followed suit and let Chaz take back his desk. "You're doing great," he said, his hand warm on my shoulder.

When I parked on Jamie's block a little after eleven, his car was still in his driveway. According to Daphne, Jamie was a late riser, and it looked like I hadn't missed a thing by going into the office. Shortly after noon, he came out of the house dressed in jeans and a red flannel shirt. I followed him to another lunch, with yet another friend, at a busy café in Los Feliz. It was amazingly busy for a Monday afternoon, full of young people who could afford the luxury of sit-down weekday lunches without submitting to the drudgery of the nine-to-five grind.

After he ate, he drove up to Joe Tilley's, and I grabbed a torta from a taco stand on Hillhurst. I took a walk around the neighborhood and circled back after an hour. Jamie left a while later and went straight to a happy hour downtown.

After three days of constant surveillance, I was beginning to get frustrated with his packed, unstructured schedule. I felt no closer to my actual goal, and Jamie's volume of social activity was making me almost ill with anxiety. There was something about the sheer level of apparent *fun* that I wanted to scorn, and I had to wonder if I was jealous. I hated the idea of it, that after all I'd been through I could envy the lifestyle of the popular kid in the lunchroom.

It was almost eight in the evening when Jamie went home, and as I sat in my car outside his house, my mind circled in a miserable funk of self-evaluation. When he reemerged fifteen minutes later, I rolled my eyes and wondered where he was going to dinner.

He walked toward his car with a slump in his step, hands hooked into his pockets, shoulders raised. He got in and smoked a cigarette, and then he was on the move.

We drove at the speed limit, crossed town to a house in Encino, where Jamie pulled up to an intercom and entered through an electric gate. The street was quiet, a wealthy, suburban street, and most of the house was walled away from view. I parked behind an empty car on the other side of the street and waited.

There was something promising here, a break from his pattern. Jamie had no family in Los Angeles, and his friends were unlikely to live in a mansion, even if it was in the valley. He'd driven across town on some errand, and if I paid attention, I thought I might find something interesting.

Ten minutes later, the gate opened and his car nosed out, spilling poor light on gray asphalt. I let him leave the street and caught up to him on the on-ramp to the 101.

The Monday-night traffic was light, and I kept him at the edge of my vision for the whole stretch of the freeway. There were a few other cars on our commute, falling before and behind me for miles. When Jamie signaled to exit, I followed, not far behind. One car signaled between us.

It was a white Audi A4 with a scuffed bumper, and it drove steadily between me and Jamie, all the way home.

We drove for a good mile and a half off the freeway before I conceded that it could be following Jamie. I thought, for a moment, that it might be following me, but it never made an effort to fall behind me or stay out of my sight.

I didn't see it leave the house in the valley, but I hadn't been paying close attention to other cars at that point. If this person was tailing Jamie, odds were good that he'd started at or near that house.

When Jamie pulled up at his apartment, the Audi slowed down and cleaved to the curb a half block away. I drove past, trying hard not to drop my pace. I got a brief look at the man in the driver's seat—a Latino man in his late twenties or early thirties, sitting alone. It was hard to know for sure from my split-second glimpse, but I thought he was staring right at Jamie, who was sitting in his car with the engine off.

The man didn't seem to notice me as I circled the block and drove back onto Jamie's street, hanging back far enough to avoid raising suspicion. Or so I hoped. The white Audi was still there, presenting, to my eyes, a predatory gleam. I smirked—I had no real standing to make that judgment.

After another minute, Jamie left his car. Detecting his presence, a light turned on in the driveway, showing him in outline like the lone figure on a stage. He slouched as he approached the door, then cast a casual gaze behind him. If he'd meant to check if anyone was watching him, he didn't do a great job. His survey was too fast, not paranoid enough. On one shoulder, he carried a black backpack I hadn't noticed before.

Not ten seconds after Jamie went inside, the white Audi started up. I followed it back onto the 101, and when it exited at White

Oak, I knew exactly where it was going. Even so, I tailed it to the Encino mansion, where the man in the Audi buzzed in at the gate, identifying himself over the intercom. I sped away and called Daphne on the way home.

Jamie's Monday night adventure reenergized me, and I spent the next two weeks observing him, on Daphne's request. I developed something of a routine, stopping in the office every morning and following Jamie from around eleven to eleven each day. I spent a lot of time in my car. I got a lot of reading done, and I spent hours talking to Daphne, mostly right before bed. Some nights we had a drink over the phone while she filled me in on Jamie's behavior from her end.

"He's buttering me up now," she told me one night. "He's been calling every day, asking, 'Baby, how was your day?' and 'How's your painting going?' like there's nothing more important in the world."

She laughed, and I laughed with her. "Well, good. If he knows he's in trouble, maybe he'll stay on his best behavior."

"Oh yeah, he knows he did wrong. He sent me roses yesterday. He *only* sends flowers to say sorry. Some men are like that, I guess."

"Sure," I said. "So you've forgiven him for now?"

"I'm not giving him the boot quite yet. I feel a little more relaxed now that you're on him."

Jamie's weekdays were no less social than his weekends. He spent time working at Joe Tilley's, but outside of those hours he kept himself busy fluttering across the streets of Los Angeles, hanging out with good-looking people in handsome venues.

But over the course of two weeks' surveillance, I'd come to

the conclusion that Jamie's life was not all brunches and beers and trips to the beach. I had to give Daphne's speculations a fair hearing.

After his errand in Encino, a number of people dropped by his house at odd hours throughout the week, a whole string of guests, male and female, ranging widely in age, None stayed for longer than half an hour, and everyone left with a look of self-conscious hurry, stepping so fake cool I could almost see their chilly sweats, hear their guilty whistles as they bustled with full pockets to their cars. The same pattern repeated the second week, complete with another Monday night visit to the same house in the valley. It seemed likely that Jamie was slinging something. If he was a coke addict, it might as well be coke, and probably everything lower on the pyramid.

The white Audi reappeared twice, once on a Friday, when Jamie was on his way to work, and once again on Monday, when he visited the valley. I ran the car's plates and found that it belonged to a fifty-year-old woman in North Hollywood named Guadalupe Perez. She was not the driver.

Daphne didn't know who he was, either. "Some lowlife, probably. A new friend, maybe. I hardly know anything about my boyfriend that you don't tell me."

"Do you want me to find out more about this guy? He kind of worries me."

"Yeah, me, too," she said, and I heard her take a long swallow of her wine. "Keep on Jamie, though, and if this driver tries to hurt him, you can intervene."

"I'll engage him in hand-to-hand combat." I poured more rye into my glass.

I hoped Jamie wasn't actually dealing drugs, and that if he was, he wasn't attracting undue attention. Maybe it was his dopey boy face, or just the soothing pull of continuous familiarity. Maybe it was just the small debt of a parking space on a miserable day. He was my first target who appeared to be a halfway decent human being, and I recognized, with a little shock at my sentimentality, that I was growing fond of him. I wanted him to keep his nose clean and prosper, for both his and Daphne's sakes.

If it didn't look like Daphne was right on the money, I might have disliked her for putting me on Jamie's tail. I had a duty to clients to respect their wishes, their privacy, to heed their instructions while they paid for my services. I had no such duty to like them. In fact, most of the people who walked into Lindley & Flores were despicable in at least a few ways, defined by jealousy or scheming on top of the normal spectrum of personality flaws. But Daphne, as they say, was different. She wasn't paranoid or angry or even overreaching. We got along.

We talked intermittently throughout each day, and she called me every night before her East Coast bedtime, usually after she'd talked to Jamie. I issued a full report of my day's findings, of Jamie's movements and interactions, more often than not with Jamie's front door in my field of vision. I gave her my impressions, facts first, hunches second, sprawling speculations if and when she prodded. We analyzed together, and when we were done with my report, she gave me hers. I listened, and I listened well.

Somewhere in those hours of shop talk, we found room to get to know each other. We found small things we had in common, not least of all a shared interest in detective fiction—she'd always wondered what it would be like to hire a private investigator. My work for her was intensely personal, both of us knew, so there was a built-in closeness there, a sharing of secrets and problems, the polite restraint of recent acquaintance cut away like an opaque smear of fat. I even told her a fair amount about myself, narrated some of the worst events of my life in calm, stoic tones while my heart pumped loudly with pain and a release like pleasure.

For two weeks of quiet surveillance, I gave my whole life to the follies and misadventures of this strange, dysfunctional couple. I let them seep into my thoughts and lay claim to my emotions. I should have known then, that was never a good idea.

Three

On the Thursday of my second week of surveillance, I followed Jamie from his apartment to Joe Tilley's house, where he swapped his car for the yellow Ferrari and played the chauffeur right back to The Roosevelt Hotel. They checked in a little after 8:00.

I valeted my car, killed time in the lobby, and took my ticket to the valet stand a half hour later. I asked the parking attendant if I could grab something out of my car, and he gave me my keys and directed me to a lot across the street. It was an ugly parking structure, plain and grimy in a way antithetical to The Roosevelt's nostalgic glamor. The yellow Ferrari stood out like a brand-new lemon in a litter box.

I snapped a picture on my phone and sauntered back to the hotel for a leisurely drink. I called it a night after one. I had a feeling they weren't leaving for a while.

When Daphne called, I was getting ready for bed, nearing

the end of my last rye before brushing my teeth. I moved fast to pick up my phone, and I realized with a pathetic pang that I'd been waiting for her call for the better part of the night.

"He never called," she said.

I glanced at a wall clock. It was rounding midnight. "I was afraid of that."

"What is he doing, Song?"

"Last I saw he and Tilley checked in at The Roosevelt."

"Goddammit. What an asshole." Her voice was soft, exhausted.

"You don't sound surprised."

"I can't say I am. What do you think I should do?" she asked.

"You mean right now or in the larger sense?"

"Should I just dump him?"

"I don't know, Daph. Do you really want to keep paying me to follow him around, though?" I smiled, and felt a little tipsy. "I mean, I'm not going to tell you not to, but I don't know if I would if I were you."

"Just a little longer. I want proof he can't deny. And besides, he could be in some shit, you know? What does Jamie know about dealing drugs? He's a doofus. He might get himself killed."

"You want to fix him up? Save him from the whirlpool and towel him clean? I mean, come on, you know how that story goes. You've tried already. You won't change him."

She sighed. "I need another drink. Will you have one with me?"

I shook the half-melted ice cubes in my little glass. They made a lonely, musical sound. "Sure."

When we hung up the phone, it was almost three in the morning. The sun might have risen in New York. She didn't want to talk about Jamie, so we talked about everything else instead.

I had three more ryes and went to bed, spent and close to laughing.

I woke up late Friday and drove back to The Roosevelt in the afternoon. I parked on the street a half block away and walked straight into the valet lot to find the Ferrari, unmoved since the day before. For the third time in two weeks, I made myself comfortable in the Roosevelt's lobby. It was four o'clock when I sat down with my first drink. I decided to stick around until I got hungry, then check back in the next day. I had a feeling Jamie and Joe weren't going anywhere.

I was contemplating a second drink when my phone rang.

"Song." Daphne was breathing hard. "Jamie needs your help."

"What? What's going on?"

She sniffled, and a sound came out of her like lips parting against a humid room. "I told him you were in the lobby. He called me panicking and I told him he had a friend there."

For a second, I felt caught, even minorly betrayed. Then I remembered—despite all the time we'd spent together, Jamie had no idea who I was until this hour. He had as much reason to expect my loyalty as he did a wedding invite from the Queen of England.

"Okay, what's going on?"

"Something . . . happened. Jamie's going to come down and get you in a minute, okay? He'll explain everything." She started to cry freely. "Song, I'm so glad you're there."

I barely had time to protest the cut connection before Jamie Landon pinged out of an elevator, alone. There was something uncertain and fragmented about his gait, like I was watching him on a bad Internet connection. He was so clearly agitated I could almost hear him twitching across the lobby.

He flitted his eyes around the room. I stood up, bent at the waist, and got my arm into position for a tentative blind-date wave. I had my fingers curled in a limp, motionless paw when he saw me and approached. He stopped walking and stared at the floor when he saw me move toward him.

"Hi, Jamie. Song. What's going on?" I asked. He didn't offer me a hand, but raised his oblique shuddering eyes to meet mine.

I felt his gaze descend on my skin like a nervous sweat. I'd spent almost two weeks with Jamie, but this was the closest I'd come to him, including that brief meeting in that other life. His face almost startled me in such high definition. A pretty face, boyish and compelling, with full lips stained a berry pink. I saw now that he'd peeled off layers of flaky skin, exposing the soft unaccustomed flesh underneath. He had light brown eyes with dark brown borders that made them pop like a tiger's, and these were open wide, manic, with a clouded light dancing in huge ink-pot pupils. They beamed desperation.

"My friend," he said, halting suddenly, as if his tongue tripped against the roof of his mouth. "I found my friend Joe."

He didn't have to tell me that something was wrong with Joe. The way he relayed the discovery was message enough. After all, finding a friend is rarely an unpleasant surprise.

"Jesus," I said, gulping nothing. "Is he dead?"

Jamie clamped his eyes shut and matched his top and bottom teeth like puzzle pieces in a picture of pain. Without a word, he turned toward the elevators, and I followed.

I followed almost without thinking, and looking back, later, I realized that despite my premonitions it didn't occur to me to leave. I knew I was choosing to walk into something awful, and I knew that it wasn't a mess I'd signed up for. But Daphne had asked for a favor, and I wanted to shoulder the weight of her dependence. And then there was Jamie, a man who'd been kind to me once, who I'd watched from a distance until his life had brought him to this. He led the way into that elevator assuming I'd follow, not out of presumption, I thought, but because he would have done the same for anyone in need. I saw his shivering back and felt attached to it by a hundred little ties.

He forced the doors closed, clapped both hands over his mouth and dragged his cheeks down, revealing the wet red flesh in his eyes. He shook his head and for a second I thought he was going to cry. Instead, he lowered his hands and took a deep, gasping breath, a single cycle of hyperventilation. "I just found . . ." He let out a screech through clenched teeth, like he was working through an attack of sharp physical pain. "Everything is fucked."

I wished I had a drink to dilute the flavor of his misery. "I know the feeling."

He touched a key card to the elevator panel and pressed an unmarked button beyond the highest indicated floor. The ride up was swift and airless.

The doors opened to a short hallway and a grander set of doors. Jamie keyed us in, and for a moment, I forgot we were in a hotel. We stood in the foyer of a modern mansion, decorated like a multimillionaire's bachelor pad. White furniture, impractical and attractive; white, furry rugs on a varnished hardwood floor. It would have been some magazine editor's vision of edgy, stylish, moneyed, masculine interior design, if it weren't for the cans, bottles, and dirty glasses covering the numerous small tabletops. Several parts of the floor glowed ominously, glazed and mucky with spilled liquid of uncertain origin. There were traces of white powder on a glass coffee table. The room smelled of cologne and bodies and cigarette smoke.

"Is anyone else here?" I asked.

"No. They were all gone when I woke up." He shook his head and rubbed his wrists against his thighs, started clawing at a small rip at the knee of his jeans. "Is it freezing in here?"

He was trembling, and I felt something sad and protective stir deep in my chest. I wanted to tuck him in and let him sleep for a long time. Instead, I asked, "Where is he?"

He crossed his arms and brought one shaking hand up to cover his eyes. His lips curled broadly into the shape of a rigid smile, and he sobbed. The sobs left his open mouth with the sudden ugly volume of new sneakers squeaking against a waxed floor, and they came faster and faster until he had to sit down to keep from falling.

I sat with him on a well-stuffed couch, moving clothing and crumbs and other detritus from the cushions. I hesitated for just a few seconds before touching my hand to his back, and he didn't shrink away, just let his body heave under my palm.

I thought of the strangeness of sitting here, watching a man I'd just met break down with the abandon of a child. It seemed fitting, somehow, like I was his dark guardian angel, accruing trust and familiarity in my two weeks of surveillance. I knew many things about him his own mother wouldn't know.

"Fuck," he said. "I . . . everything is shit. Everything is fucked."

I patted his back lightly, like I was coaxing a baby to sleep. "It'll be okay," I said, and felt like a liar.

"I—I can't go back up there."

"Are you sure he's dead?"

He rocked and made choked sounds of affirmation.

"Did you check his pulse?" I asked.

He shook his head. "Couldn't. Couldn't touch him."

"Oh Jesus Christ. Did you call 911?"

"No, I—I called Daphne. She said you would know what to do."

I cursed silently, the air of it breaking inside my cheeks. "Jamie, if he's still alive, we have to call 911. Have to, understand?" I stood up, willing courage into my every muscle. "I'll go check, okay? Where is he?"

He squeezed his eyes together and small wrinkles emerged all around them. "Upstairs," he said. "There's—there's blood."

That made me stop for a second, but before I could start following up, Jamie was sobbing again. I turned toward the stairs that led up to the rest of the penthouse. I steadied myself; I had seen dead men before, and I was in better shape than Jamie was, anyway.

I took the stairs slowly, gripping the cold metal of the rail. The penthouse was huge, and its emptiness rang in my ears like the soundtrack to a slasher movie. When the second floor came into view, I took it in with some wonder. Where the downstairs was trashed by the revels of many, the upstairs looked ready to show to any wealthy buyer: a glass coffee table weighted with magazines; a tremendous, expensive-looking modern chandelier. I studied the peaceful effects of this outer room, and walked in to see a set of silver curtains, parted but not tied back, hanging like a luminous gate, left open. Beyond them was a bedroom, the bed made.

I was looking for a movie star with more coke in his veins than blood. If he wasn't near the party, chances were good he was in a bathroom.

And that's where I found him.

He lay naked in the biggest bathtub I'd ever seen, a titanium gray free-standing novelty shaped like a deep soap dish. It was part of the master bedroom, no wall between, a bachelor-pad feature for the bold seducer. Tilley was very much alone—by the looks of it, that was the way he wanted to go.

I blinked hard and got closer. There was no smell of death, no smell of anything at all. The bathtub looked like a sterile thing, hewn from a block of cold metal. Only the blood told the story, the red in the water thick enough to mask his nakedness. His head and neck rose out of the water, his eyes frozen half open, casting a milky stare over the tainted bath.

This was no overdose, and it didn't take a Sherlock to deduce as much. I walked up to the body with unease growing in my belly. Halting, I lowered two fingers to touch the skin of his exposed neck and looked, with diligence, for a pulse. There was nothing there, no report of life, just cold skin going waxy with its own irrelevance. My fingers smeared with a film of death, I lowered my palm to the surface of the water. No heat rose, and with one dread-filled fingertip, I tested the bath. The surface broke, and the bloodied water wrapped around my finger. The temperature matched the room, and all at once I felt that the room was very cold.

I looked hard at the crimson water, tried to find the shape of the body inside, but the blood thickened the bath to a gruesome opacity. I swallowed hard and lowered my hand into the water, my breath skipping as I picked up Joe Tilley's dead arm. I heard myself let out a squeal as I extracted it from the water. It was heavy and rigid, and as I raised it diluted drops of blood dripped onto the tile floor. A deep gash ran from his wrist to an inch above his elbow. I stared at it with nausea and somewhere, a tingle of fascination.

I didn't need to know whether there was a twin wound on the other arm—the artery was severed, the blood loss from the one wrist more than sufficient. Jamie and I were hours late. It couldn't have taken long for Joe's life to pour out.

An open doorway led to a full bathroom, and I washed hands and arms with Shakespearean vigor, long after the watercolor strands had swirled down the drain.

I scanned the bathroom and without much effort, found pill bottles and traces of cocaine. The counter was otherwise undisturbed, the towels folded, the small hotel toiletries yet unused. I spent a few minutes searching for a note, but found nothing. There was no weapon in sight. Chances were, it was sunk inside the bath with the naked dead man. I felt little desire to find it.

It took Jamie another ten minutes to compose himself when I came downstairs. I smoked a couple of Lucky Strikes without asking permission, and when he was stable enough to communicate, Jamie copped one, too. What did cigarettes in the living room matter, after all, with a dead body upstairs?

"Are you high?" I asked. "Right now?"

He put his head in his hands and nodded.

I almost laughed. There was Daphne's answer, packaged in that sad little nod. Not that I'd needed it, sitting right next to him—it was clear enough he was high as a saint.

"Before or after you found him?" I asked.

"Before," he wheezed through his fingers. "God, I'm so fucked. Everything is fucked."

"Okay, calm down. When did you find him?"

"Half an hour ago? I don't even know, man. I called Daphne right after, and we talked for, maybe, fifteen minutes."

I nodded. Tilley had been cooling in that bath long before Jamie had found him. "Where were you before that? Here?"

"I have my own room. We come here sometimes, to hang out, party and stuff, and it's big enough that I get my own room." He looked around the penthouse with devastated awe. "He pays for it. Obviously," he added, head sagging between his knees.

"And you woke up—"

"We were partying last night, and it went pretty late. I don't know when I woke up this morning, or afternoon or whatever, but I went back to sleep without leaving my room. I just woke up again and when I went to see how he was doing . . ." He broke off with a dry sob into his palms.

I watched his hung head and his trembling shoulders, collapsed in toward his neck. Part of me felt like I knew him, and something in me answered his grief. A lock of wavy hair bobbed up and down by his ear, and I wanted, quite badly, to smooth it away.

"I had a younger sister who killed herself." The words spilled out, almost coolly. I heard them leave my mouth with something akin to surprise. "Almost ten years ago now."

He sniffled, looking at me with mournful interest. "I'm sorry."

"It's a terrible thing, I know. You can't blame yourself. It was his decision. You don't have to live with it." I buttoned my mouth against the other possibility. "Jamie—to your knowledge, was Joe Tilley depressed?"

"I don't know. He had his problems, yeah, but I don't know."

I sat down and closed my eyes, let the surreal texture of the afternoon settle around me.

"We have to call this in, Jamie. We'd better let the hotel know, too. This is serious."

He turned so white I thought he'd have to faint or puke to go whiter. "Oh Jesus. I have to call his manager."

He stood up and pulled a cell phone out of his pocket. As the ring tone played in his ear, he looked at me with fear and nerves collecting in his eyes.

"Do you want me to leave?" I asked.

"Oh God, please, no," he said, and he grabbed at my shoulder like it was the only hold on a steep and dangerous mountain.

Alex Caldwell stood with his eyes closed and the bridge of his nose pinched between the fingers of a small hairy hand.

"Jamie," he said, his voice muffled in his forearm. "Who the fuck is this?"

He'd been in the penthouse for fifteen minutes without ac-knowledging my existence. To be fair, he had other things on his mind. I thought he might cry at the sight of his famous client, dead and ugly, but he refused to look at the body. Instead of sad-ness, he projected a volcanic anger. Jamie shrank from him, avoid-ing its spew.

"Juniper Song," I answered instead. "I'm a friend."

I put out a hand, and he pretended not to see it.

He was a stocky man, about five-eight, barrel-chested, with two-hundred-dollar jeans bunched tight around the crotch in an intentional cowboy way. His hair was a pale butter blond, gelled into soft peaks by someone with expertise. He looked like the kind of man who could cook a good meal, but would only get started if there were no women around to do it for him. There was no ring on his finger—I guessed he was in his late thirties, and that his greatest love was a very nice car.

"Jamie," he repeated. "Who is she?"

Jamie glanced at him with trepidation, looking small and childish before the shorter man. "She's a friend."

"Yeah? And what's she here for?"

Jamie turned to me and gave me a helpless shrug. "I . . ."

I'd almost forgotten that I wasn't his friend at all, that I was a hired probe sent to watch him by his girlfriend, an entity somewhat hostile to his interests. It was true that I'd become fond of him, but that was my own doing. I shrugged back at him, let him know that he could say what he pleased.

"She works for a private investigator," he mumbled.

Alex cupped a hand to one ear and blinked. "What?"

"A private investigator."

"You're fucking kidding me."

"It's a long story."

Alex looked at me and put one pudgy finger in biting distance of my face. "What are you, working for some newspaper? Lawyer?"

"No."

"Who, then?"

He was so close and so angry I thought he might spit in my mouth. I felt my own ire rise to meet him. "None of your business. Would you please get out of my face?"

"Get out," he demanded. "This is no place for an outsider."

I looked at Jamie. He squirmed, but I knew he wouldn't insist on my staying. I didn't like bending to the will of this odious man, but he was right: Joe Tilley was nothing to me.

I went down to the lobby and sipped a rye while I processed the events of the afternoon. This job was turning out to be more interesting than I'd expected. In the investigation business, this was rarely a good thing.

It took some effort to remember why I was there—just an investigator's apprentice checking out a boyfriend's bad behavior. Daphne wanted to know what kind of trouble Jamie was getting into, but she was afraid of drugs, not death. Then again, death was that final, bulging fear, just a scratch beneath the surface of every other.

As I sat and drank and simmered in thought, the people in the hotel lobby began to stir. My first thought was that a celebrity had walked in the door, but as my attention came alive I noticed sirens. The paramedics came first, then the police, all wearing dour masks on excited faces. I didn't stick around to see the reporters, but I knew they couldn't be far behind. They'd vie, every one, for the big break, the quote of misery from the manager, the unknown friend. Somewhere, maybe in that big house on the hill, Tilley's third wife was crying. I hoped numbers one and two found out before his death hit the news.

It was a sorry story, the whole thing, and I wanted nothing more than to see myself out.

Four

I called Daphne on my way home but she didn't pick up. I could think of a few reasons she might be busy, but I was worried, my nerves strung, plucked, and vibrating. I tried her twice more before I gave up and called Chaz instead.

I got him on his cell. One thing I liked about Chaz, he always picked up my calls.

"What's going, girl detective?" There was something about his cell phone that brought out the cheesiest qualities of his cool act.

"Oh, Chazzie. You don't even know."

I'd been keeping him loosely posted on my assignment, but he gave me enough credit that he didn't press me for details—micromanagement was not, he claimed, his style. Some developments, though, deserved a full report to the boss. I suspected the death of a movie star in close proximity to my target had to qualify. I decided to give him the long version.

It felt strange to tell him Joe Tilley was dead. Chaz didn't care much about celebrities, but he knew who he was, and knew what it meant. Tilley was a big enough name to top the news, invoke speculations about rules of three. This was not a quiet story, and it would be everywhere in a matter of hours. When I told Chaz what had happened, the words buzzed on my lips and left a sting of shame. I had no particular feeling for the man, but I was in awe of his death and bothered by this reaction. He was more than an abstract to me, no longer a celebrity figure made inhuman by the waxy gloss of fame—yet I couldn't speak of him without feeling like a cheap purveyor of tabloid gossip.

Chaz listened, grunting here and there to let me know he was still on the line. When I was done, he exhaled like he'd been holding his breath for minutes. "So," he said. "This girl puts you onto her cokehead boyfriend and you win the corpse lotto while you're on the job. Congratulations."

"Thank you."

He sighed. "I don't like it, Song. It's always bad news when someone turns up dead, and it doesn't help that this someone is famous as the Pope."

"I am aware of this, Chaz."

"And you haven't talked to the client yet?"

"She isn't picking up."

"Well, let's just pray she got the answers she needed so we can get paid and move on with our lives."

"Yeah," I said, without conviction.

"Here's hoping, anyway." He sighed again. "Maybe this isn't our problem."

When I got home, Lori was out, and I cracked open a beer and sat down with my laptop. My workday had been short but tiring.

I tried Daphne again, and this time my call went straight to voice mail.

The news of Joe Tilley's death didn't wait for morning. By the time I'd fed myself dinner, Twitter exploded with halfhearted eulogies, a hashtag in honor of the dead man. I scanned the RIPs, misspelled, articulate, glib, occasionally heartfelt. It felt eerie, seeing the online explosion, the frenzied dust cloud generated by the fall of a celebrity. It made me feel like I'd witnessed something large, that I was somehow privileged by this morbid brush with fame.

The few details were murky—found dead in a Los Angeles hotel room in Hollywood or Beverly Hills or Laguna Beach, cause of death widely speculated. No official statement. I pictured manager Alex, that angry man with his finger in my face. I guessed someone was still paying him to keep busy.

A celebrity death was a public event, and I could see it all, the way it would play out over the next week, the next month. There would be tributes, a memorial service on television, YouTube remembrances by famous friends. And in the meantime, there would be a toxicology screening, a coroner's report, a thorough police investigation.

I wondered where Jamie Landon would fit into it all. I wondered if the poor boy was ready.

I woke up early the next morning after a night of sticky dreams. Lori was in the kitchen—I could smell eggs frying from my bedroom.

The kitchen was narrow, with a refrigerator door that swung out the wrong way, blocking everything. I peered in from the threshold separating the kitchen from the living room, my hands on the sides of the doorless doorway.

Lori was folding an omelet onto a clean dinner plate, its yellow fluff studded with white and red and green. She was humming to herself, her face fresh, her tiny body tucked into her pinstriped pajamas.

I knocked on the doorjamb and she looked up with a surprised smile, her crooked tooth gleaming at me. "You're up early."

"Slept badly," I said. "Is Isaac here?"

Isaac had been over until I went to bed the night before. I'd heard the two of them laughing in the living room while I drank and read in bed. I had no desire to interact with other people after the events of the afternoon. Even their light, playful chatter sounded irritating and clueless and I resented them, these two innocent people who'd touched no dead bodies in the past twelve hours. I doubled my nightcap to drown them out, but I still couldn't get good sleep.

"Oh *unni*." Lori blushed. "You know I wouldn't let him sleep over."

I smiled. Lori was a virgin for Christ, and I teased her about this once in a while.

I took two Advils and caught her watching me as she cracked eggs for another omelet. "What is it?" I asked, wiping my mouth.

"Are you hung over again?" Her wide eyes held a gleam of importunity.

"I have a little headache." It came out terse, and she looked back to the frying pan.

The eggs sizzled, cutting across the silence. Lori asked, "Did you hear about Joe Tilley?"

The name surprised me for a split-second, but of course Lori had heard through the usual channels. I never talked to her about my work. There were confidentiality issues, and on top of that, my job was a sensitive subject. I was shadowing Lori when we first met, and though we became friends as a result, that was not a happy episode in either of our lives.

"Yeah." I nodded, and realized I hadn't checked the news in several hours. I tried to keep my voice nonchalant, with some success. "What's the latest? Are they calling it a suicide or what?"

"I don't think they know."

She set a brand-new omelet on the table and waved for me to sit down. I did, and felt chastened as she asked me if I wanted coffee. "How's Isaac?"

"He's good," she said.

"Things are going well, I take it? You guys are boyfriend-girlfriend and all that?"

She smiled and raised a knuckle to her cheek like she was taking its temperature. "As of yesterday, yeah."

"Congratulations," I said. "He seems like a swell guy."

"He is, *unni*. Very swell."

She chattered about him while I ate the omelet, and I gave her my full attention. It was nice to see her happy, and seeing it, this once, let me know how rarely she'd been happy as long as I'd known her.

I didn't know why, but it made me feel cautious.

"Whatever happened with that other guy? Did you talk to your uncle about him?"

She bit down on her lower lip and shook her head. "He's been texting every few days. I respond politely, but that's it."

"You're being nice."

"I think so."

"If you think so, you definitely are. You haven't seen him again, though?"

"I haven't been by the garage in a while."

Lori saw her uncle at least a couple times a week, and most of the time she met him at T & J. She'd been avoiding it.

"Lori—are you scared of this guy?"

"He makes me uncomfortable." She shrugged and added "That's all."

I must have drifted off, because when my phone rang, it yanked me awake. The screen showed a 917 number.

"Hello?"

There was a moment of silence on the other end, long enough that I thought I'd been dialed by accident.

"Hi, it's Jamie. From yesterday?"

I sat up. His voice came through sleep-deprived and frantic, but he sounded much more collected than I'd left him. "Yeah, hi, of course. How could I forget?"

He gave a pathetic laugh, half snort and half sigh. "Thank you. For helping me. That was really nice of you."

The body in the bathtub flashed before my eyes, red and awful. "What did I really do?" I asked. "I'm guessing Alex handled the hotel and police and all that?"

"Yeah." He took a deep breath. "Listen, Daphne told me what you were doing for her."

"I figured as much."

"I don't care. I deserved that. I just—I want you to know that I'm not a bad guy. I mean sure, I get high, and I sling a little sometimes. But I would never hurt anyone." A wheezing quality crept into his voice, and I wondered if he'd been crying, and whether he was about to start again.

"I didn't think you would, Jamie." I prepared myself for any answer, and asked, "Why?"

"After you left, two cops came to the room and looked around. They questioned me up and down."

"That makes sense. I think it's standard procedure to interview the person who finds the body."

"But the way—the way they were questioning me, they thought I was this scumbag, I could feel it. Alex—he wanted us to clean up the room before we called the manager, before the cops would come, but I thought that was a bad idea, you know? Compromise the scene or something."

"Sure."

"You saw what the place looked like. It was trashed." He cleared his throat. "They knew I was partying with him, that I was doing drugs, and the way they were asking me questions, I could see their wheels turning."

"Oh, no. Jamie—it was a suicide. Wasn't it?"

He was silent for almost a minute. "They haven't ruled any-thing out."

There was a part of me that had felt this coming the moment I heard that the man was dead. It was the reader in me, the per-verse voice that sought out the direst contingencies in the cor-ners of my imagination.

Joe Tilley was dead, and it wasn't a clear-cut suicide. If there was foul play, Jamie was fucked.

"You were with me. You saw how I was yesterday. Did I look like a guy who'd just murdered his friend in cold blood?"

"No," I said. "Not at all."

"I told the cops they should talk to you. Is that okay?"

"Of course. Anything I can do." I chewed my lip and sighed. "Are they really treating you like a suspect?"

"They haven't come out and said so, but come on, yes. I mean, I was in the room with him," he whispered. "There's my fucking alibi. *I was there.*"

I thought about Jamie Landon, snorting coke in his room while his friend lay dying beyond his door. I thought about where I would look, if I were a thinking cop. "So what is it you want me to do? Call in?"

"I'll have the police contact you. They'll probably want you to go in for questioning."

A few hours later, I drove to the LAPD Detective Bureau downtown. I'd been to the building once before and I didn't like the place one bit.

"Thank you for coming in, Miss Song. I'm Detective Veronica Sanchez and this is my partner, Detective Milo Redding."

Detective Sanchez was a big, sturdy woman, almost as wide across the waist as she was at the hips, with breasts suffocating beneath a buttoned-up navy blue polo shirt. I was five-foot-nine in my flat shoes, and she towered over me. She wore her hair buzzed to a few stiff inches that projected a monkish discipline. Underneath her hairline her face was soft, with sweet, droopy brown bloodhound eyes. She didn't smile, but she wasn't unfriendly.

She led me to an interrogation room, followed by Detective Redding, a small balding man with large blue eyes and a dark blond mustache. Detective Sanchez must have been the bad cop by default.

"Coffee?" he asked, before I could even sit down.

"Sure," I said.

The coffee was weak and grainy, and I lapped at it without enthusiasm as Detective Sanchez watched me.

"State your name for the record, please."

"Juniper Yoon-Kyung Song."

"What do you do, Juniper Song?"

I bit down on the inside corner of my lip. There was no way this wouldn't come up. "I'm an apprentice at a PI office."

Detective Sanchez raised one black eyebrow and turned her head to nod at Redding. "PI as in private investigator?"

I nodded.

"What's the outfit?"

"Lindley & Flores, in K-Town. It's a small shop."

Sanchez tilted her chin, then her face relaxed. "How's Art Flores treating you?"

"You know Arturo?" I felt a flutter of kinship at the unexpected connection—I hoped she did, too.

"We used to work together. He quit the force in a blaze of glory. How's he doing?"

"Good, I think. I work for Chaz, mostly, but Arturo's a good boss."

"Ah, the goofy one." She smiled, and I saw her face change when she caught herself doing it. "And what do you do for Lindley & Flores?"

"This, mostly." I picked up my half-empty cup of sludge coffee and shook it from side to side. A few brown drops fell thickly on the table. "Man the desk. Sometimes I get to do stakeouts, stuff like that."

"Were you working when you were at The Roosevelt?" Her tone was steely now, as if she were overcompensating for her display of fond feelings.

I thought about the last couple of weeks and wondered, with

disgusted amazement, how it had come to this. I was working when I was at The Roosevelt, but I went beyond strict duty when I walked into that room.

Detective Sanchez was sniffing, but I could tell she knew nothing about my assignment, and I doubted she knew a thing about Daphne. She suspected, correctly, that I had information she might want for herself, but I wasn't about to oblige her. Sitting there, in that interrogation room, I saw the stubborn lines of my allegiance. Daphne was my client, and on top of that, she was my friend. Detective Sanchez was just a police officer asking after her business, and I saw no reason to involve her.

I plopped an elbow on the table and rested a cheek on a fist. "Hey, do I need to answer these questions?"

Sanchez turned back to Redding, who stopped his pacing behind her. "Technically, no," he piped up. "But this is an important investigation, and we would appreciate your cooperation."

"I'm happy to cooperate, but I'd rather leave my work out of this. You guys called me in to talk about Jamie."

Sanchez leaned forward and narrowed her eyes at me. "What were you doing at The Roosevelt?"

"I was having a drink."

"What is your relation to Jamie Landon?"

"I just met the guy."

"Funny." The way she said that word, like it wasn't funny at all, made something slip in my chest. "Jamie said you were his friend."

I cursed in my head. I should have asked Jamie what he'd told the police. "I did just meet the guy."

"But you consider each other friends."

"Maybe we do. Maybe we're friends." I smiled broadly, and she gave me a tight smirk in response. "Look—am I in trouble here? Do you want me to help you or not?"

"How do you know Mr. Landon?"

"I barely know him. I'll swear to it in front of any court."

"Why were you with him?"

"That is my business." I cracked my knuckles, as long as I was annoying her. "I don't mean to be difficult, Detective Sanchez. I want to help, honestly. But if you ask me any more about my business, I'll be leaving."

She sighed, running her palm across the gelled tips of her hair. "At about what time yesterday did you first see Jamie Landon?"

The interview lasted for half an hour, and I told no more half-truths. I thought, by the end, that Detective Sanchez had even taken a liking to me.

Then she walked me out of the station and put a hand on my shoulder, a hard grip that felt almost wonderful. "There's a lot of heat on this case, Juniper Song. If you have anything else to report, I guarantee you'll hack it up, one way or another."

"If you talk to Arturo, tell him I did good, will you?"

She chuckled. "I'll let him know you were a pain in my ass."

I met Chaz for lunch at a diner near Sunset Junction, one of those brand-new restaurants designed to look eighty years old, with muted orange vinyl seats and vintage ads boasting twenty-five-cent coffee. I called him, my adrenalin running high on my way home from the station, and he took the opportunity to show me his magnanimity. "I'll buy you pancakes and we'll talk, okay? Tall stack of pancakes, butter and syrup. That should cheer you up."

I wanted to talk to him and I didn't have the heart to tell him I'd eaten, so here we were, Chaz scowling at my salad while he drowned three Frisbee-sized pancakes in a storm of maple syrup.

"So, girl detective, you can't handle one stinking cokehead boyfriend case by yourself?" He put a smile in his voice so I'd know he was joking, but I knew he hated to think about work on the weekend. He had a wife and two kids at home, and he liked doing dad things like taking his kids to the park and embarrassing everyone.

"Joe Tilley, Chaz. A straight-up Hollywood death scandal. Some easy assignment."

"So what, it's not a suicide?"

"The way they questioned me? I don't think they're going with suicide, at least not yet."

"Murder, huh? Jesus. Some luck. Why are they looking at Jamie?"

"They didn't exactly fill me in, but my guess is wrong place, wrong time, right?"

"Let me make sure I have this straight: Tilley bled to death in his hotel bathtub after some big drug party. Is that basically correct?"

"Yeah, his wrists were slashed."

He nodded, frowning slightly, telegraphing deep thoughts.

"I'll tell you why they're after Jamie," he said.

"Why?"

"If I had to guess? They probably have shit beans in the way of hard physical evidence. Think about it."

"Any party guest could've smeared DNA all over the penthouse at any time for any reason."

"Right. And I'd be surprised if they found a murder weapon with usable fingerprints or anything like that."

"I didn't see a weapon near the tub. I was thinking it was probably in the water."

"And it would've been easy enough to wipe prints before dropping it in. Not too suspicious."

"So you think they have squat, so they're just going after Jamie because he was there?"

He shrugged. "It sounds weak when you put it that way, but what else are they supposed to do? This is a high-profile case. Academy Award for Murder of the Year."

"That's not good for Jamie. I mean, shit, it isn't good for me either. Detective Sanchez thinks I'm holding out on her."

"Well, you did hold out on her."

"Was I wrong?"

"No, you're within your rights there, but—" He laughed. "This Jamie kid might be their primary suspect, but they must have a file on you now."

I rummaged a fork through my salad, which was looking pale and unappetizing. "Shit."

"I know *I* would."

I looked up at him, searched his broad face for some easy answer. "So what do you think I should do?"

"Be ready." Deadpan, heavy and enunciated, like he was giving me advice of immense practical importance.

"Okay, something more concrete, maybe." I resisted an urge to roll my eyes. "Come on, Chazzie. Help me out here. I'm look-ing to you for your wisdom and experience. Regale me."

I laid it on thick and he smiled, lips glazed with syrup. "Call Daphne. Explain your situation, and Jamie's, too."

"And tell her what, I need to talk to the cops about her? You want me to give a client's name to the police?"

"She needs to know there's pressure. If this is a murder inves-tigation, you can't just lie to the cops." His face darkened, a scowl hitting his sticky lips. "And if this is a murder investigation, Daphne Freamon should probably be investigated."

I set down a forkful of wilting salad. "How's that?"

Chaz gave me a look that said he knew I was playing dumb. "Come on. This girl sends you on some endless quest and suddenly there's a dead body? Tell me what's not suspicious about that."

"Stranger things have happened."

"Sure. A dozen of them, probably. I'm not saying she had anything to do with it. But good God, the police would be interested in talking to her."

I nodded slowly. The logic was sound, if upsetting. "You're probably right. But is it our job to make sure that happens?"

"I trained you in PI ethics, didn't I?"

"Yeah, you did."

"Good. Art would kill me if I hadn't." He wiped mock sweat off his sweaty brow. "So you tell me, then."

"Client confidentiality—I don't have to tell the police shit."

"That's right. But I'd call Daphne. As soon as you finish that sad little salad."

Five

Daphne called me first, late in the afternoon.

"I've been trying to get in touch with you," I told her before she could get in a word. "Where've you been?"

"On a flight to L.A. Sorry, I should've told you, but I left in a hurry."

"Oh." I felt an inappropriate rush of pleasant surprise, as if she were just an old friend. "You're in town?"

"Yeah. Just got in. It's been a hectic day."

"Yeah, I believe you. Jesus Christ."

"Jamie told me you had to talk to the police. I'm sorry I got you into this."

"Look, uh," I clicked my back teeth. "They asked what I was doing there with him."

"What did you tell them?" she asked after a pause.

"Nothing, but they know I work for a PI, and they gathered that I was there on an assignment."

"You must not have mentioned me. I haven't been contacted."

"No, I didn't."

"I appreciate that. I mean I'd rather not get tangled up in all this if I can avoid it."

"Understandable. But one of the cops, she seemed to think I was hiding something. She might be in touch again." I waited, hoping she'd make things easy for me.

"I don't like cops." She spoke softly but with emphasis. "If there's a way to avoid it, I'd rather not have to deal with them."

It was clear enough to both of us that I had wanted and expected her to yield, and there was a moment of tense silence as we worked out the disagreement in our goals.

"Yeah of course, but—" I said, keeping my tone non-confrontational.

"Please, Song," she cut in. Her voice was a little stronger now, but still even, unaggressive.

"Well, she shouldn't have much more use for me anyway. It was a pretty thorough interview, otherwise," I said, dropping the subject. "So I guess Jamie and I are friends now, huh? That's a weird turn of events."

She managed a cynical chuckle.

"So I guess I'm not chasing him around town anymore."

"Guess not," she said. "Are you glad?"

"Well, I am sorry that it turned out the way it did." I paused. "Did he tell you that yes, he's been using crazy amounts of cocaine and that yes, he's been slinging a little while he's at it?"

"Yeah." She sighed. "But what the fuck do I do, dump him now?"

Jamie's face popped up in my head, terrified and sickly and vulnerable. "I guess he probably needs you now, more than ever."

She groaned. "God, though, really, fuck that guy. He gets so high he doesn't even notice a man dying five feet away? And now I'm supposed to stand by him?"

"It's not a great situation."

"So here's my choice—do I want to be a doormat or a cold-hearted bitch? There's nothing in between."

"It's not fair. I'll agree with you there."

"What would you rather be?"

"Me?" I laughed. "I'd choose coldhearted bitch. But, you know, I'm basically a cat lady without a cat."

"I guess I'm not quite cold enough. I feel too sorry for him to leave."

"So you're sticking with him, then?"

"For now, anyway. He also says this thing with Joe was a real wake-up call. I mean, I believe that."

"So," I said, feeling slightly hopeful. "That's that then, huh? You got your answers. Was my performance to your satisfaction?"

She sucked in air and said, "Oh, Song. You must know I still need you."

"I was hoping . . ." I offered. "He's really in trouble, then, isn't he."

"Song, they think he killed Joe."

"That is trouble."

"Will you help him?" Something in me responded to the plea in her voice—the powerful human instinct to help a friend in need.

"How do you want me to do that?"

"Find out what happened in that hotel room."

I arranged to meet Daphne and Jamie at the Lindley & Flores office at seven o'clock. I got there a little earlier, readied the paperwork, and cleared some room on Chaz's desk. I decided to hold the meeting in his office instead of between my desk and the overstuffed green corduroy sofa Chaz had gotten for free from his sister.

I called Chaz to ask what I should do, and he told me to hold this first meeting without him. Daphne had asked for me specifically, and Chaz trusted me to take good notes so he could catch up later. He sounded busy on the phone. He was at his sister's for his niece's birthday.

I paced the office when I ran out of little tasks to keep my hands busy. I was running at high speed, with dread and anticipation prodding me in equal measure. Despite the circumstances, I was excited to meet Daphne.

At five minutes to seven, there was a knock at the door, and when I opened it, I took a startled step back.

Daphne Freamon was a bona-fide model-grade knock-out. She was about my height in heels, and she looked right at me with wide, clear brown eyes set deep between heavy black lashes. Her cheekbones were high and so well defined they nearly pointed. The swelling pout of her lips softened their effect, and all her features resolved in a round, angelic face the size of my palm. Curly black hair formed a halo fanning out to her ears, which glinted with gold button earrings. She wore a fir green sweater dress that followed the dizzying curves of an athletic body. Her dark, burnished brown skin shimmered like stretched satin.

It took me a second to see Jamie behind her, and when I did, he looked incongruous with his beautiful girlfriend. Jamie might have been handsome most of the time, but today he looked tired and haggard, like he'd surrendered five pounds since I'd seen him only a day before. His cheeks had a hollow look, giving his face the contours of a dented melon.

Daphne spoke first, and her voice made her instantly familiar. "Song, it's good to finally meet you."

"You, too." I gave her my hand and she gave me a hug. "Though it would've been better if you'd had no reason to come."

Jamie gave me a limp smile, his lips barely holding their shape.

"Come in," I said. "Want coffee?"

They declined, and I led them into Chaz's office where they sat across from me, separated by Chaz's messy desk.

I asked Daphne about her flight, and she talked freely, like she did over the phone. Jamie was silent and visibly nervous. White tabs peeled away from raw red around his cuticles, and he started biting at them before we even got started.

"So," I said to him after a few minutes. "You're in some trouble, huh?"

He nodded. "You've got to help me. I didn't do anything."

"Sure, man. I believe you, okay? That's the default. I believe you."

"Thanks."

Daphne put a hand on his knee, and he squeezed it like he was getting a tetanus shot.

I tapped a pen on Chaz's desk and uncapped it to take notes. "What do they have on you?"

"I was there, and they know it wasn't a suicide."

"They know that, huh? How?"

He ran his free hand through his hair, twice, in quick succession. "There was no way he could've done it. He was on too many drugs."

"Weren't you on the same drugs?"

He shook his head. "There was Rohypnol in his system. A lot of it."

"You mean the date-rape drug?"

"Yeah, the roofie. But that's not its only use. It just has that bad association."

"Educate me."

He looked sideways at Daphne, who rolled her eyes gently. "It's a downer. You know, like a sedative. Have you ever tried coke?"

"No."

Something like disappointment swirled around his eyes. I felt strangely inadequate, a vestigial twang from early adulthood, when drug abuse seemed edgy and cool.

"Well there's a reason people get addicted, but there are some bad side effects, too." He gnawed on his lip. "Like you get real jumpy, and sometimes it comes with a bad crash that just makes you want to, I don't know, stab yourself in the chest."

"Sounds delightful."

"Yeah, well, there are things you can do about it. For example, Rohypnol shaves some of that down, and it feels good on its own, too, or just with alcohol. Actually, some people will take it with booze to get drunk faster. Especially around here. You know, less calories."

"Can't be good for you."

"No, and apparently Joe, he took some stupid amount. Enough to make sure he was knocked out cold."

I rested my chin on the heel of my hand, piano-played my cheekbone. "So their theory is that someone—probably you—used Rohypnol to knock him out, then slashed his wrists open."

"Yeah."

"Does anything strike you as particularly idiotic in that theory?"

His eyes widened at me, clueless and hopeful. He looked like a teenager. "That I didn't do it?"

"No, not that. It makes sense that they'd suspect you. Look. I'm no expert, but isn't it pretty easy to overdose on cocaine? Especially if you're mixing it with Rohypnol and who knows what else?"

"Yeah, it happens."

"And premature celebrity drug deaths are . . . well, they happen. More often than murders."

"Yeah."

Daphne leaned forward in her chair, perked up to catch every word.

"So, if you killed him," I said, savoring the conclusion, "why on earth would you give him just enough drugs to knock him out, then slash his wrists instead of giving him a little bit more?"

He clapped his hands and stood up, the most energetic I'd seen him since we'd met. "You're right! I'd have to be a grade-A idiot."

"The thing is, a lot of killers *are* idiots. So there's that." I watched him deflate and sit back down on the sofa. "Do you know if they have anything else on you? Fingerprints on the weapon, anything like that?"

"I don't know. They haven't told me."

Daphne chimed in. "I'll bet they don't. I mean they haven't arrested you yet."

"Okay Jamie. I'm going to ask you some questions, and you have to be as honest with me as you can if I'm going to help you."

"Sure," he said, the small shreds of relief falling out of him like feathers from a slashed pillow.

"How would you describe your relationship with Joe?"

"He was my friend. Sort of. As much of a friend as an ultra-famous man twenty years older could be. He treated me like a sidekick. We'd smoke cigars together and he'd point out girls to me, make dirty comments about them and kind of nudge me like, *you know what I'm talking about.*"

"Sounds like a wonderful man."

"He was an asshole," Daphne said.

Jamie shot Daphne a look of hurt that made her bite her lip. "I know what he sounds like. But I'm trying to tell you something about him. He didn't like how old he was. It was weird, you know? Like he had kids and everything, he was forty-eight, I think, so edging up on fifty, but I guess because he was this heartthrob for so long he had trouble accepting that he wasn't a young man anymore. He had pictures of himself in his house, from when he was younger. I've seen him staring. And he didn't have that many good friends. You'd think he would've had more, but he didn't. And I think he wanted to be friends with me because I was the age he wished he still was, and he could act my age around me and I wouldn't really care."

"So he was immature."

"Yeah."

"Not the paternal type."

"No, not to me. He didn't even seem to want to mentor me, really. Just wanted to hang out."

"Did you like that?"

"You have to understand this, Song." He turned those eyes up at me, sad as a dog's. "I loved the man. He was a great friend."

I nodded. I wanted to pat him on the shoulder. "How did you meet him?"

"Well I've been writing and producing for a few years, since college, basically. Freelance, you know? But I built up my resume a bit doing shorts, that kind of thing. I went to Cannes one year." He smiled and his eyes grew dreamy, thinking of starlets and beach weather in the south of France. "And then one day I heard

Joe Tilley was interviewing writers. Daphne knows his personal assistant, and she told me to apply. So I did."

I turned to her. "Who's his personal assistant? Not Alex?"

"No," she said. "We used to waitress together, back in the day."

"So, Jamie. Listen. Where did Joe get his drugs?"

He looked nauseous, and Daphne shook her head at him.

"Okay, hey—I'm not here to get you in trouble for dealing. You just have to be honest with me. Were you Joe's drug dealer?"

He lifted his chin and his Adam's apple quivered as he swallowed, then nodded.

"How did that happen?"

"I kind of stumbled into it," he said. "I was getting stuff for myself, and then Joe liked what I was getting, so I would buy for him, too, and then a few other people gave me money to buy, so eventually I was buying in large-ish quantities. My dealer started asking if I was reselling, so I kind of told him I was in with this Hollywood crowd."

"Did you mention Tilley by name?"

His eyes fluttered, and he looked sheepish. "Yeah," he said. "I might have mentioned that I worked for him."

"So, what happened? They cut you in?'

"Yeah. My dealer put me in touch with his supplier, who talked to his boss, et cetera, et cetera. They figured out I could move top-grade shit to people who didn't mind spending money. So I became this low-level dealer, I guess."

"Who's your dealer, Jamie? What's his name?"

"Well he's not my dealer anymore, but a guy named Drew. He's on the same level as me, though, now."

"Your supplier, then. Who lives in that house in Encino?"

He blinked hard and gave me a dazed smile. "You followed me all the way out there, huh?"

I nodded. "It was my job."

"No one lives there, I don't think. It doesn't look lived-in, anyway."

"What is it, then?"

"Like an office, sort of. People meet there, leave shit there, do pick-ups and drop-offs. The only person I ever talked to there was my supplier. He's a guy called Tin Tin."

"Like the cartoon character?"

"I don't know his real name."

"Any other names I can follow up on? Nicknames, even?"

He started to shake his head, with a look of deep thought on his face. "The guy who wanted to bring me in, they call him Young King. I've never met him, though."

"Jamie—did Daphne tell you that you were being followed?" I paused and added, "By someone else, I mean. Latino guy in a white Audi."

"Yeah," he said, lowering his voice. "She mentioned that."

"Do you have any idea who he might be?"

"I wish I knew. I don't like it at all."

"Does anyone in that whole drug ring have any reason to be unhappy with you?"

"Not that I know of, no."

"Any reason to be unhappy with Tilley?"

"Oh," he said, turning pale. "I don't think so. As far as I know, Joe never met any of them. He had me for that. But do you think—I mean, I don't know many people who could murder a guy."

"But no reason to think any of these people would want to kill him." I sighed. "So okay, you got Tilley drugs for the party Thursday night. Did you invite the crowd?"

"No," he said. "I invited some of my friends, but I didn't know half the people there."

"How many people were there anyway?"

"I don't know. A hundred? I have no idea."

I shook my head. Not exactly a locked-room mystery. "Did Tilley have any enemies that you know of?"

He shrugged. "Probably. There were a lot of people who didn't like him. But I don't know of anyone who really *hated* him, you know? Who would want him dead so bad that they'd kill him?"

"Someone obviously did. We know he was murdered. Given that, do you have any educated guesses?"

He peeled at a white tag of skin on his lip. "See, that doesn't feel right."

"What do you mean?"

"Speculating about people I know, wondering if they might be murderers."

"I get where you're coming from," I said. "But look, plenty of people are speculating. Plenty of people think it was you."

He nodded and yanked the strip of skin from his lip. A drop of blood welled up in its place.

"Was there anyone at the party who might have wanted to hurt Tilley?" I continued.

He looked at the floor, and for a while I wondered if he'd even heard me. When he finally spoke it was in a guilty mumble. "His son was there," he said.

"His son?"

"Theodore. From his first marriage."

"How old is he?"

"Twenty-three? Twenty-four? Joe had him young. Married his high school sweetheart."

"How romantic," I said. "What was this kid doing at his dad's drug party? Was he invited?"

"Of course not. He found out about it. God knows how."

"Wait. Let's back up for a minute. What kind of weirdo kid tries to crash his dad's parties?"

"They don't have what you'd call a normal father-son relationship."

"Sure. Explain."

"Well, for one thing, I don't think Theodore's really lived with Joe since he was six or seven, when his parents got divorced."

I nodded. I was five when my dad died of liver cancer, and I knew a thing or two about father pangs.

"For another," he continued, "Joe has been very famous for most of Theodore's life. So think of what that might have been like. He knew his dad was absent, and he guessed, kind of correctly, that he had almost no interest in him. He also knew what his dad was up to, thanks to the hard work of the paparazzi."

"Did he not see him at all?"

"A few times a year. Pretty bad, considering. Theodore grew up in Calabasas and went to USC. I mean Joe traveled a lot, but still."

"Theodore grew up resentful?"

"You could say that. It's not like I've talked to him about it."

"Did Joe talk about his son?"

"Sometimes. When he was wasted, he'd talk about how guilty he felt."

"He has other kids, too, doesn't he?"

"Yeah, two daughters with his second wife. They're much younger, though."

"Do they have problems with him?"

"They're six and nine. I'm sure they'll have crazy issues in a few years, but my guess is that'll be because their dad was murdered, not because he abandoned them."

"How long did his second marriage last?"

"Eight years? A decent while, in Hollywood time."

"So for eight years, he lived with his new family with a neglected son twenty miles away."

"Yup."

"Do you know him?"

"Sort of. Not well. We've met a few times."

"Including the night Tilley died."

He nodded and pulled at his lip.

"What?" I asked.

"Huh?"

"You look like you have something else to say."

He hesitated. "To be honest, I don't like the guy. I feel a little bad for him that his dad treated him like shit, but he sure never handled his lot with any grace. And Joe might not have been at his soccer games or whatever but he gave him everything anyone could possibly want, stuff and money-wise."

"And?"

"He picked fights with Joe. It got ugly sometimes."

"And that night?"

He shrugged. "I didn't see anything, but I know they talked, and they almost never talk without getting into something. That kid is pretty dramatic."

"They argued, then? And hours later, Joe was murdered?"

"Yeah, I guess."

"Did you tell this to the police?"

"No," he said. "I don't like him, but I also wouldn't feel great accusing him of murdering his own dad."

"That's not how it works," I said. "The police want anything that could be relevant. When you're investigating something, you have to look at every possible clue, even ones of the mildest interest. You don't know what's going to pan out, and you have to sift through a lot of noise and bullshit, but if you don't do that, you get nothing. So this fight, it could be noise and bullshit, but it's more interesting than the average nugget."

He swallowed. "Okay."

"With that in mind, can you think of anything else that might be of interest? Any other enemies present?"

"Not that I know of, no. I'm sure not everyone there was a fan, though. Part of being famous is that people come to your parties even if they don't like you."

"What time did everyone leave?"

"Around three, three thirty." He pressed fingers into his eyelids. "After that, it was just me and Joe."

"What did you do after everyone else left? Did you go straight to bed?"

"No," he said. "We did a little coke and stayed up for a while, talking. He was upset about Theodore showing up."

"Did he seem scared, anxious, anything like that?"

"No. Just vaguely sad. We ended up spending more time talking about work stuff, the great movie we were going to make together." He smiled. "It was about fathers and sons, the soul of America, all that. It would've been great."

"Did he seem like he'd taken enough Rohypnol to knock him out at that point?"

"No, he was too alert."

"Did you go to bed before him?"

"Around five in the morning he said he was tired so he went to bed, I thought, and I passed out in my room. Next time I saw him, he was dead."

"You didn't hear anything?"

He shook his head. "I slept like a log."

"And as far as you know, you were the only two left, at that point."

He nodded.

"But it's not like you did a sweep, right? There could've been stragglers. In all likelihood, the murderer was in the penthouse while you guys were having your heart to heart."

A cold pallor came over his face, and his eyes contained a ghastly brightness. "What do you mean? I could have stopped him?"

"Oh, no, that is not what I was implying. Jesus, no, it wasn't your fault. What were you supposed to do anyway, to someone who got into a famous man's penthouse with the purpose of killing him?"

"But who could it have been? Song, as far as anyone knows, I was the only one around when he died."

"Well, it doesn't sound like you were the only person with opportunity. It sounds like about a hundred people had opportunity. Once they were in the party, it might not have been that hard to stick around somewhere." I drummed the table. "Even so, maybe you should line up a lawyer. Just in case."

When we left the office, the night was thick with a cold, watery dark. I pulled a cigarette from my purse and held it unlit while I started to say good night.

"Wait," said Daphne. "Have you eaten?"

"No," I said, suddenly hungry. "Have you?"

"I'm starving," she said, and Jamie nodded weakly. "Why don't we get dinner? We're not going to get anything done tonight, so let's try and make the best of it. At least I'm out here visiting, right?" She smiled faintly, not even trying to convince anyone. "You know anywhere good?"

I took them to Park's Barbeque on Vermont near Olympic, the southern end of Koreatown. It was a popular spot among Koreans and non-Koreans alike, where Daphne and Jamie wouldn't feel out of place.

It was after nine already, but the restaurant was busy, alive with chatter. We waited inside and scanned a wall of signed photographs of the owners posed with an impressive range of celebrities, both American and Korean, of several levels of fame. Most of them featured a smiling Korean woman about my mother's age, and I wondered if she had a good eye for famous faces, or if the less recognizable patrons piped up and offered themselves. I thought of Joe Tilley and his sad, suffering narcissism. I scanned the wall for his face and concluded he'd never eaten at Park's.

I caught Jamie studying the same pictures with a look of loss. He was about as hard to read as a Kabuki mask. I was relieved when our table was ready.

Our waiter spoke English, and we ordered three portions of *galbi*, thick strips of marinated short rib, a dish so iconic in Koreatown that Seoul restaurants had *L.A. galbi* on their menus.

"If you want anything to drink, we can get Hite," I said. "It's kind of like beery water, but it's good with the meat."

We got two tall cold bottles and three plastic cups. I was grateful for the liquid support. It was nice to be out on a Saturday night with people I liked, but as I struggled to find a neutral topic of conversation, I started to regret tagging along. I could have been at home now, pants off and under the covers, with a book and a glass in my hands. Instead I was socially engaged with two clients, one all but accused of murder. It wasn't exactly professional.

"So," I ventured, after a minute's silence, "I mean, Jamie, I've heard so much about you."

"Yes, I've gathered that." He laughed, and his laughter was surprised and mortified, but not devoid of humor. It broke some thin membranous strain in the air, like a finger pressed against a soap bubble. "I have no right to be upset about it, you know? So I'm glad it's all just out in the open now."

We grilled beef at our table and I gave them the rundown of *banchan*, the dozen side dishes to go with our meat and rice. I showed them which sauces to dip the *galbi* in, and when they showed interest, I even threw kimchi on the grill, a nifty trick I'd once heard described as a Korean secret. We ate well, and by the time we were done with dinner, we'd had a few beers each.

An hour later, we ended up at Gaam, a Koreatown lounge, drinking soju and smoking cigarettes while Korean pop blared above us. I hadn't been there in a while, but it had once been a hangout, before I lost my closest friends to death and betrayal. I remembered against my will my last drunken visit, a fun, rowdy night, just eight or nine months past. The nostalgia left a bitter taste, and I did my best to blow it out of my mind.

We shared one bottle of soju, and when it was time to order another or leave, we agreed to split one more, shrugs all around. I taught them a drinking game I used to play, and we took turns flicking the peeling coated aluminum of the green soju bottle cap until a long strip separated from the coil, a hot potato command to drink.

About an hour in, I started feeling good. The music sounded softer, and I looked at Daphne and Jamie with an overwhelming sense of kinship and benevolence.

I caught Jamie staring at me and said, "What?"

He smiled. "This is going to sound creepy," he said, "but I'm pretty sure we met, like before any of this happened."

I felt a sharp thrill of happiness, like he'd just paid me an enormous compliment I only half deserved. I hoped it didn't show in my face.

Daphne raised an eyebrow. I hadn't told her about the parking incident after all. "What's this about?" she asked with placid curiosity.

"On Rodney. I swooped in on your parking spot?"

The heat settled evenly on my cheeks, and I tried not to look too sheepish. "Yeah, that was me," I said. "I remember. Daphne, your boyfriend is a saint."

"I think you're using that word wrong," she said, smiling. "What did he do?"

I told the story and she looked at Jamie with an expression of mock admiration.

"Well, God knows you couldn't have a pretty girl walking around mad at you."

He laughed. "Oof, you've really got me figured out."

The tone was suddenly celebratory—we drank soju and ignored the terrible things that had brought us together.

"*Unni*," someone said. "*Unni!*"

It took me a few seconds to consider that the voice was calling me.

I turned around, and there was Lori, standing on high heels four feet behind me. She looked tired but overjoyed to see me, and it took me a startled second to notice the man at her side.

He wasn't Isaac. This man was older, between thirty and thirty-five, with coarse sun-worn skin and hair cropped close to disguise the retreat of his hairline. His features were distinctly Korean—thick eyelids, square jaw, flattish nose. A white scar cut across one black eyebrow. He was almost handsome, in a rugged way, but the sight of him repulsed me. This was Winfred, then, the un-wanted admirer, with one large hand claiming Lori by the waist.

I stood up, unsettled, and the outer layer of my buzz flaked off. "What're you doing here?"

"I'm here with my friend," she said. Her voice was soft and sunny but her eyes sought mine with purpose. She was relieved to see me, but she didn't want to show it. When I bent down to hug her, she clung to me, and I waited for her to whisper in my ear. She didn't.

"Hi," I said to the man, when Lori let me go. "I'm Song, Lori's roommate."

"Winfred," he said. He held a hand out for me to shake and almost crushed my fingers.

"Come join us." I motioned to our table. There were a few leather stools scattered nearby, and I started to gather them, hold-ing Lori and Winfred in the corner of my vision. He whispered something in her ear.

"Come on, *oppa*. I want you to meet my friends," she said.

The sweetness in her voice made me cringe. She called him *oppa*, the male equivalent of *unni*, an address for older brothers that turned disturbingly flirtatious when deployed outside of family.

Lori used to make a living pretending to like strange men. She worked in her mother's hostess bar just a half mile from Gaam, pouring drinks for men who paid for her company. She didn't sleep with them—they weren't even supposed to touch her—but she learned the prostitute's art of false enthusiasm, the shell of love where there was none to enclose. It was a handy skill, one she could use to get her way.

I asked Jamie and Daphne if they minded a little extra company, but they were drunk enough that they didn't mind the intrusion. I made introductions and we ordered two more bottles of soju.

"It's a party, then," I said. Lori sat close to me, her knees touching mine. Winfred clung close to her other side with a dark, sullen look in his eyes.

When I looked at Lori, she was staring at Daphne with evident admiration. "How do you know *unni*?" she asked.

Daphne blinked back with a polite smile. "Who?"

"Oh." Lori blushed. "Song, I guess."

"Let's see," said Daphne, putting a hand on Jamie's shoulder. "How do we know Song?"

The two of them fell into a shared fit of laughter.

"I know them through work," I said. I nodded at Daphne. "Is that about right?"

"Song's helping us sort some things out," she told Lori. "But let's not get into *that* mess. We're here to have fun tonight." She reached across the table, filled a shot glass to the brim, and handed it, sloshing over, to Lori.

Lori's eyes went big as Daphne motioned for her to down it.

I'd almost forgotten about Winfred until he said, with a lewd lilt, "Don't even act like you don't want it."

He was smiling now, a slight snarl that bore no teeth. I couldn't tell if he'd meant to be funny, and I was still studying his face when Daphne interrupted my train of thought.

"Wait, was that a joke?" she asked, turning the full force of her attention on the man. She wasn't shouting, but her voice pulsed at a level above the noise of the bar.

The smile dropped off his face, but he answered, "Yeah, so what?"

"It wasn't funny."

He rolled his eyes and took the shot glass out of Lori's hand, spilling half on the table and half down his throat.

"Daph," Jamie said. "Not now, huh?"

She gave him a sharp glare, but Jamie's face was so tired and beseeching that even I felt my heart soften. She let it go.

It was a strange night. No one was actually happy, and to cope with the large miseries hulking in our shadows, we let the soju flow. After another hour, you wouldn't know that we weren't celebrating. Even Winfred grew boisterous in a way that no longer made me flinch.

We stayed until closing and walked over to an even shadier bar with a long Korean name, none of it written in English. It was the kind of after-hours bar that only existed in Koreatown, serving booze long past two with no pretense at legality. The waiters stood ready to pack it all up at the first sign of cops—I'd seen it happen before, at other bars just like this one, all long since found out and closed for business.

I kept an eye on Lori and Winfred, and every now and then she found and squeezed my hand—an assurance that she was in control. Lori was a lightweight, but I could tell she was the most sober of all of us. She had ways of making alcohol disappear without actually ingesting it—another trick of the trade.

I wasn't the only one watching her, either. Winfred must have pinged Daphne's Spider-Sense. Her gaze flicked over to him and Lori every few minutes, like she was guarding both cat and canary. She shook her head when she saw me notice, and I felt a thrill of sisterhood.

Despite the tension, the night passed in a rather enjoyable blur, the shutter speed of my brain falling by the minute. At one point, we joined forces with a group of Korean boys, fellow voyagers stinking of tobacco and soju. The last thing I remembered was a stranger's tongue in my mouth, rolling around like a pig in mud. It felt good and I didn't mind him, though I didn't like him, either.

Six

❧

When I came to the next morning, I was lying under the covers with just my underwear on, a trash can right next to my bed. It was light out, and as soon as I moved my head, a world-class hangover throbbed against its walls. I closed my eyes and tried to fall back asleep, knowing I should at least get up to take a dose and a half of Advil.

And then I heard the deep, sleepy breaths coming from over my shoulder. As I turned to see who was there, my chest went tight with panic.

Relief took over right away. Lori lay on top of the covers, curled up in a kittenish ball, her rounded back turned away from me. I stroked her hair and got up to put on a T-shirt and administer to my headache.

She woke up when I thudded off the bed. "*Unni*," she said, her voice clouded with sleep. "Are you okay?"

"I feel like shit," I said. My throat rasped and my mouth tasted putrid. "How did we get home last night?"

"Do you not remember?"

"No," I said, deciding it was easier to speak than to shake my head.

"I drove."

"Were you okay to drive?"

"Easily," she said. "I had, like, two drinks all night."

"Smart girl. I had at least three."

She laughed. "Oh *unni*. You had at least three before I even got there."

"Did I get sick? I feel awful."

"You puked on the sidewalk, and you puked a lot more at home." She sat up and crossed her arms. "I held your hair and then I made you sleep on your side so you wouldn't die in the middle of the night."

"Thank you, Lori. You didn't have to sleep here. I've gotten sick before."

"Oh. I mean, your friends are still here. I let them sleep in my room," she said.

"Darling, you're almost *too* sweet," I said, rummaging for the bottle of Advil I kept on my dresser.

She got out of bed and left the room. When she came back, she was carrying a tall glass of water. "Drink it all."

"Thanks." I gulped and it hurt my head. My brain felt three sizes too big. "So, how'd you get rid of the creep?"

She twisted her mouth into a grimace. "I said I had to get you home."

"That was enough?"

"And Daphne helped me say so more forcefully."

I smiled. "Was I useless?"

"A little bit. I think you wanted to say something but you weren't really moving at that point."

"So, am I right in thinking you didn't love his company?"

She sighed. "I don't really know what to do about him."

"What was that yesterday, anyway? A date?"

"That's not how I was thinking about it."

"Did he ask you out for a drink?"

"Yeah."

"And you said yes?"

She chewed on her lip. "He asked me like right after we first met. I kind of skirted it, but then he kept texting me."

"He wore you down?"

"Not exactly," she said. "I talked to *samchun* about it."

"What did he say?"

"He said what he told me before. 'Be nice to him.' He just kept repeating that like it meant something until I finally asked if he wanted me to say yes to the drink. Then he practically begged me to go."

"That's fucked up," I said. "Winfred must have something on your uncle. Do you know what it is?"

She shook her head. "I don't know. Money?"

This seemed likely, now that I thought about it. Yujin Chung was being tried for murder. The stakes were about as high as they could get, and Taejin and Lori made the decision to hire the best lawyer they could. They sold Yujin's house, but it was entirely possible that that wasn't enough. Taejin lived in an apartment over his shop, and I guessed he had little in the way of valuable assets.

"You think he borrowed money from Winfred?"

"I don't know."

"Well," I said. "You don't have to cover his debts. That's his problem."

"His problems are mine. That's how family works."

Lori left for church and I went back to bed. When I woke up, the apartment smelled like coffee. Daphne handed me a cup as I stumbled out of my room.

"Lori said we could help ourselves. Hope you don't mind," she said.

"Of course not. Thank you." I sat down and pinched my brow. "Jamie still in bed?"

"Yeah."

"He do any better than me last night?"

"Just barely," she said, sighing. "But I think he had a good time."

"Listen, I'm sorry I got so sloppy. Unprofessional of me."

She laughed. First thing in the morning, her face unmade, and she looked like a skincare model. Marlowe had a line about women like her—he said he only knew four in his life who could throw back their heads laughing and still look beautiful. I remembered the line because it made me feel self-conscious about laughing for a while, back when I laughed often and gave a shit about such things.

"You kept saying 'Please don't tell Chaz. Please don't tell Chaz.'"

"Jesus Christ, really? I'm sorry."

"I don't care, Song. It's better this way anyway. We're friends now. All this stuff we have to deal with together? I'd rather you were my friend than a stone-cold professional."

The coffee warmed me, and it mingled with a surge of gratitude in my chest.

"Aw, shucks," I said.

"Don't worry, though. We'll still pay you." She twisted a lock of hair around one finger and tugged at it with a curious look on her face. "One question, though."

"Sure, shoot."

"Why didn't you say anything about meeting Jamie before?"

The grumpy, aching clouds in my head dispersed in a snap. I opened my mouth to say something defensive and closed it before I could say anything patently insincere. I gave her a guilty squint and smiled.

"I'm sorry about that," I said. "Honestly, if I thought it mattered, I would've mentioned it. Do you think it matters?"

"What, to the case at hand?"

"Yeah."

"No, obviously not. I was just wondering why you didn't mention it, since it's a pretty funny coincidence. We could've had a good laugh."

I sighed, rubbing at my eyes in bemused embarrassment. "Okay, sure, fine. Don't get mad, alright?"

She smiled and leaned back, folding her hands on the table. "Oh, I see."

"It was kind of a charming encounter, and I thought you might think it was weird I remembered his face after meeting him for just the one second." I panned my hand in a small voila gesture. "There it is—I thought your boyfriend was cute."

"Thought?" She was grinning now, with good humor and mischief in her eyes.

"Oh, come on," I said. "I think lots of people are cute. You're cute, I'm cute. That guy I made out with last night, I think he was cute, wasn't he?"

"He was. Not that it would've mattered."

We laughed, and for the moment, I felt remarkably at ease. My attraction to Jamie was a trivial thing, but it was apparent now that I'd been carrying it like a secret. There was release in putting it out there and finding it was nothing to worry about. I felt that much closer to Daphne, and in spite of the mess all around us, I found a measure of lightness and pleasure.

"That Winfred, though," she said, her voice suddenly dry. "Not so cute."

Her expression was somber now, and my humor dissipated with hers as I remembered the way he'd touched Lori. I rotated my coffee cup in my hands and stared into the slow swirl of liquid.

I didn't have time to respond. Jamie stumbled out of Lori's room with mussed hair and uneven steps, like he'd left one foot behind in sleep.

"Great, great, great," he said, half mumbling. "There's coffee."

I was about to say something about Winfred, but when I looked back at Daphne, there was a simple, cheery smile on her face. Whatever her thoughts were on Winfred, she didn't mean to share them in front of Jamie. I kept my mouth shut and wondered why. After all, Jamie had witnessed the same things we had—was it just a subject best kept between us girls?

Jamie helped himself to a cup of coffee and looked from me to Daphne with a quizzical tilt of the head. "Why so quiet all of a sudden? Were you guys talking about me?"

Daphne and I made eye contact and the silence dissolved into a new round of laughter, its minute, strained quality nearly forgotten.

It was eleven o'clock when the three of us took a cab back to Koreatown to pick up our cars. It dropped us off at Sixth and

Mariposa, where our cars had cooled on the street overnight. My hangover had more or less cleared up after a long shower, and I did my best to emit an aura of competence as we stood on the sidewalk and discussed our immediate plans.

"I'd like to talk to Theodore Tilley as soon as possible," I said to Jamie. "Do you know how I can get in touch with him?"

He thought for a moment and started fiddling with his phone.

"Ha," he said. "I thought I had his e-mail. He e-mails me once in a while to stalk his dad." He showed me the address on his phone.

"Thortilla?"

He rolled his eyes. "Thor Tilla. He gets upset if you say it like *tortilla.*"

"What's a Thor Tilla?"

"It's Theodore Tilley's stage name."

"Stage name?"

He smiled. "I hope you do get to meet him. I'll leave it at that."

"I guess the odds are good he's swamped or depressed. Both, probably."

"Yeah, I feel bad for him," he said, sounding chastised.

"I didn't mean to imply you didn't. I'm just wondering if I'll be able to get to him."

He bit down on a peeling part of his lower lip. "Don't tell him you're working for me. Be vague, maybe hint that you're connected to press and you're interested in hearing his story."

"You think that'll get him to talk to me?"

"Honestly, yeah. Like I said, I don't know him that well, but what I do know is that he's desperate for attention. I don't think that changes because his dad gets murdered. He might be grieving, but I'll be shocked if he passes up this chance for the lime-light out of some notion of class."

It was a damning portrait, but I hoped, rather selfishly, that it was on the mark.

"Try and relax today," I said as we parted. "I'm going to try and track down Theodore. I'll do my best to find out more about Tilley, with or without his help. In the meantime, you can always call me if you need anything. I'm also going to see if I can find you a decent lawyer."

"That bad, huh?"

"I don't know, but it can't hurt to line something up, can it?"

"She's right," Daphne put in, taking his hand. "We might as well be prepared."

We swapped hugs and agreed to meet at the office again the next day.

I sat in my car and sent off an e-mail to Tilley's son, with my phone number and a request that he get in touch as soon as possible. I told him I was an investigator interested in his father's murder—I kept it vague and suggestive, but there was no need to lie. I left enough room for him to draw his own conclusions, and I indicated that I was particularly interested in talking to him. If Jamie was right, my e-mail should have been enough to spark Theodore's interest. Then there was the other element, which Jamie had all but ignored. Theodore was the son of a murdered father, and he might be itching to talk to anyone who might give him information about an investigation. If he was the murderer, that was doubly true. Whether he'd see the e-mail anytime soon was another question. I imagined he had a lot on his mind.

I googled Thor Tilla and found a YouTube channel with a handful of videos with view counts ranging from four to six figures. The most popular one was a music video for a song called "Hollywood Pimp," and I watched the first thirty seconds with mild fascination. The production value was evidently high—nifty camera work, beautiful extras—but the song was terrible. Thor Tilla was on-screen in a low V-neck and flashy chains, rapping slowly about living the life of a celebrity. I looked for him on Wikipedia. He didn't have his own page, but he was mentioned in a note on Joe Tilley's, as part of his personal life. Theodore was a twenty-three-year-old USC grad pursuing a career in "musical performance and production." I found his Web site, his Twitter feed, and a pop-culture blog that covered every one of his music videos with snarky, explosive delight. His name never came up independent of his father's, but he had used that association to carve out his own shitty niche in the cultural consciousness.

And here I was, a nobody waiting to hear back from this tiny eminence. I waited with my head leaned back against the seat rest, my phone in hand, puzzling over my next move. Theodore Tilley might not even call today, and I didn't like being idle.

I dialed Jackie Diaz, the widow of my best friend, my college boyfriend, who'd been murdered for looking out for me, not a year earlier. When Diego was alive, she was wary of me, and there was no way she didn't blame me for his death. It was straightforward enough—if I had never been born, Diego would never have died trying to help me. I blamed myself, every day. It was a miracle she didn't hate me now. While Jackie would never call me her friend, there was a bond between us that calcified when we lost Diego. I never thought of her without a spike in emotional activity, of remorse and affection and longing.

She picked up. She always picked up when I called. "Song," she said. "How are you?"

The last time I saw her was in December, two days after her daughter was born. Cristina had Diego's dark eyes and even newborn, his curly black hair. I fell apart crying before I left the hospital, and Jackie and I hadn't tried to see each other since. I couldn't tell if she was happy to hear from me.

"Not bad," I said. "Work's been interesting."

"Is that a good thing?"

"Oh boy. " I let out a dry laugh. "I mean, no. I guess not. How are you? How's Cristina?"

"She keeps me up all night, so she's good and I'm tired." She sighed heavily, a sample of her exhaustion.

"Are you home now?"

"Yes. Always home."

"Can I stop by? I'll bring you lunch or something."

"Sure." I couldn't tell if she was deflated or just tired, but her voice sagged. "I'd like that."

Half an hour later I was at her place on Kings Road with two turkey sandwiches in a take-out bag.

Jackie came to the door with a finger to her lips. Her face looked pale and unrested, but she smiled when she saw me. "She's sleeping," she said quietly. There was a note of mischief in her voice, as if she were getting away with something, as if I might help her.

She'd lost weight since I'd seen her last. It didn't surprise me—even nine months pregnant, she'd made a point of hitting the gym. She'd gained the recommended amount of baby weight and not a pound more, and now she was almost thin and insubstantial, the fatigue fuming off of her like cold air from a ghost.

I'd dropped by like this on the day Diego died, and I still

thought sometimes that he must be coming back. Jackie had installed a nursery, but otherwise, the apartment was unchanged. She could have moved easily—she didn't. She slept in the bed they'd shared, with the same art on the walls. Even his clothes stayed hanging in the closet.

He haunted the place, but only in whiffs until the baby came along. I wondered what that was like for Jackie, spending every minute attending to the child Diego had left behind. I wasn't brave enough to ask.

The baby gave us plenty of material for small talk as we ate lunch. Jackie told me about her nursing schedule, and about the stream of friends and family who had come to help out and visit. When we were done eating, she asked about my job.

"Actually, that's why I'm here." I knew as soon as I said it that this was a half-truth. I also knew that I needed it to feel comfortable. "I need a lawyer."

With Diego gone, Jackie was the one attorney I knew. She worked for the ACLU, and I thought chances were good she might know a decent criminal defense lawyer. "Oh no," she said. "Why?"

"I have a client who's in a bit of trouble. He's being investigated by the police and it might just be a matter of time before he's arrested."

"For what?"

"Murder." I took a sip of water and mumbled into the glass. "For what it's worth, I think he's innocent."

"Murder? How?"

"It's a long story," I said. "I shouldn't get into it."

"Is everything all right with you?" She gave me a hard look, and I strained under it like a pinned bug.

"Yeah. It's fine. It's just work."

"I can give you a couple names and numbers," she said. And just like that, her phone was out and she was sending me an e-mail. My phone made a little noise and I forwarded the message to Jamie and Daphne with a short note.

"Thanks," I said. "I'll make you coffee or something."

"Are you saying I look tired?"

I shrugged, and she smiled.

"I'm about to collapse, honestly, but the coffee won't help."

"Why not?"

"Because it's some decaf organic crap that won't make me a bad mother."

"Do you want some anyway? Maybe you'll get a little placebo effect."

I made us coffee and we sat in companionable silence scattered with languid plops of conversation. At one point, she fell asleep, her lips parted and her neck bent back. When the baby started to cry, she jolted awake with a flustered, snuffling sound.

"I can hold her or something if you want," I said. "You look pretty comfortable."

"No. It's okay." She stood up with an athletic burst I hadn't expected. There was a knee-jerk defensiveness to her reaction that seemed to freeze the room. She felt it, and so added, "She won't shut up unless I go to her. But you can say hi."

I followed Jackie into the infant's lair, where Cristina lay on her back, mewling in her crib. She'd grown, of course, but she looked, as ever, like Diego's child. The thought of him filled me with the familiar sadness, and I wondered if I had any right to touch Cristina, this girl who would grow up fatherless as a direct result of my actions.

"She got bigger," I said stupidly.

"Doctor says she's twenty-fifth percentile in height, seventy-fifth percentile in weight."

I wiped a tear from the side of my eye and smiled. "Babies are supposed to be fat."

"I don't know," she said, with a mock grimace. "What kind were you?"

"I was skinny and I looked mean. No one thought I was cute."

She laughed and paced around the room, patting Cristina on the back. When the baby fell back asleep, I gave Jackie a hug and left.

Seven

❧

I jogged my phone to check the time and found a text message waiting on my screen. "Yo its thor. Can u talk?"

I texted him back immediately, and was gratified to find he was more or less waiting by his phone. He was home, he said, and told me to swing by. He gave me an address on the Venice Beach boardwalk. He didn't ask a single question.

I drove across town with swift purpose, skimming through light, scattered Sunday traffic. It took a good half hour anyway, and I kept the radio off and plowed into thought. I spent most of the ride feeling sorry for Theodore Tilley. Over six months had passed since my best friend was murdered, and there wasn't a day that went by without the pain of that loss squeezing me for breath. Theodore and his father may not have been close, but the shock and injustice of murder tended to amplify grief. I knew I had no words to console him, but I practiced them anyway. I even teared up for a bit, but I got my sympathies under control by the time I made it to the beach.

Back in the day, Venice Beach earned the slick name of the "Slum by the Sea," and I always thought of that phrase whenever I came through. It wasn't a slum anymore, but it wasn't exactly a sparkling beach town. The Boardwalk was its most salient landmark, a crowded, colorful stripe of pathway just inches from sand and ocean. It was an institution of sorts, an eccentric cultural center characterized by the so-called "street"—street artists, street performers, and street ballers all found their stations amid the cheerful grime and noise of the Westside's dingy promenade.

I parked in a public lot and walked through a dense portion of boardwalk to get to Theodore Tilley's address. Venice was a long, arduous drive from Echo Park, and I realized I hadn't come anywhere near a beach in a couple of years. I remembered the last time, a full day's outing with friends since departed. I tried, unsuccessfully, to put that out of my mind.

The ocean rolled beyond a smattering of surfers and Sunday beachgoers, a few of them glistening in swimsuits despite the chill of early March. I gazed out at the water, my thoughts reaching into the past, and almost tripped on an unsupervised toddler. His mother came running and yelled at the child in Spanish, sending an angry glance and a muttered string of language my way. I shook my head and walked on, looking straight ahead. The Boardwalk required concentration. Rollerbladers whooshed by, and pedestrians weaved in illogical directions. Artists and craft vendors sat on both sides of the path, building statues of sand and hocking jewelry made of soda-can tabs and seashells. A white man with dreadlocks rang a bell outside a pot dispensary, shouting, "The doctor is in!" I wondered how many of the people

I passed knew about the murder of Joe Tilley. I remembered when Michael Jackson died, sharing an elevator with a man I'd never know, who whistled the tune to "Billie Jean." In my direct dealing with Tilley's death, I'd almost forgotten that it was a public event. And now, as I prepared to meet his son, I thought about the millions of people who shared tiny shreds of that private grief.

It would have been nice for Jamie if Theodore Tilley were on the lam. Instead, he was smoking pot on the couch in his beachfront condo. He was wearing basketball shorts with nothing on top, and his six-pack seemed to smile at passersby. I stopped in front of his address and saw him through the glass wall, where he sat in full view of anyone bothering to look. I gathered that his address wasn't public, and that his face was not widely known. That would change if he was the perpetrator of the patricide of the year. He didn't look like a murderer, but he didn't look like the son of a newly murdered father either.

I dialed his number and saw him stare at the cell phone on one arm of his couch. He set his pipe down on a coffee table and reached for the phone.

"Yeah," he said.

"I'm right outside. Korean lady, blue button-down shirt."

I waved and he waved back. "One sec," he said.

He disappeared from view and when he came out he was wearing a ribbed black tank top that clung to his musculature. Better than nothing, anyway, for an interview in his bachelor pad.

"Hi," he said. "I'm Thor."

"Right, Thortilla."

"No, Thor Tilla. Like Ghostface Killah?"

"I'm Song," I said. "Nice to meet you."

Theodore Tilley was a handsome boy with none of the powerful magnetic quality of his father. He might have stood out in a bar, but he would have blended in with any assortment of good-looking faces. He had his dad's strong jaw and a nice pair of blue eyes rimmed dark with lashes. He was on the short side, about my height with the spike in his hair, and his biceps were stiff and wide as melons, inked up and down with hard-to-read words in terrible fonts.

"What's that say?" I asked about a prominent line of text on his right arm.

"*Dulce et decorum est,*" he said. "It's from one of my dad's movies. It's Latin."

"War movie?"

"Yeah, *The Trenches.* Did you see it? He only had a small part, actually."

"No."

"Wow, then how'd you know?"

I shrugged. "Lucky guess."

He led the way into the condo, which was much bigger than I'd thought from outside. It was a beautiful place, spacious and modern with enviable views. The décor was straight Crate&Barrel, and I had no doubt that an interior decorator was well paid for the job. The effect was somewhat dampened by the mess of dirty plates and discarded clothing strewn across floor and furniture. Everything reeked of weed.

He gestured toward the couch and I took a seat. I looked out at the pedestrians on the boardwalk and felt oddly self-conscious, like I was taking the stage. Still, it wasn't a bad place to see a man about a murder.

"Nice house," I said. "It's just you here?"

"Yeah. My dad gave it to me when I turned twenty-one."

"Not bad."

His eyes were red and they turned redder still before filling with tears. The change was sudden, but I'd been too eager to miss the signs of grief before.

"I'm sorry about your dad," I said, feeling somewhat chastised. "Why are you alone here? Where's your mom?"

"She's coming. I couldn't reach her until yesterday, and she's coming from Thailand, so . . ."

"Do you have friends coming by?"

"I'm okay. I got girls in and out." He picked up his pipe. "Do you want some?"

"No, but do you mind if I smoke a cigarette?"

"Sure."

We lit up and sat for a while, smoking in silence. The weed visibly relaxed him, and he sat slumped against the couch, looking blank and a little bit dazed.

"How are you holding up?" I asked after a while.

He shrugged. "My dad got whacked, so . . ."

"Were you close?"

"Yeah, we were close. I'm his only son, what do you think?" He spoke rapidly, with a bit of an edge, and I saw him hear his own voice before breaking into a weird guffaw. "Maybe 'close' isn't right."

"But you loved him."

"Worshipped, is more like it."

"I wish I had a dad," I said. "I was so young when mine died, I barely remember him. I can picture his face, but it's this static face, and I'm pretty sure I nabbed it from a photo."

I hadn't longed for a father since I was pretty young, but I had enough true sentiment to magnify into common ground.

"Half the time I think about my dad, I see him as one of his

characters, or I put him in clothes he was wearing in a magazine."
He shook his head. "It's messed up, but I'm pretty sure he didn't
think about me."

My knee-jerk thought was to tell him that wasn't true, but I
kept my mouth shut. Jamie had conceded that Joe was a terrible
father, and I saw that what Theodore said was possible, and that
I had no grounds to refute it.

"How well did you know him?" I asked instead.

"Better than you did, probably."

"What was he like?"

"Want to hear my favorite story?"

"Sure."

"He took me to Disneyland for my eighth birthday. It was
one of the happiest days of my life. We rode everything I wanted,
and he let me hold his hand. I hadn't seen him in a while. Don't
know how long, but I feel like I must've been younger. 'Cause
this was the first time I noticed how people stared at him."

"When did you figure out your dad was famous?"

"Before, I guess, but I didn't know what that meant. But that
Disneyland day, I saw everyone looking at us, and I remember
feeling really proud, like everyone was at Disneyland to see us or
something. Goofy asked for his autograph, and all the princesses
smiled at us."

"I'm sure that made an impression."

"Yeah, no shit. My dad was more famous than Mickey Mouse.
We didn't wait in any lines, and I strutted around that theme park
all day. But then he met this lady," he said. "She was gorgeous,
even prettier than the princesses."

"Ah," I said. "What happened?"

"Dad was buying me a Goofy hat, and there were these three
women trying on Minnie ears nearby. At the time I thought they

were real adults but I bet they were twenty-two, tops. They were giggling and taking pictures, and at some point they noticed my dad and stopped talking. He walked over and started talking to them, and after a minute I could tell he was just talking to the blond one." He shook his head and continued. "And then he came over to me and said he was going to ride Splash Mountain with the nice lady, and that the other nice ladies would buy me ice cream. I looked over and saw the blond one talking to her friends. One was giggling and the other one was rolling her eyes."

"Your dad really left you with them? To ride Splash Mountain?"

"Yup. They got me a Mickey Mouse ice cream sandwich and it was so cold it made my lip bleed. And I cried and made a scene at the ice cream cart."

"How long were you with them?"

"I don't know. A long time, it seemed like. It takes a while to ride Splash Mountain."

His tone suggested a euphemism, and I didn't ask.

"But he came back, and everything was perfect again. I still remember that day as one of the highlights of my childhood." He took another hit off his pipe and smiled with a wistful glint in his eye.

"How about more recently?"

"What?"

"Tell me about your dad as you know him now. It's been fifteen years since you were eight."

"Now?"

He gave me a confused look and I could tell he was gearing up to point out that his father was dead.

"I mean until Friday."

"He was Joe Tilley. He was a movie star. Everyone loved him.

He had a scandal here and there. He went to Haiti for a few days when there was that earthquake."

I didn't feel like correcting him. "I don't need his tabloid dossier. I mean what was he like to you? As a man and a father?"

He closed one of his eyes halfway and looked up at me without a hint of recognition. "I guess he was pretty shitty." He laughed. "Hey that's a sweet rhyme."

"Shitty how?"

He shrugged. "He wasn't much of a father. He was shooting during my high school graduation, I guess, but for my college graduation he didn't even make an excuse. He said he'd come and then he straight-up just didn't come."

"When did you see him, then?"

"When he felt guilty enough. My birthday's in April, and sometimes he'd call me up in June and take me to lunch or something, talk about making it up to me. But he never did, so . . ."

"You partied with him, though?"

"Not really."

"Wanted to?"

His face turned red. "He had these legendary parties once in a while. Filled with drugs and famous people and beautiful girls. I was never invited, but I have friends, you know, who are famous. I went to Julian Lillywhite's bar mitzvah. You know, lead singer of The Mooninites?"

I shook my head.

"Anyway, we're still sort of friends, but he's also friends with my dad now. Not close friends or anything, but they're in the same circle."

"So he kept you in the loop?"

"Yeah."

"And he told you about this party Friday?"

"Yeah."

"And you went, I heard."

He stiffened. "Who from?"

"Jamie Landon."

I realized as I said the name that Theodore hadn't asked me who had hired me. He seemed, now that I thought about it, oddly incurious about my mission.

His shoulders relaxed, but his mouth formed into a scowl. "Oh, that guy."

"What about him?"

"I just don't like that guy. He's a smug asshole, and I never trusted him. And now, look, my dad is dead."

"You think Jamie did it?"

"You're the investigator. What do you think?"

He looked at me with a pressing eagerness in his clouded eyes.

"It's too early to say," I muttered.

"Well, give me a reason, and I'll go knock that guy's lights out."

"So what happened at this party?"

"What have you heard?"

"Not much," I said.

"Who else have you talked to?"

There was a mounting agitation in his voice that was starting to make me nervous. I decided to test him for a tender spot.

"I talked to Jamie, and I talked to the police."

His eyes widened, clearing and coming fully awake. "What about?"

I shrugged. I had no reason to disclose that I was working on Jamie's behalf, much less that I saw his father's dead body. "This and that, just getting information."

He scratched one eyebrow, covering his face with his moving hand. "Did they say anything about me?"

I searched my memory for any mention of his name in my interview with Detective Sanchez. Nothing came up, but I didn't need to tell him so right away.

"Why?" I asked.

"It's nothing."

"Sure it is."

We sat in silence for a while, and I stared at him openly while his face grew queasy with unease. I felt kind of guilty when it crumbled and he started to cry.

"We had a fight," he said. "It was fucking awful and now he's dead, and I can't make it right."

"I'm sorry. What happened?"

"I showed up at the party, hung out with Julian and a few other people I'd met before. I didn't want to go talk to him right away. I knew he might not like me being there, so I just hung out for a bit."

"Was this your first time at one of these things?"

He nodded. "Yeah, actually. I never managed to get in before. Isn't that crazy? My dad threw all these parties where most of the guests were closer to my age than his, and he didn't once think to invite me?"

"Not that crazy if you think about it. It sounds like they were drug-fueled ragers. Not exactly kid friendly."

"I would've felt better about it, you know, if I thought he was excluding me out of concern. But I'm pretty sure he wasn't excluding me intentionally at all. I think he just forgot I existed most days."

Again, I thought of the usual platitudes about all parents loving their children and blah, blah, blah, but what good were platitudes in the face of lived experience?

"And if he'd thought about it for one second," he continued, "he would have figured out how much it would mean to me if I could be one of the hundred or so people partying in his penthouse."

"You'd asked him, too, hadn't you?"

"Yeah."

"And he said what?"

"Usually he just ignored me. It's not like I saw him in person too often. When I cornered him he'd say something about it being 'weird' to have his kid around."

"Maybe you made him feel old."

He snorted. "If I made him feel old it's 'cause he was old."

Joe Tilley was between Chaz and my mom in age. I tried to picture them partying with Lori and her friends, dressed in flashy duds in some glamorous room. The image almost made me laugh.

"So, tell me about this fight," I said instead.

"The police didn't mention it, huh?"

I nodded.

"I'll tell it to you straight. I know there were people who overheard the fight, and I don't want anyone getting any ideas. If you're running a story or whatever you can say you got the straight dope from me. Okay?"

"Sure."

He took a deep breath and looked at his pipe before turning to me with an earnest sheen of suffering in his eyes.

"I was talking to this girl, a model. We were hitting it off, kind of, though now that I think about it I guess she was only interested 'cause she figured out who I was. Anyway, I was talking to her, and then my dad came barging in the room. He cut in and started talking to her, 100-percent cold-shoulder ignoring me. There was no way he didn't see me. I know he didn't give two shits about me, but I wasn't, like, straight-up invisible."

"Jesus."

"He was trying to get me to leave. He wanted me gone, and that was how he decided to try and make that happen. I was so mad I almost did leave, but I didn't want to give him the satisfaction."

"So what'd you do instead?"

He rubbed his eyes vigorously, and spoke while they were hidden. "I shoved him. Hard. He stumbled and almost knocked the model right over."

He paused, and I waited a minute for him to continue before nudging him on. "Is that it?"

"No," he said, breathing heavily. "He turned around and slapped me across the face. In front of everyone."

I winced. That was a tough last memory to carry of anyone, let alone someone who should've been biologically programmed with a measure of parental love.

"He got in my face and told me to get out of his house, like we weren't in a fucking hotel room. I spat on the floor and said he'd be sorry."

"You said it like that? Like, 'You'll be sorry'?"

"I said, 'One of these days, you'll be sorry.'"

He was trembling, and I understood, now, why he'd been eager to talk to me. He'd had something to confess, and he'd been waiting, behind the transparent walls of his house, for a confessor to come and find him.

"Honestly"—he sniffled—"I know the word is he was murdered, but I can't help thinking he killed himself. Maybe it was all my fault."

"The police haven't asked you any questions?"

"No." He shook his head broadly and looked at me with wide eyes pumped full of something like innocence. "Why?"

*   *   *

The interview petered out after that, and I left Theodore's house without coming to any solid conclusions. The conversation had been illuminating in a lot of ways, but if he had any real information to give, he'd certainly kept that light under a bushel. As I drifted back across the peopled canal of the Boardwalk, my head swam with a turbulent blend of pity and suspicion for the murdered man's son. I had to wonder why the police seemed to favor Jamie when there was a more obvious suspect to clear, and I debated whether to give Detective Sanchez a call. I got in my car and called Jamie instead.

"They had an actual fight?" he asked after I shared my report. "The night of the party?"

"That's what he said."

"It's that fucking kid. He fucking did it." He was amped up, and though the same thought was skipping across my mind, his enthusiasm caught me off guard.

"Why the sudden change? You already knew they argued."

"Yeah, I know, but I've been thinking about it ever since we talked, and it just makes sense. And man, I didn't know it got physical. That's another level."

"He seems to think *you're* the most likely suspect. Though he also mumbled something about suicide, so maybe he hasn't quite picked a theory. He seemed pretty confused."

"Or maybe he was trying to confuse you."

"I have to say, he was pretty forthcoming, as things go. It was almost surreal."

"He was probing you because you talked to the cops. Not a bad move for that doofus."

"Come on, there's no need for that. His dad was just murdered."

"Yeah—by him, probably."

I could almost hear him pacing. "Hey, calm down, man. We don't know that."

"Fine, fine, fine. But look, someone killed him. If I had to pick a favorite, I'd go with Thor." He paused. "Did he tell you he has a standing relationship with every gossip rag in the country? Did he volunteer that?"

"No, but you already said he'd talk to me if he thought I might be press."

"It's extreme, though. He would ask Joe to lunch, and the paparazzi would show up. It's why Joe stopped seeing him."

I was almost embarrassed by how pathetic that sounded, but I remembered Thor Tilla's videos and thought he must not embarrass too easily. Still, it was hard not to feel bad for him.

"Look, I'm not defending that or anything, but it sounds like Joe stopped seeing him in any meaningful sense when he was eight years old." I caught the rebuke in my voice and filtered it out. "I mean, I'm sorry your friend died, but pretending he was any better than he was is just not going to help us find his killer."

He was silent, and in that interval, with some relief, I decided on my next move.

"I was thinking of making my way over to Los Feliz," I said. "I want to talk to his wife."

"Willow?" There was a note of alarm in his voice. "I know spouses are always suspect, but—"

"Not because I think she killed him, Jamie. I'm just assuming she knows more about him than most."

"Right," he said, the "t" lost in a falling sigh.

"Maybe she'll have more insight on Theodore, and either way, I'll be surprised if she has literally nothing to contribute."

There was a pause on the other end of the line. I thought I could hear him sawing dead skin off his lip with his teeth. "Do you want me to call her and set it up?"

It only occurred to me that moment how hard it might be to access Tilley's widow without some sort of in. "Oh, sure, yeah, that'd be great. You're friends?"

"Yeah, sort of. Call you back in five minutes."

What I knew about Willow Hemingway, I'd gathered from the Internet, pulling facts and credible gossip to form a mental file. Though most notable for her marriage to a newly deceased A-list actor, she was moderately famous in her own right. At thirty-two-years old, she had a long career behind her. She started out as a teenaged model, then acted in soaps, picking up minor spots on sitcoms and crime shows here and there. At twenty-three, she landed a regular supporting role on a teen drama that was popular when I was in high school. That was the pinnacle of her acting career. Over the next several years, she collected a small number of credits, and when she was twenty-nine, she married Tilley, who was sixteen years her senior. As far as I could tell, she stopped acting after the wedding, but her prominent marriage saved her name from obscurity.

Jamie called back with a gate code and an all clear. Willow was at home, and she'd agreed to see me. Forty minutes later I was outside of her house, smoking a cigarette and watching the scene. A hundred other people had had the same idea, and I was grateful that Jamie had covered my lapse of foresight. For as long as Tilley's death was news, Willow Hemingway was the most famous actress in America.

I walked down the street with my hands in my pockets, and

got past several parked cars before a murmur rose behind me. By the time I'd reached the gate, car doors were opening and equipment shifting, and a few people asked who I was. I ignored them, feeling heat rise to my head, and covered the keypad while I pressed in the code. The gate gave a rattling buzz and the background noise rose to a flashing, shouting frenzy. Somebody touched my arm and I swatted away a meaty hand, its knuckles matted with dark hair. I walked into the driveway without turning around.

I rang the doorbell, and after half a minute, I heard the muffled metal sound of a turning lock. The door opened just enough to let me know it could be pushed, not a crack of visibility for the photographers waiting outside.

I slipped through the narrowest entrance I could manage. Willow Hemingway was waiting ten feet inside, watching me with a dull curiosity in her eyes.

"You're Jamie's friend," she said, her voice flat and raspy.

I nodded and tried not to stare.

She was a beautiful woman, her features so smoothly unimpeachable I would have believed they were computer generated. She was a blond, of course, and she had the kind of wide blue eyes that occupied billboards across the world. Her nose was small with a sharp, thin-skinned bulb; full lips pouted over a dainty chin, slightly dented in the middle like soft fruit pressed by a thumb. I might have seen her face in a magazine when I was young and felt ugly and inadequate with my small dun eyes, my dark lank hair.

At this moment, her looks were compromised, though not by much. Her skin was stretched and her eyes shot red with the residues of an angry cry. She wore makeup, but only a little—only to camouflage, unsuccessfully, these very effects. A black silk robe hung on her fragile frame. Even with its soft shimmer and its short hem, it had a rumpled blasé look, the millionaire actress's equivalent of sweatpants.

"Come in," she said, and led me out of the foyer.

The house was magnificent and overstated, far enough over the top to veer back toward tasteless. Chandeliers dripped from high ceilings, and a winding marble staircase climbed toward a glazed atrium. Every piece of wall displayed either some tapestry or painting or mounted pottery, or a framed portrait of Joe or Willow. The number of these was astonishing, and in most other situations, it would have taken some effort to suppress a laugh.

I followed her to a living room where she installed herself on an oversize couch draped in brocade. She indicated the other side with a panning motion, and I sat down.

"Who are you supposed to be, exactly?" she said, the question delivered without rising intonation.

"You talked to Jamie, right?"

"He said you were working for him, and that I should see you to help him, but why?"

"Jamie's the—" I closed my mouth and started again. "What have you been told about your husband's death, Ms. Hemingway?"

"Just call me Willow, please. Don't make me sound so dusty."

"Any relation, by the way?"

"To Papa?" She floated a smile that was meant to be ambiguous. "There's some relation, but it isn't clear where."

"So what have you been told?"

"Something about my great-uncle, a bad marriage maybe."

"Sorry," I said, a little embarrassed. "About the other thing."

She sighed and pulled at a handful of her hair. "Not a lot. The police officer in charge of the case is this fat dykey chick. I think she hates me."

I was tempted to say I wondered why, but I held my tongue. "Have they mentioned anything about foul play?"

"They've danced around it. Maybe they think I killed him. They'd *love* that." She nodded toward the front of the house, where reporters and paparazzi buzzed in squirmy discontent. "They'd call me the Black Widow. I'd look amazing on trial."

I didn't doubt it. "So Jamie—"

"Yeah, so what's the deal? Why is he in trouble?"

"Well if Joe was murdered, it looks like Jamie's the favorite suspect."

She rubbed one eye with a sharp knuckle and laughed. "Jamie! Murder Joe!"

"I work for a private detective. Jamie hired me to find out what really happened."

I watched her, to see if she would pale or tremble. If I wanted to clear Jamie, I needed some alternate suspects, and she was a more likely candidate than the average chump on the street. She didn't flinch, though it occurred to me, almost reflexively, that she was an actress.

"Poor Jamie," she said.

"Do you know him well?" I asked.

"Pretty well. He comes here often, and he's always so sweet and helpful."

I wondered whether there was a flirtation between them. Jamie was good-looking, even next to Joe, and he was closer to Willow's age. I kept the wondering to myself.

"I'm sure he appreciates you seeing me. As do I. It must be a tough time for you." I paused and tried to sound sincere, even though the feeling was there. "I'm sorry for your loss."

She nodded. "It's been hard. Joe was an asshole, but he was still my husband. I can't believe I don't even get to yell at him anymore. If someone really killed him, though, I'm sure he had a good reason. Fucking Joe. I wonder what he did this time."

A cigarette appeared out of some fold in her robe, and she lit it with a silver lighter. I thought about going for one of the Lucky Strikes tucked away in my purse, and decided against it.

"I understand he had a rocky relationship with his son Theodore."

Willow was not quite ten years older than her stepson, and I doubted they knew each other very well. I was genuinely curious to hear what she had to say about him.

"Oh that poor child," she said. "Believe me, I told Joe he should be nicer to him. But it's not *all* Joe's fault. Theodore's mom is such a damn space cadet, how else was he supposed to turn out?"

"What do you mean? How did he turn out?"

I sat at attention, half expecting to hear about school expulsions, a troubling history of violence.

"I just mean he's such a"—making a megaphone out of one hand and whispering across her thumb—"*loser.*"

"Do you think he could've . . ."

"What, killed Joe?"

"Yeah."

"Maybe," she said. "Better him than Jamie."

The way she said "better" struck me as particularly cold, but I realized I'd thought the same thing. Then again, I wasn't married to the dead man.

"I feel bad for him, but he was always a little shit."

"Do you know if he ever threatened your husband or anything like that?"

She shrugged. "Nothing like that that I know of. You know I only met the kid one time, right?"

I wondered how on earth she expected me to know that, but I didn't say so.

I watched the white smoke rise from the end of her cigarette and moved to another line of inquiry.

"Did he have any enemies?" I asked.

"Oh, tons, I'm sure."

"Any you know by name?"

She narrowed her eyes. "I probably know several, but it's hard to know who likes him and who hates him, even among his 'friends.'" She used air quotes there and rolled her eyes. "Comes with being famous, I guess. People hang around even if they wish you'd fall off a roof, or fade away."

"Joe had lots of these friends?"

"We both did. I still do, I guess. So many people have called or texted or written on my wall or whatever, and I'm sick of it. It's like—sure, maybe some of them mean well, but I don't even *know* most of these people. They're not concerned. They're curious. They want me to make them feel special. They're fame vultures."

I nodded and listened as she complained about her fame. She wanted me to know that she suffered, and there was a certain relish in her voice as she listed these woes. "But not Jamie?" I asked.

"No. Jamie's the real deal. He loved Joe. Which is why I know you're not going to turn around and vomit this conversation to *Us Weekly* or whoever's waiting for you outside."

"The party at The Roosevelt Thursday night—were you there?"

"Of course not. Joe didn't believe in inviting his *wife* to *parties*. I don't do blow anymore, and I'm not some chick he can go after and hook up with, either." She sighed heavily, her lips parted, pouty and thick. "Sometimes I wonder why he bothered to marry me."

"How did you meet?"

"We worked together. On *Hot Air*." She smirked. "Have you seen it?"

"No, sorry, I haven't."

"Terrible movie. Even I know that. Anyway, I played his side-kick. We got terrible reviews. People said we had no chemistry." She laughed bitterly, and I could picture her reading online message boards and getting very angry. "But we were great together offscreen. Joe romanced me, really did his best to sweep me off my feet. I was so flattered I fell in love with him. We got married after four months."

It was clear enough that the honeymoon didn't last, but I let her tell the rest of the story.

"He was so wonderful those first months. I've read the tabloids, I know what people say about me, but I was so in love with him. I hadn't been in love like that since I was in high school."

A film of tears formed over her dry red eyes.

"I'm sorry," I said.

"No." She sniffled and tilted her head to catch the one tear big enough to roll out, a wet bead that dispersed on a red fingernail. "I'm glad we had at least that. I'll try to remember at least that."

I nodded.

"The night he proposed, he had this party at this house with, like, thirty of his friends. We hadn't been dating that long, so I hadn't met a lot of them and I was just starstruck." She catalogued the guest list, and I recognized most of the names. "And they knew who *I* was, and it was just incredible. Then Joe opened this incredible champagne and, with everyone looking, he gave this incredible speech and got down on one knee. I didn't stand a chance."

"That sounds special," I said. "Did you know it was coming?"

"Not at all. I mean, it was stupid of me to say yes, but you know, *George Clooney* was there."

I almost smiled. "The key to any successful proposal."

"I'll never forget that night. No matter what he did after, Joe got that right."

I tried to picture a room filled with faces from movies, and I had to admit, I couldn't claim immunity to the disorienting vapors of fame. Talking to Joe Tilley's widow about her A-list dream life injected me with some strange, heady sense of self-importance. I didn't like it.

"So what happened after that?"

"We got married, and again—*everyone* was there. You can see my wedding photos if you look online. Some photog must have wedged himself in the bushes. We were trying to be discreet, you know? Anyway, after the honeymoon—we stayed in a castle in Bordeaux. After the honeymoon, things started going south."

She frowned, and her shoulders slumped in a crumbling way that said she'd had a drink or two since morning.

"There was this one night. We got in a fight because he flirted with a waitress while we were at dinner. He said I was being crazy, but he touched her hip. The far hip. So like, his arm had to go across her back. *That*, in front of your *new wife*, who's already way younger and more attractive than you—sorry, it's true though. Anyway, *that* is crazy. Ugh, sorry, this wasn't the point."

She dropped her head and raised her eyes, staring at a blown-up photograph of Joe hung up on the opposite wall. It was a good portrait, a close-up of his head and shoulders, taken when he was in his twenties. Next to it was a portrait of Willow, and motionless, silent, side by side on this wall, husband and wife were the same age and, suspended in that false dimension, they made a gorgeous couple.

"So after this fight, we're just sitting in bed. We've both been crying, and there's snot all over our covers. He's wearing this stupid fucking burgundy kimono with a dragon on it that I just— maybe I'll burn that thing or put it in a shrine now that he's dead. He loved that thing and it was so terrible. Anyway, there's snot all over that, just shining. And I don't even remember who says it first, but we agree that we've made a huge mistake."

She took a long smiling drag on her cigarette and released smoke with a dry, punching laugh.

"And then we stayed married. Because I don't even know. We were embarrassed? We made such a big deal out of everything. He proposed in front of George Clooney! And plus, I was Joe's third wife and he'd already gotten plenty of grief about that. Talk about red flags, right? Oh—you should talk to *her*. His ex. She hated Joe more than I ever did."

"He had two ex-wives, didn't he?"

"Yeah, but he married Flora Rae young and they parted on okay terms almost twenty years ago. She's like a Buddhist monk or something now. Bald head and everything. She lives in Taiwan or Thailand, one of those."

"So tell me about the other one. What's her name?"

Her mouth opened and her tongue showed gray and pink like something dying. "Abby Hart." There was snide disbelief in her tone. "You can read all about her on Google."

I almost laughed—the third wife was proud of the second wife's fame. I made a note to read tabloids on Joe Tilley and his ex-wife, who did sound familiar.

"Willow, I'm going to ask you something personal."

"Do you want to know who I'm fucking?"

I raised my eyebrows and put up my hands, then brought them back down again. "Yeah, I guess. I was planning to be more delicate about it, but yeah."

"That dyke cop asked me already," she said, rolling her eyes. "I'm not seeing anyone, and I guess I should count myself lucky for that."

I sat quietly for the next hour as she recounted her romantic history, her blue eyes probing mine whenever she dropped a full name. I was starting to get restless, and at a logical pause in the interview, I asked to use the restroom.

The guest bathroom was the size of my bedroom and much more opulent. The sink was a deep, tall bowl of veined black marble that received water with remarkable quiet when I washed my hands. Guest towels sat stacked in a ceramic tray, thick, mono-grammed things that were nonetheless meant to be disposable. The mirror on the wall was ripped out of the Evil Queen's bou-doir, a huge oval of glass with a heavy, ornate border. As I looked into it, I felt like a sloppy tourist who'd wandered into a fancy hotel just to relieve herself.

And then my eyes landed on the painting on the wall behind me. I whipped my head around with my hands still wet.

It was a large oil painting, covered in layers and layers of rich hot colors. Paint curled with the texture of rose petals, flame pet-als, and it ate up the canvas with small, hungry licks of vermillion and scarlet, blood orange and blood red. Four long black streaks cut across the lake of fire, diagonal gashes that revealed a neutral, outer-space black, an alternate dimension peeking in through portals rent by a hero's sword.

There was a violence to the painting that sent a chill of rec-

ognition up my spine, but it took me a paralyzed minute to recognize why.

My eyes found the signature in the bottom right corner. It was
black and almost illegible, but I made out a sharp L, four knife
strokes of a W.

I dried my hands methodically, gripping my palms together
until they almost hurt. I gave my knuckles a thorough crack and
looked back in the mirror until my face looked peaceful again.

When I went back out, Willow was lighting another cigarette,
and this time I asked if she minded if I joined her. She shrugged,
so I lit up and took a long pull.

"Nice bathroom," I said.

"Should be," she said. "You don't even want to know how
much it cost to remodel."

"I like that painting. The red one."

"That one?" She made a face like I'd mentioned seeing her
robe in a JC Penney catalog. "Joe had it from before we got married. Some young artist he basically sponsored. I think he paid
six figures for that dumb thing."

"Really," I said, and took a casual drag on my Lucky Strike.
"Who's the artist?"

"Something Waters. Latoya . . . Latisha . . . something like
that. Never amounted to anything, as far as I know." She ran her
nonsmoking hand through her long blond hair. "If you want to
see some real art, Joe has, like, a Rodin."

I started to demur politely and gathered up my purse.

"Had," she interrupted, her voice soft and dreamy. "I guess it's
all mine now."

Eight

❖

As I drove to the office, I felt the hot lump of a hunch turning and taking form in my stomach. It was a familiar feeling, dull-edged and vaguely sickening, and I tended to it carefully, the radio off, gripping my steering wheel in relative silence.

The office was empty when I arrived, and the light turned on with a yellow buzz as I sprinted to my desk.

I booted up the desktop and opened InvestiGate. It was a good tool, one we relied on, that we refrained, as a practice, from using on clients without cause. It wasn't courteous, and more to the point, it wasn't free. With it, though, I had access to the kind of information Philip Marlowe risked his life for a dozen times over. These days Google was pretty comprehensive for things like birthdays, addresses, little bits of information released into the wild of the Web, more often than not on purpose. But with InvestiGate, I could pry out the nuggets that wanted to stay hidden. I could plug in a name and learn employment information, criminal history. Even changes in identity.

Daphne had given me no reason to distrust her. I liked her more than most of the people I knew, and she'd been fully cooperative the entire time we'd been working together. But the painting in Joe Tilley's house might have been torn from her portfolio. There was too much similarity there to ignore, and too little else, so far, to go asking strange questions.

I typed Daphne Freamon's name into InvestiGate and ran a background check. I'd done it before, on people I'd never met, found things their closest friends would never know. This—using this tool on Daphne—was an invasion. It was worse than reading her diary, the facts of her life displayed without her participation, exhumed without her knowledge. I hoped I would find nothing important, that I could tell her about my crazy suspicion and my breach of trust, one future night, drinking confessional wine. I held that hope for a precious twenty seconds.

Lanya Waters was born in Watts, at the southernmost tip of Los Angeles, when her mother, Tatiana, was twenty years old. Her father was unknown. When she was five, her mother married a man named Rudy Roberts, who died when Lanya was nineteen. Rudy and Tatiana had two sons, Colson and Samuel. Both boys were now in their early twenties.

When she was in sixth grade, Lanya showed up at school with bruises on her neck, prompting a home visit from a social worker that generated an incident report. The report was skimpy, and there was no follow-up.

After high school, Lanya moved to Hollywood, where she

waited tables and obtained a SAG card. It was hard to say how many young women in L.A. shared that profile at any given time. Between the ages of sixteen and twenty-two, she worked at bars and restaurants at every level of service. There was some advancement in her service career—by its abrupt end, she was the hostess at a trendy restaurant in Beverly Hills. Her acting career saw less motion. Her employment records showed a couple short gigs—a TV commercial, a photo shoot with a stock-photo company, and one for a print ad.

And then, one day, she sold a painting to an anonymous collector. Its title was listed as *Beware Beware*, and it sold for a cold one million American dollars.

Shortly after, she changed her name and moved to New York, where Daphne Freamon launched her own artistic career. Five years later, her boyfriend was working for Joe Tilley, and within months, the man was dead.

It took me an hour to cull through all the information, to piece together the story of Daphne's life from mismatched patches of fabric, many of them torn and holey. I opened a window and smoked a chain of cigarettes. I thought about checking Arturo's and Chaz's offices for liquor, but I knew I'd get in trouble even if I did find something to drink.

That Daphne had lied to me was clear enough—if not directly, then certainly by omission. She lied, in that passive, comprehensive way, to just about everyone who came across her. Her Web site offered a false biography, complete with made-up credentials she must have used in her career.

I googled Lanya Waters and found a lot of noise, with no likely matches for Daphne. The name was more common than I would have guessed, and it looked like she'd met little success as an actress. There was no hint of employment beyond what I'd found in her records, no IMDb page. She had the Internet presence of a young person who came of age right before overexposure became the norm.

It was remarkable how little trace there was of the sale of her painting. An unknown twenty-two-year-old artist made a million-dollar sale, and somehow, this escaped public notice. Even with the buyer's identity suppressed, this stretched credulity. If I hadn't seen it an hour earlier, I would've had a hard time believing the painting ever existed.

Searching both of her names together yielded nothing—her change in identity was unacknowledged in the public sphere.

Maybe Jamie knew. I couldn't decide whether it was better if he did.

I shifted in my chair and reread everything three times. It was starting to hurt my head. I was about to call Chaz when my phone rang. I jumped like I'd been caught with my pants down.

It was a 323 number neither my phone nor I recognized, and on most other days, I would have let it go to voice mail. But alone with my discoveries, everything around me felt heightened and prickly with potential importance, so I picked up.

"Juniper Song?" The voice was female, clear and stern as a schoolteacher's, one with God on her side.

"Yep," I said, sitting straighter. "Sorry, who is this?"

"It's Veronica Sanchez."

"Ah," I said. "How're you doing?"

"Good. I was wondering if you had anything to report."

"Why? Should I?"

"Sounds like you do."

A large part of me felt the draw of her invitation, and I knew it would feel good to hand everything over to this law-enforcement professional. What did I owe to Daphne, after all? She was my client and friend, but she was a proven liar, capable to a frightening degree. I didn't trust her, and she clearly didn't trust me. How much loyalty could she expect from a friend she wouldn't trust with her own name?

But maybe I owed her this much—to resolve these discrepancies between us first of all, to keep cops out of a crisis that could just be personal.

"Nothing to report," I said. I massaged my temple with the heel of my hand.

"Well, I talked to Jamie Landon today, and he said you were working for him."

Her tone ticked me off. It was nonchalant in a phony way, calculated to put me on the defensive.

"That's true. I am. And he's free to talk about that as much as he wants."

"And what are you doing for him, exactly?"

"If he told you anything, I'm sure he told you that."

"You know, Juniper, we're on the same side here."

"Sure."

"I'm not out to put Jamie in jail. I'm after the truth. You seem like an upstanding citizen, more or less. I'm sure you'll help me out if you find anything worth reporting."

There was just the smallest hint of admonishment in her voice, like she was trying to extract guilty secrets from a child.

I made a vague humming sound that could be taken as assent.

"Do you know any Lanyas?" she asked.

I paused, and regretted it. "Should I?"

"Maybe." I could almost hear her shrug. "If you're any good at your job."

*　*　*

I called Chaz for advice when I got rid of Veronica, and he told me to stop by his house on my way home. Chaz lived in Van Nuys, which was farther from Koreatown than Echo Park, and in the opposite direction.

"How's your house on my way home from the office?" I asked.

"You come here, and then you go home, that's how." He chuckled, apparently pleased with himself. "It's up to you, girl, but I can't go out on a Sunday. Molly's making dinner."

I realized I was shaken enough that I wanted to see him, and I agreed to drive over, grunting my acquiescence. Sunday afternoon was disappearing into a quiet cast of gray, and I made the drive in twenty minutes through scanty traffic.

The Lindleys lived in a part of the valley that wasn't holding its breath to gentrify. Sherman Oaks bordered Van Nuys to the south, and it guarded that fence with disdainful jealousy, a haughty, superior neighbor. Pockets of Van Nuys seceded over time, choosing neighborhood names that were not Van Nuys, and thus increasing their property value.

The Lindley home was in the heart of Van Nuys, a four-bedroom house built in the fifties. Chaz and Molly had bought it in 1997 and they had no plans to leave. It was a nice house, with an old look that wasn't shabby, brick and stucco with an inviting front yard. Chaz approached landscaping as a hobby, and he'd planted an orange tree that made the house look like a picture.

I parked in the driveway and rang the doorbell. Molly came to the door and ushered me in. She was a plain woman with a sweet, doughy face that maintained the smoothness of youth. She had brittle dark blond hair that knotted easily, and she wore a Mickey Mouse sweatshirt over big faded jeans. Her eyes were small and kind, and they shone like marbles when she smiled. I could tell that she liked me—we'd only met a handful of times, but she approached me with a warmth that would have seemed exaggerated from a less earnest source. I had no doubt that Chaz had apprised her of my background, and that my very image filled her with pride in her charitable husband.

"Chaz is in the office," she said. "Go bother him. He's not busy."

I thanked her and found Chaz watching a talking dog video on YouTube with Opal, his younger daughter. Their laughter filled the house.

The office was one of the fourth bedrooms of the Lindley home, and it served every family purpose unmet in the rest of the house. Two desks held two computers, and the remainder of the space was given over to play space, covered in a disarray of toys. It looked like Opal and Ruby had built a fort with small blankets and stuffed animal bricks.

"That was fast." Chaz mussed his daughter's hair. "Opie, go play with your sister. We'll watch more later."

She gave me a shy, impish smile and dashed out of the room.

I sat down in the empty desk chair and Chaz closed the door.

"You need my help again?" he asked.

"Yeah. It's almost like this is my first solo case and a murder happened."

"I'm just giving you a hard time, Song." He reached over to pat my shoulder. He miscalculated the distance and had to bend in a diver's stance to tap me with his paw. "It is a little more complicated than advertised, I'll give you that. So what's going on now?"

I told him about the painting, and the call from Detective Sanchez. He stuck his head out like a turtle's while I talked, and when I was finished he pulled down on the loose skin around his mouth.

"Well you don't have to tell that cop a damn thing. She can do her own investigating. She probably has the same resources we do."

"I agree."

"But this definitely changes how you deal with your client."

I pinched the inner corners of my eyebrows. "So here's a question: Who is my client? Jamie or Daphne?"

"Good question. On paper? I guess it's Daphne."

"But I'm trying to keep Jamie out of jail, aren't I?"

"Because that's what Daphne wants you to do."

"I don't know if Jamie even knows."

"About any of it?"

"Yeah. I mean he's made no mention of any real connection between Daphne and Joe, and I don't know if you really share past identities with your significant other."

"Well, that would depend on the relationship."

"Sure," I said. "But I shouldn't assume, should I?"

"No, definitely do not assume."

"So, what do I do?"

"I guess you talk to Daphne."

"That's what I was thinking."

"Good girl. Good instincts." He reached forward and patted my shoulder again.

There was a knock on the door, and Chaz said to come in. Molly opened it and leaned against the wall with a solicitous smile.

"Sorry," she said. "Am I interrupting?"

"No," he said brightly. "Song just needed a little help."

She beamed at me and asked, "Would you like to stay for dinner? We're having mac and cheese, and there's enough for all of us and leftovers."

I started to object, but Chaz stopped me. "It's fine, Song. You should join us. Meant to have you over one of these days anyway."

The dining table only had four chairs, so Chaz brought one of the desk chairs over and sat in it himself. Opal and Ruby looked at me with overt interest and I smiled at them with what I hoped was friendly warmth. They were six and nine, and I didn't know how to talk to people under twenty.

Molly served me a full plate of mac and cheese with steamed broccoli, which I ate gratefully. I told her it was delicious.

"It's their favorite," she said.

"The girls'?" I asked.

"All three of them," she answered, and Chaz high-fived both of his daughters.

Molly asked me polite questions that were so carefully worded I knew Chaz had warned her not to pry. I tried to be extra sunny in my responses, but I was relieved when the conversation moved to the girls. I asked them about school, and they chattered enthusiastically. Opal was especially talkative.

During a lull in conversation, she looked right at me and asked, "Are you Chinese or Japanese?"

"Opal!" Molly dropped her fork. It clattered like a spun and falling coin, and her voice surged with dismay.

"It's okay, Molly." I laughed. "I'm Korean. But don't ask your classmates that. It might make them feel sad."

Opal toggled her gaze between me and her mother, and confusion built in her round eyes. "Why?"

"Because it isn't polite," said Molly.

Chaz let out a rumbling belly laugh.

Nine

Daphne was at home with Jamie when I reached her after dinner. I told her I needed to talk to her, without Jamie there, and she didn't ask why.

We arranged to meet at the office at 9:00 P.M. That gave me time to stop at home, and I was glad for it. I wanted a moment alone, a chance to lie down and breathe.

As I walked in the door, I realized I'd forgotten to let Lori know Chaz was feeding me. I had an apology ready to go, but I found the apartment dark, with no signs of cooking. This was unusual for a Sunday night.

A keen sense of worry crept into me, and I was relieved when I heard Lori moving in her room. The door was closed—also unusual—and when I got closer, I heard her crying.

I knocked, and the crying intensified into a long, animal moan. I cracked the door open. "Can I come in?"

She didn't say anything, so I went inside and sat next to her on her bed. She grabbed onto my arm like it was a lifeline.

"What happened?" I asked.

"Isaac—" she sobbed. "Isaac—"

I stroked her back, shushing softly to calm her down. After all the trauma we'd been through, I thought I could walk her through a broken heart.

"Isaac is in the hospital." She got out the words and started to wail.

A chill shot through me. "Oh, Jesus," I said. I put an arm around her and she cried into my shoulder.

When her sobs subsided, I ventured the horrid question. "What's wrong with him?"

"He got beat up," she said.

"Do you think it was Winfred?"

"I don't know. Do you?"

"I believe in coincidence," I said. "But only up to a point. Winfred certainly seems like the kind of guy who would do something like that."

She hung her head and it swayed, thoughtfully. "It was three men," she said. "What kind of guy would that make him?"

Lori stood up and went to the bathroom to wash her face. When she came back, she announced she was going to see Isaac before visiting hours ended.

"Do you want me to come with you?" I asked.

She said no, and it was just as well—I had plenty else to take care of before the night was through.

I got to the office five minutes late, and Daphne was waiting outside, leaning against the door frame of Lindley & Flores, a perfect picture even in the dirty hallway light. She wore an orange blouse over fitted blue jeans and brown boots, and she gave the impression that she never looked less put together.

She looked up when she heard my footsteps, and smiled.

It took me a few seconds to construct a smile to telegraph back, and I wondered if this interview was in my control. I needed to make the shift between new friend and accuser, and I was going in with unsteady hands, too sweaty to take a firm grip.

"Hey," I said, and I led her into the office.

When the door shut behind us, my mind screamed with an expansion of paranoid imagination. I'd let myself get comfortable with a client—I'd let her occupy a place of confidence in my life, given her the privilege of private access in this quiet, closed room. But if Daphne wasn't Daphne, all my assumptions about our relationship were bunk. Lanya Waters could be anybody.

I was good at hiding emotions, at least. Better, anyway, than most. Discomfort was easy, and fear—I knew the only fear I had was lurking and paranoid, so I let it shout its faint protest and sat down behind Chaz's desk. I opened his window and lit a cigarette, knowing he'd forgive me.

"How's your hangover?" she asked, crossing her legs and taking a friendly tone.

"Fine," I said. "More or less."

"How's Lori?"

"She barely drank anything." It was a truthful answer, if incomplete.

"I noticed. That's not what I meant, though." She paused. "What was the deal with that guy?"

I thought about Isaac in the hospital and Winfred's hand claiming Lori by the waist. "Did she say anything about him last night?"

"A little bit."

"Really?"

"I asked."

"Who he was to her?"

"No. If she was afraid of him."

Daphne impressed me. It had been clear enough that Winfred was a tool, but I wouldn't have thought Lori even noticed if I were an outsider looking in. She was an open book when her guard was down, but she was working hard last night. I knew something was wrong because I knew her, and I knew her brief history with Winfred. Daphne went on intuition alone, and it bothered me that she sensed fear, and with it, implicitly, danger.

"What did she say?"

"She pretended not to hear me, but when I didn't look away, she did this." Daphne mimicked Lori's tentative nod. It was so spot on I almost laughed.

"Well, she should be scared of him. It looks like he might have beaten the shit out of her new boyfriend."

Her eyes went wide, but a split second later they turned dull and jaded. I read the quick acceptance in that quiet transformation, the way she engulfed the surprise like an ocean welcoming a fat but single raindrop. It sent a shiver down my back. I wondered why I'd told her a thing, this woman I hardly knew. She'd fled a whole life, become entangled in a murder, and that was just what I could verify. What would shake a woman who had seen so much?

"That kind of man," she pronounced with a subtle throb in her voice. "That kind of man will do anything to get what he wants."

"Do you know many men of that type?"

She shot me a bitter smile. "Everyone does, Song. Every last one of us."

We sat in silence for a while. I finished my cigarette while she looked out the window, watching the dark nothing outside.

"Is Joe Tilley that kind of man, Lanya?"

She took her time turning away from the window, then raised one hand to her forehead and skimmed her fingers across it like she was sweeping away bangs that weren't there. She let her head collapse into the dropped palm and sighed.

I gave her a calm, serious look, and I knew I had managed to take the upper hand.

"My own mother doesn't call me Lanya anymore," she said.

"Does she call you Daphne?"

"She doesn't call me anything."

The air in the office was stale and oppressive, the silence thick enough to stir. After a minute, she spoke again. "I didn't expect that not to come out."

"What do you mean by 'that'?"

"My history. My past life." She shrugged, and a shiver glided across her shoulders. "My lies. Whatever you want to call it."

"If you knew I'd find out anyway, why didn't you just tell me?"

She gave me a cold, incredulous look. "I didn't *know* you'd find out, and even if I did—why should I volunteer? I didn't go through the bother of moving across the country and changing my name so I could spend my life thinking about who I used to be."

"The police know, too," I said.

"They know what?"

"At least that you're not who you say you are."

"That's a dramatic way to put it," she said. "I am exactly who I say I am."

"Why did Joe Tilley pay a million bucks for your first painting?"

"Because," she started, without missing a beat, "it was worth that much to him."

I didn't know much about art, but I knew enough to recognize blatant irregularity. "What did he owe you?"

She smiled, a little sadly. "You doubt my talent," she said.

"No, but I'm not an idiot." I took a drag from my cigarette and kept my eyes on hers. "Come on."

She stared at the smoke with a faraway expression, like she was watching a balloon fly into invisibility.

"Want one?" I offered her the pack.

She shook her head. "We were involved," she said. Her voice was measured, her diction careful.

"When?"

"About five years ago. I'm sure you figured as much."

I nodded without commitment. That they had dated seemed a logical enough conclusion, but I wondered if even the wealthiest men made seven-figure presents to every paramour. Joe Tilley had a penchant for marriage that didn't speak to financial shyness, but there was something so transactional about an art sale that I had a hard time seeing it as a gift. It promised more secrets than the flashiest diamond necklace.

"Tell me about it," I said.

She pulled at a lock of hair, extending it down past her nose. When she released it, it bounced back like a spring.

"We met at a party," she said. "He was married to Abby Hart at the time, and they were throwing this elaborate catered thing at their house. I was trying to make it as an actress. Did you know that?"

"I know you have a SAG card."

"Well, let me tell you something. It is as hard for a black woman to make it in Hollywood as it is for a camel to pass through the eye of a needle."

"Amen, I'm sure."

"I gave it an honest shot. It was miserable. I only went to auditions when the directors wanted a particular 'look.' I don't think any of the casting calls said 'Negress' but that was my niche. Tiny little niche."

"But you went to parties at Joe Tilley's house."

"Sure. As a cocktail waitress." She smiled, and her teeth gleamed white and wet. "You should've seen my uniform. Most jobs, it would've been classified as 'not safe for work.'"

I bit my lip. I should have guessed she wasn't there as a guest, and I felt a flash of embarrassment, which subsided when I saw that she wasn't embarrassed at all.

"So, what happened?"

She shrugged. "What would you think?"

"He hit on you?"

"You could say that," she said, passing a hand through the dense curls of her hair. "It was this huge party, at this huge house. I doubt most weddings are half as nice, and this was for some minor occasion I can't even remember. I was one of four girls slinging cocktails in gold fringe bikinis, and I recognized one of them from an audition. We exchanged a look, kind of like 'What are we even doing here?'"

"Job's a job."

She shrugged and continued. "It was a decent gig, paid better than most, I guess. There were a lot of famous faces, but you get used to seeing those if you work service in L.A. long enough. Joe

Tilley was one I'd seen before, though I'd never talked to him before that night. I have to admit I was flattered up a mountain when he said he recognized *me*."

"Did he, really?"

"He did. He named the restaurant I worked at. He'd eaten there three months earlier."

"So it wasn't just a line."

"You can't get away with a line like that when you're that famous."

"What happened next?"

"We flirted here and there the whole night. I was working, and he had guests, so it's not like we enjoyed a long, involved conversation. At some point he looked at me casually and said, in a low but normal tone of voice, 'I want you to stay after the party.'"

"Pretty bold, I guess. You said his wife was throwing the party with him?"

"Yeah. She was barely ten feet away, but it's not like she paid any attention to that exchange. Her husband was just getting a drink from the hired help."

"But you were able to stay?"

"I wasn't able *not* to. Have you ever met anyone very famous?"

I thought of my afternoon with Willow Hemingway, and decided not to derail the conversation. "Not really."

"I've only met a few in any real capacity. Look, I'm about as jaded as it gets when it comes to celebrities. Used to see them all the time, and a lot of them were assholes. But when someone mega-famous looks at you, and sees you, and acknowledges you, and *wants* something from you that no one else can give—well there's real power there, real magnetism. I did stay when Joe asked me to. I didn't have a choice." Her eyes vibrated with something dark and earnest, and I could do nothing but nod and ask her to go on.

"What happened?"

"He must have known by the time he asked me that his wife would drink herself useless by the end of the night. When he walked away I started to watch her, and the way she floated, I could tell she was on her way. So when the party wrapped up I lingered, and when everyone left without looking in my direction, I felt a thrill at my invisibility. I'd been decoration all night, and that wasn't about to change."

It was hard to imagine a room where Daphne Freamon could hide her light, but I took her word for it. "So you stayed over."

She nodded, gravely, and I didn't press for details.

"Did your relationship continue after that?"

"Sexually? No. But we were not done with each other."

The office was soundless and stifling. I tapped a long finger of ash into the mouth of an empty soda can.

"Daphne, did you blackmail him?"

Her chest rose and her jaw stiffened at the word. After a pause, she exhaled with a sigh. "I wouldn't call it that. He never did."

"How did it happen?"

"Let me make one thing clear, at least," she said. "I was trying to make it as an actress, yes. But I'd discovered by the age of twenty-two that my talent lay in painting. *Beware Beware* was my first sale, but it wasn't some made-up way to get money. I was serious about it. As serious as a twenty-two-year-old could be about anything."

I nodded. "I've seen it," I said.

Her eyes grew wide and she blinked once, her dark lashes fanning her high cheeks.

"Joe Tilley's house. I interviewed Willow Hemingway. I thought I recognized your hand in one of the paintings, but the initials were wrong."

Her jaw came undone. "He hung it up in the house?"

"Right in the guest bathroom. I have to tell you, it's a striking work of art. Might not mean much coming from someone like me, but I'd only really browsed your portfolio once, and my mind made the connection right away."

"Thank you," she said. "I am good at what I do."

"That doesn't change anything."

"I know."

"So how did it happen?"

She ran a hand through her hair again. "I don't remember how I phrased it, but I told him a few days later that I was a painter, and that I'd noticed he was something of a collector."

"Just like that."

"I may have mentioned a particular painting hanging in the guest bedroom."

"And that was enough."

She shrugged. "He banged a cocktail waitress in his house while his wife slept upstairs. We could hear her snoring. He paused whenever the snoring seemed to get quiet."

I laughed, and she laughed with me before continuing.

"I approached him about the painting because he was too famous to expect to get away with that kind of behavior. But if he'd turned me down, I'm not sure I would have escalated the conversation. I might have pretended it never happened. I might have just disappeared. I don't know. I didn't have to find that out." She shrugged again. "Anyway, the way it happened, there was room for doubt for both of us. I told myself at the time that I was just taking advantage of an opportunity, that I might never meet another art collector with his means again. As for him, I think he considered himself my patron until the day he died."

"He wasn't ashamed of it, anyway. He displayed it for anyone to see. Actually," I tilted my head and disposed of my spent cigarette. "I'm surprised Jamie never put it together."

"I'm not," she said. "Jamie isn't the attentive type."

I nodded, mostly agreeing, and lit another cigarette. "So he bought your painting. Anonymously. Overnight, you became a twenty-two-year-old artist with a million-dollar sale to a mysterious wealthy buyer. And instead of letting that launch your career, you changed your name and left the state. Why?"

"Couple reasons. You just named one."

"The attention?"

"Yeah, the attention. I think when you subtly blackmail someone, discretion is an unspoken part of the package."

"Fair enough," I said. "What's the other?"

"I was tired of Lanya Waters. Lanya Waters was someone things happened to, a sorry, lost loser, and I didn't want to *be* her anymore."

"I can't say I've never felt like that, but it's never occurred to me to just start being someone else. It doesn't seem possible."

"You'd be surprised what's possible with a million dollars."

Despite the open window, the room was getting dense with smoke. "What was that like?" I asked.

She leaned back and thought for a while, her nostrils slightly pinched. When she looked at me again she projected the air of a guru. "Well, are you happy?" she asked. "Do you like your life?"

I laughed. "I don't know."

"Is it the one you'd choose?"

"Of all possible lives? God, no."

She nodded, satisfied, like a lawyer who's gotten the desired answer out of a hostile witness. "Then I'd recommend starting over. There's nothing like it."

"It's not that easy, obviously. I mean how'd you square that with your family?"

"I moved to New York five years ago. I was already losing touch with my family by then."

"They don't know?"

"I've thought about contacting my mom, but not very hard. I stalk my brothers from time to time on Facebook. I can find them if I want to. I don't want them finding me." She paused, chewing on the smoky silence. "What else did you find out about me?"

I remembered the haunted, inconclusive social worker's report, the way it hinted at disharmony between stepfather and stepdaughter. My throat felt dry and hoarse with nicotine, and I coughed once, into the sleeve of my shirt.

"I guess my next question is, does Jamie know?"

She shook her head just a couple degrees. It barely looked intentional. "You know the answer to that, don't you? It's why we're here, and Jamie isn't."

"You got Jamie this writing gig, right? Through a friend of yours?"

She colored. "I did."

"You couldn't approach Joe directly?"

"I just wanted to help Jamie. I didn't want to get into all . . . this."

"I'm not going to sit here and tell you what you can and can't hide from your boyfriend. But I can't continue this investigation with a secret of that size between you. Pretty big conflict of interest."

She nodded. "No. That's fair."

"So what do you want to do?"

"Let me think for a minute."

I finished my Lucky Strike while she sat with her face in one hand, propped up like a fashion model's. She patted her cheek with long fingers and breathed deeply for three minutes.

"I'll tell him," she said. "I should have told him earlier. This is bigger than me, after all."

I nodded. "I've found that when someone is murdered, honesty is the best policy."

"Lot of experience there?"

"More than I would like."

Daphne left to talk to Jamie, and I stayed back with my thoughts and cigarettes. The interview had gone about as well as I might have hoped. I'd gone in expecting the worst and come out with a story I could work with. I still had questions, but the biggest was one there was no use in asking: What kind of a liar was Daphne Freamon? If she'd told a few lies to protect the secrets of her past, then we were on the same page now, and I could trust her going forward. But if she was a liar at her core, then there was not one piece of her I should believe.

There was nothing to do but split the difference. I had to be cautious, but it would have been callous and unreasonable to call her a monster and shut the whole thing down. Besides, I liked her, and my instinct saw something good in her, glowing fiercely beneath every layer. Maybe it was the Marlowe in me— weary as he was, the man had a stubborn belief in people, that they could be decent, worth helping, worth saving. He suffered a lot for that belief.

Ten

I called Lori on my way out of the office. It was eleven o'clock, and visiting hours were over. She was home, alone, and I had to get back to her. Her voice sounded funny on the phone, wispy and hoarse with exhaustion.

Isaac was okay, whatever that meant. He was alive, and there would be no permanent damage. It chilled me that these were blessings.

He did have a broken rib and a smashed cheekbone, and he'd spend the night in the hospital.

That's all I found out before Lori told me we'd talk at home. When I got there, she was in her room with the door near closed, huddled under the covers trying to will herself asleep. I knocked gently and she rustled in her sheets.

"Are you up?" I asked.

Her voice came through the covers in a thin hum.

"Can I come in?"

She shuffled and turned on her bedside lamp. In the yellow glow, her eyes retreated between puffy lids. She was done now, but she had cried for a long time.

I took the light as an invitation and walked to the side of her bed. She sat hugging her knees over the blanket, and I remembered finding my sister like this, curled up with cramps and moaning for a hot-water bottle. It was a sad sight.

She wiggled over and made room for me on the bed, and I sat down and held her hand. She rested her head against my arm, and when she spoke I couldn't see her face.

"Isaac and I aren't seeing each other anymore," she said. "For now, anyway."

My shoulder stiffened, and I felt her head respond to its movement.

"He broke up with you over this?" My knee-jerk reaction was one of disgust—disgust at his weakness, his failure of masculinity. I hated that my mind set out in that direction, but I realized, too, that I was bound to discredit anyone who hurt Lori, by whatever means I could invent.

"No," she said. "It was my idea."

"What happened?"

"I went to see him at the hospital, and he looked . . . pitiful."

"It was bad?"

"They went for his face," she said. "They messed it up. You can barely see him under there."

I thought of the stories of horrid old crones, plotting in dark rooms and alleys to ruin the looks of pretty girls. As if women were the only ones capable of petty, hateful jealousies, as if women were as likely as men to exact physical revenge.

"It'll heal, though?"

She nodded tentatively. "Though to be honest, I don't see how."

"So you dumped him because he was ugly, huh?"

She colored and started to huff. "*Unni*, you know that isn't true."

"Of course I do. I was joking, sweet girl. I'm sorry." I smiled and stroked her hair. It was filmy with grease. "But why, then?"

"Because I'm scared," she said. "I don't think it's safe for Isaac if I keep seeing him."

I shook my head. "That's messed up."

"I know. But it's true. You'd do the same thing."

"I don't know. It would make me sick. I don't like the idea of buckling to a thug."

"It's not about buckling. I just won't put someone else in danger for my principles' sake."

"Did you tell him that was why you were breaking up with him?" There was a whiff of Korean soap opera to this whole setup—the selfless heroine was always breaking up with some idiot man to protect him from one thing or another, usually cancer-related heartache. She would tell him she didn't love him with a tear in one eye. The present danger was far more concrete, but I wondered if Lori had the bug for drama lodged in her bones.

"Of course I did," she said.

"And he didn't object?"

"He did, kind of weakly. I could tell he was relieved."

"Did that upset you?"

"No," she said. "He's a sweet boy, you know? Not a fighting bone in his body. I like that about him, and if he were the kind of guy who would duke it out for me with a total *ggangpae* I wouldn't even be interested."

"I'm sorry, though. It must suck."

"It does."

"Are you sure it was Winfred?"

She nodded. "He wasn't trying to hide it."

"Who were the other guys?"

"I don't know."

"Korean?"

"One of them. I guess the other one was Mexican or Filipino or something."

"How did it happen?"

"Isaac was over here today. We had a brunch date and just came back here to hang out. He went home around five, and when he got to his place and parked, another car parked behind him."

"You mean he was followed? From our house?"

A small shiver flitted across her body. "That's what we think."

"So what happened then? They just got out of the car and started whaling on him?"

"Basically. Someone, I think Winfred, asked, 'Are you Isaac?' and he said yes. Didn't even think not to."

"I mean yeah, why would he have?"

"As soon as he got a good look at them he got scared. Three big guys. Isaac's so skinny. He says he couldn't have taken one of them."

"Did they say anything else? 'Stay away from my girl' or whatever?"

"No, they just started beating on him."

"How long?"

"Not long. But any longer and they might've killed him." The whine of oncoming tears seeped into her voice. "He can't handle another beating."

"He can't just press charges?"

"I asked him that. He's too scared. We don't even know who the other two are. If Winfred gets arrested, they still know where Isaac lives."

"Do we even know who Winfred is? I mean, did you talk to your *samchun* today?"

"I called him, yeah."

"Well, what did he have to say for himself?"

"He kept asking me if I was sure, and when I said I was, he just got really quiet."

"Nothing illuminating?"

"No," she said. "*Unni*, what do I do when he calls me again?"

When. She knew he would. The fear in her voice crawled down my throat and made a fist that clenched in my chest. I held on to her hand. "Ignore it," I said. "For now, at least. I'll talk to Chaz and see what else we can do."

It was too late to call him then, so I waited until Lori fell asleep and sneaked out into my room. The poor baby, I thought. That poor fucking girl. She'd been living in dread of this horrible man, and the dread had been answered, borne out in a way that promised more pain to come.

I'd vowed to protect Lori to the best of my ability, but I wondered now what that even meant. Lori wasn't a child who needed help crossing the street. If she needed protection it was against the larger threats of the world, and I saw now how much my aegis was worth. I felt weak and defeated, pinned down by the full weight of my uselessness.

I thought I'd at least google Winfred, and then I realized I didn't even know his full name. I did nothing instead, just smoked a few cigarettes and stared at the wall until I felt like trying to close my eyes.

I had been lying awake under the covers for fifteen minutes when my phone rang. I was almost relieved. Sleep had seemed so unreachable that it took on the shape of a task, and I was glad to procrastinate even a few minutes more. I bent over the side of my bed and picked up the phone from where it lay on the floor.

"Song. It's Jamie." His voice flagged, like he was within a two-minute window of a jagged, teary breakdown.

"Christ, Jamie. What's wrong?"

"You know what's wrong. Daphne told me."

I bit down on my thumbnail and nodded, though I knew he couldn't see me.

"Can I come over?"

I looked down at the floor, where I had just dropped my bra on my way to bed. I was in my pajamas, and I could hear Lori breathing with the rhythm of sleep from across the wall.

"I mean, not really," I said. "It's like one thirty in the morning isn't it? My roommate's asleep."

"Sorry, did I wake you?"

"No, not at all. Look, I can meet you somewhere if you want."

"Great," he said. "That would be really great. I'm actually outside."

"Outside my house?" I sat up and threw the covers down. My window overlooked the street and I drew the curtain and saw him there, leaning against his car, parked slanting down the road.

He looked up and found me in the darkness, and he sent up a meek wave. "Hi. I hope this is okay."

He sounded so defeated that I couldn't raise any objection. In the bad, milky glow of the streetlight he was tiny, wan and alone.

"Just give me a minute," I said.

I let the curtain fall, picked clothes off the floor, and got dressed. I dipped into the bathroom to sneak a peek in the mirror, splashed water on my cheeks, and went downstairs.

When I was close enough to see Jamie's face, I felt a wave of exhaustion hit me like a tranquilizer. I was right—he'd been crying, and he wasn't trying to hide it.

"Hey," I said. I offered him a cigarette, and he took it in fingers that looked ghostly white in the dark. I lit his, then mine, and we stood on the curb smoking, our arms crossed against the night cold.

"What's going on?" I asked.

"Daphne broke up with me."

It was a night of broken hearts. I was half wasted with empathy. "Really?" I wondered if she'd copped out when it'd come time to tell him her story. "How did it happen?"

"I don't even know."

"Did she tell you anything? In particular, I mean?"

"Oh, yeah. She told me everything, about her name, about Joe, the whole grand confession."

"And then she dumped you?"

"Yeah, she was telling me all this and I was trying to wrap my head around it when she said she'd understand if I couldn't forgive her, and then I don't know. Somehow we broke up, and I didn't even want that but it happened and she couldn't be convinced it shouldn't."

He slumped against the hood of his car and I followed suit.

"Do you want to go somewhere we can sit or something?" I asked. "I'd invite you in but my roommate just got to sleep. She's had a rough night, too."

"This is fine. The sky's pretty tonight." He held an invisible tumbler and shook it back and forth. "And I'll bet you have something to drink."

I went inside and filled a Snapple bottle with rye. It was chilly out, so I grabbed a college sweatshirt before leaving to rejoin

Jamie. "This should fit you," I said. "I sort of inherited it from a guy I used to know."

"Thanks. Is that Snapple?" He looked at me with a small laugh in his eyes.

"No. Here." I unscrewed the cap. "We'll share."

He took a thirsty gulp, as if it were actually peach iced tea.

"You planning to drive home?" I asked.

He shrugged. "My car is comfortable."

"Suit yourself."

He passed me the bottle with an insistent nod.

We leaned against the hood of his car, smoking and boozing, a quiet little picnic of sadness and vice. The sky was an oily black, starless, chilly, portentous.

"Daphne is an odd girl," he said. "I don't know that I've ever figured her out."

"Just guessing here, but could this have anything to do with the fact that you learned she had a secret life, like, three hours ago?"

"Ha," he said. "Probably. But I've thought this before."

"Well, she had plenty of secrets before today."

"It has nothing to do with secrets. She could tell me everything and I might never know her. There are just some people like that, you know?"

"Unknowable?"

"Yeah, like you put in the work, you peel the layers, and underneath—no core, just more layers."

I shrugged. "I can't think of anyone like that. Not anyone I've bothered to get to know." I took a warming swallow of rye. "I guess that isn't a very inclusive set."

"You," he said. "You seem like that type."

"Coreless?" I laughed. "Black hole for a soul?"

He shook his head. "It's not that. More depth than emptiness, like any abyss."

I felt flattered, somehow, against my will. The booze in my bloodstream was starting to tickle.

"So where is Daphne now?"

"I don't know."

He crushed his cigarette under his shoe and asked for another. I lit it between my lips and passed it to him. In the low light I saw him watching my mouth.

"How do you do that?"

"What?"

"Light a match with your thumb like that."

I smiled, oddly pleased. I'd put some effort into learning this trick back when I first started smoking, and it was still gratifying when someone noticed. "It's easy, as long as you have strike-anywhere matches."

"Show me."

He stood close and I demonstrated on a few matches, flicking the heads against my thumbnail. I concentrated on the bursts of flame, and I felt his eyes on my hands, then on my face. I looked up and he gave me a small smile, like he'd been caught.

"Do you want to go for a walk?" he asked.

I squinted into the night and shrugged. "Not particularly scenic."

"Who can see anything anyway?"

We walked down the sloping street to Glendale, and I said, "We can take a nice walk around the lake."

"Lake?"

I pointed at the cheerless shapes ahead, chain-link fence, bulky tarp. "In all its beauty."

He laughed. It was good to hear.

We walked in silence on the narrow concrete path around the closed-off lake. As I nipped at the whiskey it nipped away at me. I looked at Jamie from time to time and grew sharply aware of the shape of him—a good-looking man at my side after midnight, sharing a stroll by a dormant park.

"Do you know how we met?" he asked, dispersing my cloud of thought.

I scanned through my long log of conversations with Daphne, and wondered if I'd heard the story—it didn't come to mind. "I don't think so, actually. You can tell me, if that's what you really want to do."

"I saw her at a gallery opening. She was one of the artists, and I was there because my friend was part of the entertainment, playing keyboard for the band."

"Right out of a *New York Times* wedding announcement."

"I noticed her as soon as I walked in. I went right up to her—and she completely ignored me."

I smiled. "I'm sure she gets hit on all the time."

"She does. And I guess I interrupted her conversation with an art critic for some big magazine."

I laughed. "So how'd that go over?"

"It didn't. I hung around the gallery, waiting for another opening, but I couldn't quite recover that night. So I left with my friend and got hammered instead."

"So when'd you see her again?"

"Well, I had her name, and I knew where she was showing, and I managed to bump into her again."

"She's not that easy to stalk," I said. "I've googled her many times."

"I'm resourceful," he said. "Anyway, I managed to bump into her a few more times, and finally, she agreed to a drink."

"You were persistent, huh?"

"That's not even the end of it. When she didn't fall in love with me right away, I painted post cards," he said. "You know like the ones they have in museums? Of Picassos and whatever? She wasn't really famous, you know, so no one made post cards of her paintings. So I did."

"Love letters?"

"Front and back. I mailed them to her, one a week, from wherever I was thinking about her."

"That's really . . ." I trailed off.

"Say romantic."

"Creepy?"

"I was afraid you'd say that. But two sides of the same coin, right?" He laughed, softly. "When you feel a connection that powerful, you have to trust it and follow through. It was like the movies, you know? I would've chased her through any airport."

He went silent. I caught the film of wet shining in his eyes and offered him a cigarette.

"Why don't you have anyone?"

I shrugged. "I have Lori."

"Not what I meant."

"I know it."

"Sorry. Didn't mean to put you on the spot. I just find you interesting."

"You and your murky compliments," I said. "Anyway it's getting late, man. I'm about to collapse."

"What time is it?"

I looked at my phone. "Jesus, it's almost four in the morning. We've been out here for two hours."

"Time flies when you're getting blitzed."

"Yeah. Are you as drunk as I am?"

"Probably."

"You can't drive home, then." I hesitated, thinking of Lori. "You can crash on our couch if you want."

He nodded. "To be honest, I was hoping you'd offer."

I laughed. "Sneaky bastard."

We tiptoed into my apartment and I grabbed a pillow and a throw blanket to set up on the couch. "It's not the Ritz or anything," I whispered. "But it beats both your car and the drunk tank."

"Hey, I drive a BMW."

"Which has a vacancy, last I saw it."

He smiled. "Thank you."

"It's no problem," I said. "Just don't bother Lori."

"Not just this. Thanks for humoring me. For everything." He sighed. "It's been a rough few days."

"Yeah. I'd say so."

He reached for me with a tired arm and I moved in to receive the hug. His head dropped on my shoulder, and he stayed there, holding me, for half a minute.

"Good night, Jamie," I said.

"Good night."

He pulled away just enough to kiss me on the lips. It was a curious, uninsistent kiss, lingering but slack, testing the waters. I let it happen with a spike in my pulse, and when we separated, it took some effort to look at his face. There was a question in it, and even confused and drunk, I knew to shake my head.

I stepped back and said again, "Good night, then."

I went to my room and passed out. I didn't dream at all, and that was a relief.

Eleven

I woke up early the next morning with the feeling that I'd over-
slept. It was unusually sunny, and my head felt clearer than it
had any right to. I found Jamie knocked out on the couch. He
was asleep in his clothes, borrowed sweatshirt and all, his
mouth hanging open like an emptied purse.

I ran the tape from last night—just four hours ago, it turned
out—and determined I had in fact engaged when he kissed me.
Without the permissive haze of alcohol, I had to acknowledge
this was clumsy at the very least. I cursed quietly.

I washed up and took extra care to look professional. I put on
mascara and a clean shirt, even busted out a black pencil skirt.
When I was almost ready to go, I woke up Jamie by standing
over him with my arms crossed. It was a trick I learned from my
mother.

"Hey," I said. "Time to go home."

He shifted his legs under the blanket, a feeble sign of life.

"Come on. I have to get to work."

He let out a long croak. "What time is it?"

"Eight thirty."

"Don't you work for me?" he asked, scratching his head. "Go back to bed."

"Actually, that's a good question. I work for your now ex-girlfriend, so I'll get back to you on that."

He sat up, eyes awake with a look of panic. "You might drop my case?"

I put my purse down and perched on the arm of the couch. "I have to talk to Daphne. But hey, let's say I do. I'm not the only PI in Los Angeles."

"I can pay you if Daphne won't."

"That's not really the issue. She's been my client this whole time, so if she doesn't want me working for you, I might not even be able to."

"I know Daphne. She may not want to be with me, but she wouldn't do anything to hurt me."

"Honestly, it wouldn't hurt you to part ways with me, get someone with a serious resume. I have yet to clear anyone of murder, you know."

"But I trust you. I need a friend for this." He spoke slowly, emphatically, with a beseeching gaze that dug into me in a way that was almost painful. "Promise you'll do what you can."

"Okay," I said, and with that I loosened my feeble grasp on any dim longing for extraction. If Jamie wanted me to play the hero, I was still willing to take that on. "I'll talk to Daphne. In the meantime, though, I have to kick you out. My roommate doesn't even know you're here."

"Right," he said. "Thanks for letting me crash."

He grabbed my hand and squeezed it with a shy smile that

brought warmth to my cheeks. I stood up and pulled back to help him off the couch.

We walked out together, and I waved to Jamie as he hopped into his car. Then I saw it, halfway up the block—the white Audi, engine off, sleeping on the curb.

I ran up the middle of the street, trying to get there before the car came to life. It showed no sign of starting, and I slowed about fifteen feet away. The driver was inside, but I couldn't see his face. It was hidden under the bill of a large cap. I glanced at the license plate—it was the same car.

I walked up to the window and saw why it wasn't moving—the driver was asleep, the cap on his face a shade from the morning light.

I knocked on the glass and he woke up with an exaggerated shake of the shoulders. He grabbed at his hat and pushed it back over his head, then turned to see me a half-second later. The window opened three inches with a rubbery moan.

I hadn't seen him up close before, and he was less threatening than I'd imagined. His wide-brimmed cap was flashy and brand-new, with a holographic sticker still attached, and a black bristly strap of beard stretched from ear to ear. His chest was visibly soft beneath the cotton of his T-shirt, and he wore baggy denim shorts adorned by a wallet chain. He looked stoned, his eyes the dull brown of dead leaves ready to crumble. "Yeah?"

I motioned for him to get out of the car with my head. "Let me buy you coffee. I think we have common interests."

"Yeah?" He looked at my breasts and I pretended not to notice. "Like what?"

"I think we're both fans of the late Joe Tilley."

He shrugged, a large motion that was supposed to carry swagger. "Never saw him in anything."

"You know his friend, though. Jamie Landon? He's a friend of mine, too. I couldn't help but notice you were following him right until Tilley got killed. He's been hanging out here, too. You just missed him."

His eyebrows formed a grave line. "Hey, whoa. I don't know what you're blabbing about, but it sounds like a thing you might want to keep quiet."

"I want to talk to you," I said. "Just coffee, okay? Nothing to lose."

He looked at his watch, a flashy thing with a gold chain bracelet and a big round face. "Whatever. You want to get in the car?"

"I'll drive," I said, with a bit too much haste. "I'm parked right up the block."

I almost jumped when he got out of the car. His obedience took me by surprise.

"What's your name?" he asked.

"You can call me Song."

"Song. That's a nice name. Really, ah, musical, I guess."

I smiled. He was kind of a dope.

"I'm Donnie. Short for Donaldo, not like Donald Duck."

We drove to a Starbucks a half-mile away, and I bought him a vanilla Frappuccino. The coffee shop was crowded, so I suggested we leave. He shrugged and followed behind, and we sat on the short plaster wall enclosing the parking lot. I lit a cigarette, and he took one, too.

"Sorry to ambush you like that," I said. "I just had a few questions."

"Are you a cop? 'Cause if you're a cop you know you got to tell me that, right?"

He spoke like someone who learned criminal law from television. I knew this because I understood him, recognized the facile line from some forgotten show.

"I'm not a cop." I smiled. "But now I know you're a criminal."

He sniffed. "I didn't say that."

"Hey," I said. "I'm not here to judge how you feed your family."

"Family? Please. How old do you think I am, girl?"

I hadn't meant to be literal—Donnie looked young. "I don't know. Twenty-one?"

He laughed. "No way, man. I'm almost twenty-four. How old are you?"

"Twenty-seven."

"No way. I would've guessed twenty-two," he said, leering.

The tone of the interview was not what I'd expected, but it wouldn't hurt if he wanted to hit on me.

"So," I said, softening my voice. "Are you a drug dealer, too?"

His smile stiffened on his face, constricting just a fraction of an inch.

"I mean, what's that like?" I powered on. "Fast cars, fast women, all that? Is it like on TV?"

The stiffness fell and he laughed. "I'm not a drug dealer. I'm much cooler than that."

I powered up my smile. "So why were you following Jamie around?"

He raised one eyebrow. "Slow down, girl. What are you supposed to be anyway?"

I thought for a second and decided it wouldn't hurt to be honest when Donnie seemed to like me. "I'm a friend," I said. "And kind of a private investigator."

"Like Sherlock?"

"Sure."

"Were you stalking me?"

"No," I said. "I was stalking Jamie."

"Some friend, huh?" He laughed again.

"Anyway, so I know you were tailing him for some reason or other, and I need to know why. Were you planning to hurt him?"

"Nah," he said. "I don't even know the guy."

"Did you know Joe Tilley?"

"Nope."

I leaned forward and said, like I might be joking, "Did you kill him?"

He snapped his head back into his neck, giving himself three slim chins. "You think I'm that gangster? Like I could just cruise into a hotel and kill a movie star?"

I shrugged. "Well you were up to something. I know that much."

"Yeah?"

"I know that you work for Jamie's suppliers. I know you were following him around when he was passing those drugs onto Tilley. That's enough to get suspicious, wouldn't you say?"

He shook his head, his eyes going bright. "No, you are way off," he said. "Shit, you're not going around saying this to cops and stuff, are you?"

"No," I said. "I'm just an interested party."

"I never even met Joe Tilley. Hand to God, man."

"Then why the interest in Jamie?"

His mouth closed and he moved his lips around like he was chewing something. I waited for him to open it again, then remembered the scant names Jamie had given me.

"Do you work for Tin Tin?" I asked.

His eyelids gave a flutter of recognition, and he smiled when he saw me notice. "Nah," he said. "I don't work for no Tin Tin."

I put out my cigarette in my empty coffee cup and gazed at him with an air of admiration. "Wait," I said. "You're not the Young King, are you?"

He burst out laughing, and I pretended to be embarrassed. "Stop that," I said pleadingly, tugging at the sleeve of his T-shirt.

"How is it that you know that name, and know exactly jack shit about him?"

"He's a man of mystery," I said, assuming that was true.

"Yeah," he said. "I guess he is, isn't he?"

He started whistling. He was a good whistler, able to carry a tune without lapses of breathy labor. It took me a minute to recognize the song: *Old King Cole was a merry old soul, and a merry old soul was he. He called for his pipe, and he called for his bowl . . .*

"So Young King had you following Jamie, huh?"

He kept whistling, his eyebrows wiggling up and down.

"Jamie said Young King was the one who got him on board in the first place. Why did he need you trailing him? Did he think Jamie was stealing or something?"

He stopped whistling. "Look," he said. "I was just keeping an eye on him for a minute. Nothing illegal. I'm innocent as a baby."

That didn't sound particularly innocent, but I let it go.

"Didn't you think it might be smart to back off after the murder?"

"What do you mean?" he asked.

"Clearly you're still chasing Jamie. If you hadn't been dozing off, I never would've caught up to you."

He gave me a look of confusion, and then he smiled. "He's steppin' out on his girl, huh?"

I wasn't sure whether to offer that nothing had happened, or that he no longer had a girl. Both options sounded too defensive, and since it was none of Donnie's business, I shrugged and changed the subject.

"Do you have any idea who might have killed Tilley?"

"Maybe," he said. "I might have some, uh, valuable information." He said "valuable" like it was the biggest word in the world.

"Care to share it?"

"Let me buy you dinner," he said. "Got to get you back for this anyway." He shook his cup, the emptied plastic lined with froth.

I crossed my arms. "Tonight?"

"Slow down, girl," he said, his tone mocking. "Let's shoot for tomorrow, huh?"

"Sure," I said. "What time? Where?"

He laughed. "Let me think on it. I'll text you, okay?"

We exchanged numbers and I drove him back to his parking spot, outside my house. It occurred to me that he knew where I lived—that everyone seemed to know where I lived.

When I got to the office, Chaz was already there, chomping on a sesame bagel. A fat seed stuck to his lip, and his voice was thick with cream cheese. "Late morning, huh?" he said. "Your client called."

"What? Here? She has my cell."

He shrugged. "It was more of an office business call, maybe."

"You talked to her?"

"Yeah."

"What did she want?"

"She said to let you know that she was still retaining you on her boyfriend's behalf. Is that news to you?"

I sat down. "Sort of. She dumped him last night. I was going to call her when I got in."

"Ah," he said. "Well, how was the rest of your night?"

I blinked hard. "Jesus, that was last night I went over to your house? It feels like it's been days."

"Yeah I missed you, too. I gather you stopped by here."

"How do you figure?"

"See, this is why I'm the detective and you're the intern."

"I'm not an intern. You pay me."

"Do I? I shouldn't." He smiled. "Anyway, it smells like a chimney in here."

"Right. Sorry. I was stressed out," I said. "Actually, it looks like Arturo isn't in. Do you mind?"

He sighed. "Go ahead. Kill yourself at your own pace. What do I care?"

"Thanks." He popped open a window and I lit a Lucky Strike. I took a deep draw and exhaled.

"So," he said. "You did talk to her."

I gave him the whole thing, as close to verbatim as I thought I could manage. He nodded along with his arms crossed.

"Smart girl, that Daphne. Wish I'd thought of that."

"Who do you have to blackmail?"

"Lots of folks."

I laughed. "Anyone with money?"

He shook his head with mock sadness. "If I'd known this case would take you to Tinseltown, I wouldn't have given it up."

"Do you want it back?" I lit another cigarette and spoke through my teeth. "I'm serious, Chaz. You're welcome to take the wheel here."

"No, the clients know you already. They seem to trust you," he said. "And besides, it's your case. You think you could just let it go like one of your oafish blind dates?"

I'd never had an oafish blind date, but I could tell he was only half joking. "Oh, come on. It's not like you'd shut me out. I'd see it through with you."

"Have some pride, Song. Do you even know why I hired you?"

"Diversity?"

"Don't be flip. I'm trying to tell you something."

"Fair enough," I said. "You hired me because I had nowhere to go, because that case destroyed me, and you're a nice man."

"That's most of it, sure, but Art had to sign off. He's not the adopting type." He waved one hand, dispelling smoke. "Song—that case destroyed you, and you let it happen. You're a sicko, but you got the job done. No stone unturned, no bridge unburned."

I felt the sting of a tear in one eye and held it off with a brief laugh.

"So that's the last you heard from her, then?" he said after a pause.

I bit my lip. "Technically, yes. But I saw Jamie after."

"After? When?"

"Daphne broke up with him when she left our meeting, and Jamie came over to drown his sorrows."

"What time?"

"Oh man, like one in the morning?"

Chaz stared at me with a cocked eyebrow. "You know boys are only interested in one thing, right?"

I rolled my eyes. "So I've heard."

"Well, what did he want with you at one in the morning?"

"A drinking buddy, mostly."

"That it?"

I hesitated. On the one hand, I was a grown-ass woman, and I had the right to fool around with anyone I pleased. On the other, there were professional limits, and I put a lot of stock in my boss's trust and opinions. "Have you ever gotten involved with a client?"

He snorted. "Who do I look like, James Bond?"

"So that's a no?"

"Believe it or not, I've had opportunities. But I've been married a long time, and that means something to me."

"What if you were single?"

"I have to tell you, I don't like where this is going." He flicked something from under his fingernail. "What time did he leave?"

"I kicked him out this morning," I said, and watched for his reaction.

He closed his eyes and massaged the inside corners of his brows. He shook his head and mumbled something about goddamn James Bond.

"Nothing happened." I added, "He kissed me."

He raised his head and sighed. "That isn't *nothing*, Song. Jesus, kids these days." Still, he sounded relieved.

"Am I in trouble?" I asked.

"You may not have broken any laws, but you know you are if I tell Art."

"You're not going to, are you?"

He shook his head and spoke in the reasonable tone of a teenager's parent. "I'm on your side here. Don't make me regret it."

"Not to change the subject or anything," I said, wanting to change the subject, "but I need to talk to you about something else."

"Molly gave you food poisoning."

"No," I said. "Actually something pretty serious."

"What is it?"

I told him about Lori's new suitor and his ungentlemanly ways, and Chaz listened with a deepening frown. He'd only met Lori a couple of times, but he knew what she'd been through, as well as what she meant to me.

"That girl," he said, shaking his head. "Trouble loves her, doesn't he?"

"Men flock to her," I said. "Most of them are nice enough, but some bring trouble. It only takes one to fuck up a life."

"So, let me guess. You want me to check up on this guy?"

"Can you?" I asked. "That would be so great, Chaz."

"I'll give you the friends and family rate."

I started to crunch numbers in my head—whatever it would cost, though, it had to be done. "Which is?"

"Molly's birthday's coming up. I want to take her out to a nice dinner."

"Sure," I said.

"I watch your man, you watch my kids."

I laughed. "You want thirty bucks' worth of babysitting?"

"I don't trust just any babysitter with my little gems."

"Thanks, Chaz. I owe you big-time."

"I know." He grinned. "Add it to the tab."

I spent the morning in the office, catching up on administrative duties I'd been neglecting. My mind needed a breather, and after that weekend, Monday morning seemed as good a time as any to relax with a pile of busy work. Chaz left soon after our meeting, with a promise to call by the end of the day.

The busy work didn't relax me as much as I'd hoped. I couldn't hit a minute without thinking about Jamie and Daphne, couldn't chase their suffering from the clean office, the sterile duties of paperwork. And I kept seeing the body—Joe Tilley in his blood bath, pale and juiced like some used fruit.

I pulled up a Web browser and googled the latest on Joe Tilley. A quick scan of headlines told me the word was out. TMZ screamed, *Joe Tilley—Murdered!* I clicked on the *New York Times* article. "Autopsy rules out suicide in death of Joe Tilley," the headline declared. The article painted the scene of the crime, and included a quote from Detective Sanchez. "We're looking at foul play now," she said. "We're investigating a person of interest."

I went cold. I had to assume the person of interest was Jamie, and I didn't like Detective Sanchez opening her mouth to reporters, even if she wouldn't dare, at this point, release his name.

The last word came from Alex Caldwell, described as Tilley's personal friend and manager of twenty years. That made him older than he looked, not uncommon in an industry that traded on youth. His statement was simple, dry, admonishing. "We are all shocked and angered by Joe's death. I've checked in with his wife and children, and they request to be able to grieve in private."

I didn't like Alex Caldwell, but there was no denying he was someone I should interview. I texted Jamie for Alex's phone number.

My phone rang a minute later.

"Let me just give you a primer on Alex," Jamie said on the other line.

"Sure," I said.

"He's a prickly guy."

"I gathered."

"He won't want to talk to you. At all."

"I can't appeal to his love for you?"

He laughed. "He doesn't like me. He doesn't like anyone who gets close to Joe. He barely pretends to tolerate Willow."

"A jealous man."

"Protective, I guess. It was his job to keep Joe in line. He saw me as a bad influence." He chuckled bitterly. "Fair enough, huh?"

"Alex and Joe—were they good friends or was it just a business kind of relationship?"

"Oh, they were great friends, from way back. Didn't have as much in common towards the end, I guess. Alex was pretty disappointed in Joe sometimes, and Joe hated that he judged him. For instance, Alex is a dad, right? Well, Joe was a shit dad, and they both knew it. That's just one example."

"But Alex cared about Joe?"

"Like a brother, I'm pretty sure."

"He didn't seem too broken up when I met him."

"That's just the way he is. He'll get angry, but he's the kind of guy who won't show weakness."

"Okay, thanks. This was helpful. So where can I reach him?"

"I'll text you his number, but you might be better off just showing up."

"You think that's a good idea?"

"He's a talent manager in Hollywood. He may not be famous, but he's a key gatekeeper. I can't imagine how many phone calls he ignores in any given hour. And today's not even a normal day."

"Good point," I said. "How about weird strangers who show up at his office without appointments?"

"Lot fewer of those. And he has a chain of admins who are pretty good at keeping unannounced visitors at bay."

"A chain?"

"Yeah. Plenty of insulation. Alex has to be available to meet clients and other important people. But he needs to keep up barriers to keep away the grasping hoi polloi."

"And that's me, right?"

"Sure, but you've met him."

"Yeah, we're real close."

"Oh, I mean he doesn't like you, but he's wary of you." He paused, like he was reviewing my file in his head. "That should be enough to get you in the door."

Alex Caldwell was one of the founders of Apex Management, a big-time talent-management operation with a long roster of A-list clients. I looked it up on my phone and found a brief Wikipedia page and a very unhelpful Web site. The site was sleek and minimalistic, a single home page with a brief description of the company and a few deft name drops that conveyed its Hollywood dominance, a small constellation implying a sprawling network of stars. There was no contact information available on the page—not a business number or a general e-mail, not even a single civilian name. Apex was an entertainment fortress, and if the site was any indication, it was built to be impenetrable.

The address Jamie had given me was in Beverly Hills, a straight shot down Wilshire Boulevard, the long artery of road and office buildings that coursed from downtown to the ocean, running right through Koreatown along the way. Wilshire didn't have a big movie to its name like Sunset or Mulholland, but it was almost as iconic, as indivisible a root of L.A. I knew a girl from high school who got a fake I.D. with her street address grafted onto a New York license. She lived in a townhouse on Wilshire—her fake got confiscated within a week.

The drive from my office to Apex was only six miles long, but it took a full half hour with only slight traffic. Wilshire got nicer the farther west I drove—the slummy exteriors of K-Town led into the wholesome line of Miracle Mile. By the time I reached

Beverly Hills, the soju billboards might as well have belonged to another country.

Apex was in a modern office building with windows like liquid mercury, wedged among the luxury department stores of commercial Beverly Hills. I parked in the underground garage and submitted, with reluctance, to the compulsory valet parking.

I rode a quiet elevator up to the fourteenth floor, and found Apex Management behind wide doors of steel and glass. They opened onto a row of young white receptionists, their tidy heads tilted down toward Apple computers. One of them looked up when I came in, and I caught his eye before he could pretend he hadn't noticed me. He was a beautiful kid, college-age with dark hair and a shapely mouth. His only physical flaw was an unfortunate cursive tattoo that spread across one side of his neck. I would have bet a lot of money that he was a connected intern, a somebody's son—he was well-dressed with an air of boredom, a little vapid in the eyes. My guess was, he was rebellious enough to get inked, but that that was the extent of his imagination. He eyed me with suspicion, and I waited for the supercilious, "May I help you?"

It never came, so I approached the desk without breaking eye contact.

"Hi," I said. "My name's Juniper Song. I met Alex Caldwell the other day and wanted to talk to him. Is he in?"

He looked me up and down, openly evaluating my appearance. It took some effort not to squirm or revolt under his scornful gaze. A few seconds later, he sat back with a smirk, a clear enough message that he found me unremarkable. I wondered if rude disregard for commoners was part of his job description. "Do you have an appointment?" he asked.

"No," I said. "This is about Joe Tilley. As you can imagine, it's important."

"Sure," he said with grating sarcasm. "You mentioned the number-one news story in America, so I'll just go ahead and put you through to Joe Tilley's manager. Do you want me to call his agent while I'm at it?"

The other receptionists had turned to look at our exchange, and the girl next to him, a pretty wisp of blond hair and blue eyes, touched his elbow. "Come on, Diesel."

A quick burn of anger flushed through me, and it was tinged with humiliation, as if I really were trying to weasel my way to a sniff of fame. I didn't like the way this kid looked at me, and I didn't like that the other receptionists seemed to think I needed their pity.

"Look," I said, much calmer than I felt. "I'm not famous, okay? But I'm not trying to get famous, either. I just need to talk to Alex about Tilley. He'll want to talk to me, too."

"What about Joe?" The hostility stayed in his tone.

I snapped at him. To hell with pleasing Diesel. "What do you think? Maybe you know he was murdered recently?"

He snapped back. "Yeah. I do. We've been broken up about it all day."

The other receptionists murmured in response, and it struck me how strange it was that they'd all shown up for work, that work went on as usual, the first business day after a major client's murder. I noticed now that the little blond girl had been crying. There was a delicate puff to her eyelids, and her makeup looked like it had been touched up in poor light. It seemed unlikely that Joe Tilley knew any of these kids by name, but plenty of people mourned him without having met him once. I granted that his murder was a shocking event in this office, and I decided to give this punk the benefit of the doubt.

"I'm sorry for your loss," I said, smoothing out my tone. "I need to talk to Mr. Caldwell about the murder. He'll want to talk to me, too."

He sensed the conciliation, and when he spoke again, he sounded like he was trying to be reasonable. "Look, Miss, uh—" He coughed. "Believe it or not, you're not the first person I've talked to today with something 'important' to say about the murder. Alex is way busy. I can't just let you see him."

I sighed. "Will you just tell him my name, and say I'm the woman he met in the penthouse? You can always throw me out later."

The crying girl looked at me. "The penthouse?" she asked.

"Yeah," I said, leaving a meaningful pause. "That penthouse."

"Were you there?"

"He was good and dead by the time I showed up, but I saw him."

All four receptionists were looking at me now, and even Diesel eyed me with a new air of respect.

"I'll tell him," he said. "But no promises."

The lobby gleamed with white furniture and walls of glass, a futuristic look out of a high-end design catalog. I waited on a white leather sofa that was much less comfortable than it looked, glancing now and then at Diesel, who was on and off the phone. I was riffling through a bland coffee-table book when Diesel caught my eye, nodded once, and looked away. Ten minutes later, another beautiful college-age admin came to fetch me, this one female, in very high heels. She introduced herself as Alex's assistant Danica and escorted me down a long hall, where her stilettos clacked like thrown stones against the white polished concrete floor. Danica was friendly and talkative, and I wondered if my admission to Alex's company came with a rise in esteem in the eyes of the Apex Management youth.

"We are all in pieces," she said, a little chirpily. "Joe was such a sweet, sweet man. Did you know him well?"

"No," I said. "I didn't know him at all."

She smiled with her lips closed, and led me to a corner office, where she knocked on the door with diffident raps.

"I have Juniper Song here to see you," she said.

"Send her in," said Alex.

I squeezed through a person-size sliver in the heavy door, and when I thought to look, the girl had disappeared without showing her face inside. I took this as a bad sign.

The temperature dropped ten degrees in Alex's office. It was cold as a cave, the kind of cold that gripped your extremities long after you put on socks and gloves. Alex sat on a high-backed chair and looked unperturbed.

"Sit if you need to," he said, flicking his wrist at a fat-cushioned chair.

I sat, though I didn't need to.

Alex looked sleep deprived but not at all softened. He eyed me with undisguised disdain. "So what exactly is it you want?"

It was all the welcome I needed.

"I'm trying to find out what happened to Joe. If you can help me at all, I need to talk to you."

"Little Miss Private Investigator. I knew you'd be a pain in my ass."

"Is it so painful to help someone find your client's murderer?"

"What do you think I've been doing, picking my goddamn nose? I told the police whatever I could."

He had a point. I didn't look quite as competent and official as Detective Veronica Sanchez.

"Here's the thing, though," I pressed on. "The police are hung up on Jamie. If they're on the wrong track, which I think they are, then they're wasting everyone's time."

"What makes you think it wasn't Jamie?"

"For starters? He and his girlfriend are the ones who hired me. He seems pretty anxious to find the real killer."

"Sure," he snorted. "That's what they all say."

"Do you think it was Jamie?"

He shrugged. "Why not?"

I thought of Jamie's boyish face, his nervous affability. "You think he's capable of killing anyone?"

"As capable as anyone else, yes."

"Of killing Joe?"

"I don't trust the kid, okay? Never have. He's a coked-up impulsive loser, and I've known enough of them to recognize a danger when I see it."

"Do you even know him?"

He laughed, and it came out sounding mean. "You women," he said. "Willow loves him, too. He's the lead suspect in her husband's murder, and she won't shut up defending him."

I flushed, and though he was making me angry, what I felt most was embarrassment. I should never have let Jamie near me, not in that way.

"He's my *client*," I said. "He wants me to find out what happened, I'm going to find out what happened. If he's the murderer, then he shouldn't have asked. Can we at least agree that there's a question here?"

He nodded grimly.

"Were you there Thursday night? For the big party?"

"Ha," he said. "No. Joe didn't invite me to stuff like that."

"What, social stuff?"

He glared at me. "We were friends, but not drug-party friends. Dinner-party friends. Our wives got along. All five of them."

He stood up and walked over to a mahogany bookcase, almost empty of books, and picked up a framed photograph. It showed Joe and Willow with Alex and a tall brunette who must have been his current wife. He handed it to me with a gruff "Here." It was less a friendly gesture than insistent evidence of his close relationship with Joe, which he'd taken me to question.

All at once, I felt a strong pity for the dead man. Nearly everyone he knew—from the kids at the reception desk to Theodore, his only son, and Alex, his personal friend and manager—wanted a piece of him, a scrap from his robe that had nothing to do with love but with ownership only, proof of communion with the star. It was no wonder Theodore and Alex resented Jamie. Tilley, it seemed, had slipped from their possession, and Jamie had him, and he had loved him without avarice or jealousy.

"How long did you know each other?" I asked.

"Twenty years," he said. "He was just starting to make a name for himself then, and I was working for his manager. We ended up becoming drinking buddies. We were close. Went to each other's weddings and all that. And we worked together his whole career."

I'd hit a sore spot, so I changed tack. "What exactly does a manager do, anyway?"

"Manage," he said, without a trace of humor.

I let it go. "And now that he's dead?"

"I still work for him, for his family. Can you imagine what would happen if every celebrity lost his team the minute he died? There would be chaos."

"So you must be stressed out right now."

"I'm grieving. I'm busy. I'm not 'stressed out,'" he said, air quoting with contempt.

"Who do you mean when you say 'his family'? Do you mean Willow? His kids?"

"I'm looking out for all of them."

It didn't seem worth the antagonism to ask who was paying him, so I left it at that.

"Look. I know finding his killer isn't part of your job, but maybe you can help me. I'm sure you want to figure out who did this to your friend."

"Fine." He gave me a curt nod. I'd cornered him. "What is it you want to know?"

"Can you think of anyone who might have wanted Tilley dead?"

He grunted. "I'll tell you what I told the cops. A lot of people didn't like Joe. He was loud and arrogant and, frankly, kind of a bastard. But I can't think of anyone who would have wanted to hurt him. And that includes his wives."

"And the son? You know, Thor Tilla?"

He blew air through his lips in disgust. "Theodore? He had as much reason to as anyone else alive, but no. I doubt it. He's too much of a pussy to do something like that."

"I met him yesterday," I said. "We talked for a while. I feel bad for the kid."

Alex, apparently, did not. "I hope you didn't tell him anything he could tell to the tabloids."

"Why's that?"

"That kid's a fucking thorn in my side." He scowled. "No pun intended."

"But you look out for his interests, right?"

"Only as far as Joe's concerned, and only as far as his interests are in line with Joe's. Beyond that, the prick's on his own."

"I gathered he talks to the press when they'll let him."

"Ha. 'When they'll let him.' Like the tabloids have standards. They'll print anything that comes out of that little snake's mouth. Do you ever read *Star*? *Us Weekly*?"

"Not really."

"Don't. It's fucking garbage. This is what it's like being famous, okay? You take a shit, and there's a story with pictures the next day, shouting, 'Stars, they shit their brains out just like us.' And then there's the idiotic write-up, something like, 'Bart Fuckface had some mean Mexican for dinner, says a source.'"

"And Theodore, he's 'a source,' I take it?"

"Yeah, a fucking gold mine. You should've seen all the trash about Joe's family life. That kid fed everything he could to the press, and when he didn't know shit, he made it up."

"Doesn't it sound like he hated his dad? I mean they even fought the night of the murder."

"It's an interesting theory," he said, his face growing dark. I could tell he was visualizing headlines and he didn't seem to like what he saw. "But I don't have anything else to say on that front."

"Alright," I said, moving on. "What about his drug habit? Did he get on the wrong side of anyone dangerous?"

"Like I said, I don't know a lot about that. He tried to keep me in the dark about the illegal stuff, as much as he thought he could."

I paused. "You must have seen most of the stuff he got into, over the years."

"More than anyone else alive. I'm sure of it."

I had one more line of questioning, one I hesitated before setting into motion. "Did Tilley ever mention Jamie's girlfriend? Daphne Freamon?"

"No. Why would he have?"

"Because he knew her, though maybe he didn't know it. She went by a different name then," I said, holding his eyes. "Lanya Waters."

His face tightened, subtly, in a way that suggested a much larger underlying reaction, like the earth moving beneath a fault line. Her name meant something to him, something bigger than I'd thought.

"You know her, then," I said.

He tilted his chin up to mimic thought, then said, "The name sounds familiar."

"I'll bet it does. I can't imagine he didn't ask you for advice about her. I'd be surprised if you never met her, really. The artist? The cocktail waitress?"

"Right," he said, leaning back in his chair. The effort was gone from his face now, submerged and no longer visible. "I know exactly who you're talking about. She's African-American, right?" He said "African-American" carefully, stretching it to the full length of its seven syllables.

"What can you tell me about her and Joe?"

"They knew each other briefly," he said. "She sold him an oil painting."

"For a lot of money."

"Yeah, it was a lot of money. But Joe was extravagant, a patron of the arts."

I shot back, "He didn't buy it because he slept with her?"

Alex scratched at his forehead, his face unreadable, but when he spoke again his tone was relaxed. I hadn't noticed, until then, that it had been tense. "If you already know the answers, why do you bother asking?"

That was it. I'd dropped the wrong name, asked the wrong questions, and the interview was over—I was locked out at the gate. Within a minute, Alex made it clear that I was overstaying my welcome, and I excused myself gracefully against my own will. I left the freezing office a little dazed and dissatisfied, but there was also a knot in my stomach, a precursor to a hunch.

It was two o'clock when I left Apex Management. The sun was out, spilling its gentle bounty on the pedestrians of Beverly Hills. I lit a cigarette and joined the crowd, walking past Midwestern families in cargo shorts, Asian men carrying shopping bags for their wives. The scene was cheerful, commercial, and the air held the calm buzz of happy people behaving themselves. It was boring, too, for anyone who'd seen it once before, and soothing, in that way. It gave me room to think.

Alex Caldwell was hiding something. The name of Lanya Waters ran through him like an electrical shock. I watched it happen, and I watched his body absorb the effect. I'd played my knowledge of the affair like a trump card, and instead of jolting him again, it stabilized him.

I thought about reentering Alex's office, of putting my finger in his face and demanding information. But I wasn't a police officer—I wasn't even a friend.

He was protecting Joe Tilley. That was what I had to go on. Alex had made a career out of being Tilley's friend, of cleaning up his messes and clearing all paths to continued success. Even now, he would continue to guard Tilley's name—he felt ownership toward it, like a sculptor who'd spent years on a single work. That name, then, was under threat.

It occurred to me, too, that if he was hiding something, there was something else to know. Maybe Daphne hadn't been as plain as she'd let on.

She told me about the illicit affair, the blackmail, the buy-off, the change in identity. What, then, was the ineffable thing?

Twelve

I needed to talk to someone who might have information on Joe and Daphne. As far as I knew, that universe of people was small. Then I remembered how Jamie got hired. Joe Tilley, like many with enough money to do away with the administrative headaches of life, had a personal assistant. Unless someone was lying—a contingency that was all too possible—this personal assistant was an old friend of Daphne's. It occurred to me now that Daphne had very few people she would call old friends. This one knew her when she was Lanya the waitress, and she presumably lived in L.A.

It didn't make sense to ask Daphne, so I called Jamie again. He didn't ask questions, just gave me a name and a number. Rory Buckner. An area code from the middle of the country.

I was surprised when she picked up after two rings, and then I realized that while Alex was busier than ever, Rory might have been out of a job. Tilley's mess needed cleaning, his reputation tending, but the man himself was dead, and all his smaller needs and demands extinguished with his exit.

"Hello?" she asked, her voice a little eager.

"Hi," I said. "My name is Juniper Song. I'm a friend of Jamie Landon's. Can you talk?"

"What's this about?"

"Jamie's girlfriend, actually." I saw no point in appending the "ex." "Daphne Freamon. Your friend Lanya Waters."

She was quiet for a contemplative second, and I waited with the strained patience of a fisherman with a tug on the line. "What about her?" she asked.

"Her and Joe Tilley—what was the deal with them? I know they had a thing, but it doesn't quite add up."

She went silent now, and I thought she might hang up on me. Instead, she asked, "Where are you now?"

She asked me to meet her at her apartment in Santa Monica, on Sixth Street about a two-minute jog from the beach. It was a glittery part of town where even the homeless were better off than their counterparts in L.A. proper. Rory's building was brand-new, with white siding and a perfect lawn. She rang me in through a glass door that opened with a soft buzz.

I took a silent elevator to her apartment on the fourth floor. The first thing I noticed when she opened her door was a powerful scent of lavender—perfume or air freshener that stormed into my nostrils like an uninvited guest. Her body came second. She wore a slate gray sports bra and matching yoga shorts that amounted to a bikini's worth of fabric. She took care of herself, that much was evident. Her arms and legs were toned, almost muscular, and her belly curved in where most curved out. Her skin was the color of a roasted almond, and I couldn't tell if it was sprayed on or achieved in a UV-radiating coffin.

"Were you about to work out?" I asked.

She shrugged. She'd been expecting me for over half an hour, and I had to wonder if she was just showing off. I knew, with sudden certainty, that she was the kind of person who posted sexy mirror pictures on the Internet.

She had an attractive face, in full makeup, with a thin nose and a high arch to her brow. I couldn't determine her age—she could have been twenty-five or forty, and neither would have surprised me. Straw blond hair sprouted out of duller blond roots that looked wild and untamed in the context of Rory Buckner.

"Come in," she said, and I followed her into a small apartment with pink walls and a bookcase full of magazines. The lavender smell was even stronger inside, and I wondered if she'd knocked over a bottle of perfume until I caught the competing odors, a garish muddle of rosewater, strawberry, and jasmine.

We sat down on a gold fabric sofa, and she crossed her legs and said, "So?"

"First of all," I said, "I'm sorry about your boss. This must be a hard time for you."

"Thank you," she said. "It's been super weird."

"How well do you know Jamie?" I asked.

"Not that well. I helped him get the job, and I've seen him a lot just with Joe. But we've never hung out or anything like that."

"Nice guy, in your opinion?"

"Yeah." She paused, then whispered, "Is it true they think he did it?"

"You mean the police? I wouldn't know much more than you."

She bit on her upper lip and nodded with visible disappointment.

"What do you think?" I asked.

She brightened, and I knew all at once how to handle her. Not only was Rory Buckner an attention seeker, she was also a gossip—the best kind of person to interview when you had no real authority.

"I don't know, but he's such a cokehead I wouldn't be super surprised."

"He's the only cokehead you know?"

She smiled. "Touché."

"What was their relationship like?" I asked.

"They were close, which is saying a lot, actually. I worked for Joe for six years, and I don't think he ever asked me a single thing about myself."

"Wow."

She shrugged. "I'm not bitter or anything. That's just how he was."

It was clear enough that she was bitter, and that could only work to my advantage. "Did you like him?"

"I did," she said. "It was a good job. Paid well, kind of weird hours, but I couldn't complain."

"As a person, though?"

She frowned. "I don't want to talk crap," she said. "But I guess you could say he wasn't a great person."

"In what way?"

"He was super self-centered and unreasonable. *Bratty*, I guess, if you can call a grown man that. Sometimes he would just smile and look at me and say things like, 'You love me, right?' Like, kind of joking? But I always had to answer."

"And you'd say yes?"

"It was part of my job, really. I've never met a man who was so into his own fame. He wanted love—he needed to be loved—but, like, he didn't want the bother of loving back."

"So you didn't love him." I thought of Jamie, sobbing that he did.

"Sometimes I thought I did. In the way you might love a kid you babysit. I'm sorry he's gone. I can say that for sure."

She put her head down and I followed suit, giving a moment of silence to the dead man. When I thought enough time had passed to change the subject, I went for it.

"So, how do you know Daphne?"

"Oh boy," she said. "The short answer is that I don't. Not really."

"I thought you were friends. I thought you got Jamie that writing gig."

She laughed. She had a salty laugh. "Is that what she told you?"

I nodded, combing over my memory for a possible mistake. There was none. "She said you waitressed together."

"We may have waitressed in L.A. at the same time, like everyone else. But I never even saw Lanya Waters until Abby's party."

"Was that the night—"

"Oh yeah," she said.

"Were you there?"

She nodded.

"Can you tell me what happened?"

"I shouldn't." She paused, chewing her lip, but I could tell I'd revived an itch, and I could see it growing irresistible as she reviewed her trove of secrets, unjustly hidden from the world.

"Sure you should," I said. "Look, this is a huge case—you know that, right? The whole world wants to know what happened to Joe Tilley. You were close to him—you know things most people don't. What you have to say might end up being important."

She didn't say anything for a minute, but I could tell she'd made up her mind.

"I was helping out with the party," she said. "Dealing with the caterer, taking people's coats, whatever. Towards the end of the night, I was also watching Abby. She was getting trashed, and I was kind of babysitting her, making sure she didn't puke in anyone's wineglass, etc."

"Did you meet Lanya then?"

"I did, yeah. She was one of the cocktail waitresses, and I gave them the rundown on how the evening was supposed to go. She was beautiful, of course. They were all beautiful. But I guess I remembered her because she was black, and like, extra beautiful for a black girl, you know what I mean?"

I didn't respond, and for a second she seemed to wonder if she'd said something wrong.

"Anyway, I remembered her. After."

She looked at me meaningfully, but I didn't interrupt.

"I didn't see her again until the next morning, which was a Sunday. I'd gone home late, and I expected to sleep in, but Alex called me at around eight o'clock. I remember looking at the clock and wondering what the hell it was Joe wanted."

"And what did he want?"

"Well, Alex got me on the phone and he was super angry, I could tell. He was cussing and breathing hard, and I just thought, 'Ugh. What is it this time?' And then he told me that this cocktail waitress from the party wouldn't leave the house."

"That's what he said?"

"That's almost the exact phrasing. 'One of the cocktail waitresses won't leave the house.' As if it were two in the morning instead of eight."

"So, what did he want you to do about it?"

"He wanted me to come to the house and talk to this waitress while he kept an eye on Abby. He thought I could convince her, woman to woman, you know?"

"Sure."

"So I went over there. It sounded urgent so I didn't even put on makeup or anything. Just threw on a sweatshirt and jeans and booked it. And when I got there, I parked outside like Alex told me to and waited for him to let me in."

"The utmost caution when the lady of the house is sleeping."

"That's when I really met Lanya," she said. "She was in the guest bedroom, alone, and naked."

"Naked?"

"She was sitting under the covers, but she was topless, like her boobs were showing and it was like she didn't even notice."

Daphne wasn't the exhibitionist type—I'd known her long enough to rule out that trait. There was something very wrong with this scene.

"So I walked in and I was thinking, 'What is wrong with this woman? She sleeps with a movie star in his own house and refuses to leave? Doesn't she know the drill?' and I was trying to figure out a gentle way to say all this when I realized she hadn't even looked at me. I started to introduce myself, and she just stared straight ahead like I was a ghost. I waved my hand in front of her face like this, like, 'Hello?' and she just blinked."

I put a hand over my mouth and breathed hard. I didn't want to hear the rest of the story, but I didn't stop her.

"I tried talking to her, saying I understood where she was coming from and all, but that she couldn't stay here. I feel like I chattered on for, like, ten minutes, and then we just kind of sat there, in total silence, for even longer. Finally, she looked at me, and she just said, 'Send in the man.' I assumed she meant Alex, and I tagged him in and spent the next hour upstairs, hoping to God Abby didn't wake up. I guess they must have worked something out, because when he came to get me, the guest bed was made and Lanya was dressed—I mean as dressed as she was going to get in that cocktail outfit."

I looked at Rory's yoga gear, but couldn't manage a laugh.

"Alex gave me a list of things to do and pushed us out of the house, together."

"What things?"

"Morning-after things," she said. "I got her some new clothes and a dose of Plan B and watched her take it in front of me. I gave her a ride home. She barely talked to me, except at the end, when she demanded my contact information."

"Did you give her any money?"

"No," she said. "But I'll bet Alex did. I never did find out how he convinced her to put her clothes on."

"Miss Buckner," I said, as serious as I felt. "What did Joe Tilley do to Lanya Waters?"

She bit her lip. "What do you mean what did he do *to* her?"

I stared at her until I was staring at my own form reflected twice in her pupils, solid and unforgiving. "He raped her," I said. "Didn't he?"

She recoiled as if I'd drawn my hand to slap her. "No," she said. "I mean he didn't *rape* rape her."

My head filled with heat and I had a hard time controlling my voice. "The fuck does that mean, 'he didn't *rape* rape her'?"

"Hold on. Calm down," she said. "I did think, maybe, it wasn't just that they slept together, okay? So I asked Alex about it."

"And?"

"He said they'd been flirting all night and that Lanya told her ride to go ahead without her. She meant to spend the night, or at least a few more hours."

"And?"

"I only know this secondhand, okay? I didn't ask a lot of questions. That's not my job."

"It's mine. Keep talking."

"Well from what I understand, they started fooling around, and then she said she didn't want it anymore. This is what *she* told Alex."

She. Like it was a dirty word.

"And then they had sex. And instead of leaving, she stayed the night. And that's where I found her. Naked, refusing to leave."

"He raped her. Joe Tilley was a rapist."

"No, come on. He wasn't perfect, but he wasn't a rapist."

"Miss Buckner, I don't know what dictionary you're using, but in mine, you become a rapist when you rape somebody."

"There's a gray area. What happened between Joe and Lanya—that's a gray area."

"That is a very *dark* gray area," I said, my eyes burning. "Some might even call it black."

I stood up and grabbed my bag in one quick motion, and she stayed planted on the couch, looking startled.

"I didn't do anything," she said, with a dazed, petulant murmur.

I thanked her for her time and let myself out before she could utter another word in her defense.

On my way home, I thought of all the questions I'd forgotten to ask. What happened next? How did she set up the art sale? How had she contacted Rory? How, and when, and why? What had happened to her, to Joe, in the years between?

But it didn't matter, not really, and I couldn't go back now. I had stormed out in my righteous rage, and the heat of it welded the door shut.

Thirteen

I was sitting in traffic with my thoughts booming in my head when my phone rang. It was Chaz.

"Winfred Park," he said. "From Diamond Bar, California."

"That's his full name?"

"Was," he said. "He's dead."

I listened, dumbstruck, as Chaz filled me in.

Winfred Park was thirty-one years old, and he lived alone in a two-bedroom apartment on Catalina, in the heart of Korea-town. He supported his mother, who lived in subsidized housing in West Adams, and had a brother, Alfred, who was twenty-nine. Both brothers were affiliated with the Rampart Boulevard Gang, a sprawling organization with a presence dating back to the six-ties. It was L.A.'s first multiethnic gang, a Harvard of the crimi-nal world. Not that that would help Mrs. Park sleep at night.

Winfred had been found dead in his apartment, after an anonymous tip to police. It had happened sometime that day, between morning and early afternoon. The cause was apparent enough. He'd been shot, execution style, right between the eyes.

"Jesus," I said when he was done with his report. "He was a fucking gangster?"

"Oh yeah, had the tattoos and everything."

"His brother, Alfred. Are the odds pretty good he was one of Isaac's attackers?"

"That would be a good guess."

"Lot of Koreans in this gang?"

"A good number. Mostly Mexicans. One of the major ally gangs is Korean, and there's some crossover there."

"What do they do?"

"Rape and pillage. I don't know, girl. Gang stuff."

"Well, what did a gangster want with Lori?"

"The same thing every man seems to want with Lori?"

"I guess the question is—what did he want with Taejin?"

He sighed noisily and asked, "Do you want me to check it out?"

Homicide was an everyday occurrence in Los Angeles. Most of these murders had nothing to do with me. I had one on my plate right now, and it was as much as I could handle, if not more.

Winfred's murder was not my problem. I didn't like the guy, and frankly, it didn't pain me much to see him gone. He was dangerous, with a lecherous ugly heart that beat, until recently, for Lori.

But if Taejin Chung was in trouble, if he was at the mercy of a gangster to the point where he'd loan out his niece in payment of services or disservices, rendered or withheld—then maybe that was my problem. Lori was as close as I had to family these days, and Taejin, by extension, was in my clan. It was clear enough, anyway, that his woes had the power to cause Lori injury.

I nodded silently before talking at my phone. "If you have time," I said, "I want to know what Taejin owed Winfred, and whether that debt stays with him now that Winfred is dead."

"Do you think Taejin could have killed him himself?"

"I don't know him well enough to say for sure. I would guess he had motive. But we can let the police solve this shithead's murder."

"That reminds me—guess how I got the scoop," he said.

"I don't know. You're good at your job?"

"I am, yeah. But we got lucky this time. The detective on the case is you and Art's mutual friend."

"Veronica Sanchez? And she talked to you?"

"She and Art go way back."

"But she hates my guts."

"Actually she kind of likes you. She said you were a ball buster. Then she said, 'It's a good thing I don't have balls.'" He laughed as he delivered the line.

We hung up, and I called Lori to tell her I'd be home soon. I spent the rest of the drive thinking about how to break the news.

It was five thirty when I walked into our apartment, and Lori was already there, watching something silly on TV. She looked up when I came in, and put her show on mute.

"Long day?" she asked.

I was rarely home this early, but the day had been harder than any all-nighter, and I must have worn its strain on my face.

"Yeah," I said. "I need a drink. Maybe you want something, too."

"No thanks," she said. Lori wasn't a casual drinker—it was an age thing, maybe. When I was twenty-three I only drank to get drunk, too.

I opened a beer and plopped down next to her on the couch. I took a cool gulp and put one hand on her shoulder. "Look. I have some important news," I said.

I told her about Winfred, and she reached for my beer. She drank a third of the bottle in one thirsty swallow.

"He was here," she said. "This morning, after you left. He was right outside, texting me to let him in, and I pretended I wasn't home."

"Jesus, really? What a creep." She winced, so I changed tack. "Lori, did you know he was part of a gang?"

She shook her head. "I had no idea, but I'm not that surprised."

"Yeah, a guy who can attack a stranger for dating a girl isn't exactly bound by things like laws or social norms." I sighed. "But here's a question: why is your uncle Taejin messing around with gangsters?"

She shuddered. "I don't know. Maybe he's short on money? It must be money, right?"

I thought about telling her I put Chaz on the trail, but it felt like an invasion, and I didn't want her objecting. "I don't have the slightest idea," I said.

Then she cried for Winfred Park, her small shoulders shaking while big tears spilled from her hazy eyes. I patted her back and brought her a new beer, which she accepted with both hands. She had seen too much death in this lifetime, too much of it too close to home.

"Is it me?" she asked, her voice thick with snot. "Am I cursed?"

It was hard to deny that, in the colloquial sense, anyway. The week I met her, four men turned up dead, all murdered in her name. Her own mother pulled the trigger on one, and as a result she was stuck with me, cursed in my own right.

"No," I said with a weak smile, denying it after all. "Whatever happened to Winfred, it wasn't your fault."

"Maybe I secretly wanted it, and God listened to my heart and made it happen," she said. "Just like with Greg." And her face broke again for another round.

I assured and comforted her, shaking my head and cooing as I'd done countless times in the last year. "Even if it has something to do with you—and that's an *if*, you know? He was a gangster who beat up innocent people with no provocation. But even if, you didn't invite him into your life. He forced his way in. Frankly I'm relieved he's dead. It means he can't bother you anymore."

She gasped between her sobs. "How can you say that, *unni*?"

"Easily," I said. "He was scum, and I was happier before he showed up. You were happier, too."

"But he was a human being."

"So was Ted Bundy. Look, I'm not saying I would have killed him, or even wanted him dead, per se. But what difference does it make to me if he died or moved to Tampa? There are lots of dead people more deserving of my grief, and I don't even know them by name."

She frowned, and I pushed my thumb into the crease in her forehead.

"Am I a bad person?" I asked her.

She shook her head with vigor, so that her curly hair whipped around her. "I didn't mean that," she said.

"Go ahead and cry for him," I said. "But when you feel better, don't feel bad if you feel light and free. Call Isaac. Work it out. You've done more for Winfred than he ever deserved."

I sat with her, rubbing her back while she cried. When she was fresh out of tears, I made dinner, clumsily, with frozen rice

cakes and a batch of sauce she'd already prepped over the weekend. Without discussion, we agreed to a bottle of wine, one of
the fruity five-dollar chardonnays we picked up at Trader Joe's.
Lori unmuted the TV, and we watched eight different couples
find dream homes that fit their budgets. Her eyes, which always
looked out of focus to begin with, glazed over from the wine and
the repetitive drone of the TV.

She turned the channel and the screen lit up with a jolty
reel of celebrity asses, every one of them young and female.
Even with the volume low, I could hear the obnoxious voiceover,
a fast-talking man using high-pitched tones that seemed to say,
"Get a load of this" as swimsuit photos flashed across the screen.
There was something frantic about the stream of images, and I
wondered how many viewers tuned in to this garbage, getting
their brains scrubbed to nothing while drool seeped from their
mouths.

I kept one eye open for any mention of Tilley's murder, though
I doubted this was the best source for solid breaking news. We
watched a full investigative report on a starlet's "baby bump,"
about the size and shape of a cheeseburger and a tall beer, not
that anyone was calling for my professional opinion. Next came
a horrible segment on a socialite whose name I hadn't heard
since the turn of the century. She'd taken a video of herself suck-
ing on the wide end of a Japanese eggplant, making bedroom
eyes at what was clearly a bathroom mirror, an iPhone held un-
steadily in her free hand. The video was sad and upsetting, and
the gleeful babble of commentary was even worse.

I was about to ask Lori if we could change the channel when
Theodore Tilley's face filled the screen. It was a mug shot. I turned
up the volume.

It was clear enough that the story didn't match the mocking, sleazy tone of the show. The voiceover was replaced with something more somber, but nothing that would ever be confused with legitimate news.

My first thought was that Theodore had been arrested for Joe's murder, and before I could register any pity for the boy, a strong relief took hold of my body, relief that Jamie had been cleared. It was followed by a flinch of guilt, but I learned soon enough that all that feeling was wasted. Theodore hadn't been arrested for his father's murder—he'd been caught assaulting the prime suspect.

"Isn't that Jamie?" Lori asked. Her voice was animated for the first time all evening.

"Shit," I said. "It is."

"What's he doing on TMZ?"

"Sorry, Lori. Be quiet for a sec."

The screen showed a picture of Jamie with Tilley, taken on some bright sidewalk on a happier day. This was followed by a picture of Jamie sitting on a couch, talking to someone out of the frame. I recognized it as his profile photo from Facebook. The montage unrolled slowly, with more pictures of Tilley and Theodore, interspersed with snippets of text, pull quotes from Twitter, and Web publications of varying reputability.

There wasn't much information available, and the TMZ reporter spent some effort trying to stretch out what he had in order to justify the length of the coverage. Jamie was attacked outside of his apartment in broad daylight, when he went out to walk his roommate's dog. Theodore had been sitting in his car waiting for him, possibly intoxicated. He chased Jamie down as soon as he saw him, and bashed him in the ribs with a baseball bat. He only had time for the one blow—two passing pedestrians had seen his swinging approach, and they caught up to him before he could inflict serious damage. Jamie was fine, from the looks of it, but Theodore was arrested.

The report ended with blatant speculation about Jamie's identity as the LAPD's person of interest. Theodore hadn't yet made a statement, but the motive was clear to the TMZ reporter, and to the mass of popcorn munchers across the world, shouting their predictions into the broad echoing theater of the Internet. Thor Tilla, they seemed to agree, was a thwarted avenger, a hapless Inigo Montoya going after the man who had killed his father, still roaming free on the streets.

I had to admit, the motive seemed to fit. Part of me had been hopeful that Theodore was the killer. He made sense as a suspect, and though I felt bad for him, I wasn't attached to his fate one way or another. I'd liked him fine, considering, but if he were a murderer, I'd been perfectly willing to give him up.

There was always the chance that this was all a stunt, designed to exonerate him preemptively in the eye of the public. But I doubted that. I might have believed him as an emotional killer, but I didn't see him pulling off anything quite complicated.

In any case, this didn't look good for Jamie.

"*Unni?*" Lori's voice broke into my thoughts with an insistent edge. "Jamie is involved in Joe Tilley's murder?"

I bit my lip. I hadn't told her much about my activities over the last few weeks. After all she'd been through, I wanted to keep her as far away from my work as possible. Not that I'd succeeded in insulating her from evil, but I hadn't wanted to involve her in the mess of a murder that had nothing to do with her.

She was looking at me now with a question in her unfocused eyes that turned, against my silence, to hurt. "This is why you've been working with him? Because he's a suspect?"

"Hey, don't be mad," I said. "I wouldn't be helping him if I thought he did it."

Her face tightened. I thought I'd never seen her so angry.

"What is it?"

"Nothing," she said, spitting the syllables.

I wanted to get in touch with Jamie, and Lori was starting to grate on my nerves. "Oh, really?"

"I can bullshit just as well as you," she said snottily.

I didn't bother pointing out this wasn't true, that even the way she said "bullshit" sounded odd and unaccustomed, like it had come experimentally out of a child's mouth.

"Why are you mad at me?"

She huffed out a scornful laugh. "You spent all night trying to make me feel better, and thank you, I appreciate it, I really do. But what am I, huh? After all we've been through, all *you've* been through, you can't talk to me?"

"Of course I can talk to you."

"Yeah? Well I would've thought dealing with another murder might be something worth mentioning."

She looked like she was about to cry, and I saw that she was right. I'd insulted her, even with my best intentions.

"I'm sorry I didn't tell you," I said gently. "I didn't want to involve you."

"Why not?" she asked. "We're supposed to be family now. You're supposed to let me into your life."

"I know. I'm sorry. But this stuff is ugly, and it's better if you don't touch it."

"Remember the part when Winfred stalked me and beat up my boyfriend and turned up killed? Remember that?"

"So why would you want to see more of that?"

"I don't! But you were there for me, and I want to be there for you. This is a two-way street, *unni*. I know you have some weird savior complex, but you need my help, too. You're even more *fucked* up than I am."

Her words sunk into me at a tender point of entry. I wanted to defend myself, but there was some truth to what she said. I did think of myself as her protector—she was so fragile, so wounded and alone—and it struck me all over again how she reminded me of my sister. I was the strong one, the perpetual survivor. I was the one who could shoulder this weight.

"I'm not a child, *unni*." She spoke softly now.

I wiped tears from my eyes with the corners of my thumbs.

"No, you're not," I said. "But neither was Diego. He was a good man, and he died because of my big fucking mouth."

"No, he didn't," she said. "You have to stop with that. He died because somebody *murdered* him. It wasn't your fault."

This was well-trod ground, an assurance that Lori had to give me once in a while. Still, I felt the warmth of it, almost painful, like bathwater poured over an open wound.

As it turned out, Lori didn't care much for the particulars, and when I told her I had to keep some things confidential, she didn't pry for the juicy details. She wasn't after gossip, though she admitted she found it exciting. She just wanted a sign that I trusted her at all. We talked until late into the night, about my involvement in the case, and my attendant feelings, my many anxieties. At some point I tried to get in touch with Jamie, but neither he nor Daphne answered my calls.

It was therapeutic, unloading on Lori, but when I told her I couldn't talk anymore, she agreed to turn the TV back on. When she stumbled on a half-hour infomercial for a juicer, I told her to stay on that channel.

I tried to tune into that low frequency, but I just couldn't empty my head. I hadn't told Lori what I'd found out from Rory Buckner, and I kept thinking about Daphne, naked and catatonic, violated by a man who had all the power she lacked. By the time Lori dozed off and I got ready for bed, I'd mulled over the scene so many times that I felt like I'd seen it with my eyes rather than Rory's. My emotions were exhausting and felt a lot like grieving, though no one had died and it had happened years ago.

Of course people *had* died, and now my mind found the image of Joe Tilley, soaking in blood. I felt a short jolt of vicious satisfaction, and thought about revenge.

As soon as the word entered my thought process, I knew I'd been avoiding it. If Joe Tilley raped Daphne, then he wasn't her benefactor, spurred to action by the lightest touch of blackmail. She must have hated him. She must have wanted him dead.

Tuesday morning I googled Joe Tilley and a picture of him and Jamie popped up in the first result. It was the same picture that was shown on TMZ, the two of them strolling on a sunlit sidewalk. Next to the picture was a headline: POLICE MAKE ARREST IN MURDER OF JOE TILLEY.

I called Chaz, fumbling for my phone without looking away from my laptop.

"Did you hear?" I asked.

"Good morning to you, too," he said. "Hear what?"

"They arrested Jamie."

"Oh good grief. When?"

"I don't have any inside info. I just found out a second ago." I skimmed through the first article, the first of many, from the looks of it. "This morning, I guess. Suspect arrested at his home in West Hollywood."

"You found out on the Internet?"

"Yup," I said, biting down on my building anxiety. "No one thought to call me."

"At this point he probably needs a lawyer more than he needs you."

I shook my head. "I guess I'm going to try and call Detective Sanchez."

"Yeah, because she's not busy right now."

"She'll want to talk to me," I said. "She thinks I'm holding out on her."

"Well you are, aren't you?"

"Oh yeah, big-time. And you haven't even heard the latest."

"Please, regale me."

I regaled him.

"Holy shit," he said. "He was a bastard."

"Yep, that he was."

"You're going to tell that to Veronica?"

"I'm not planning to," I said. "But anyway, she probably knows already."

"Do you think Jamie knew about the rape?"

"I'm trying to crunch that," I said. "Been trying since yesterday. I was going to call him today, but I guess that's not happening."

"I wonder if that's why they have him."

"Could be," I said. "It gives him motive."

"Not just him."

I closed my eyes and held my head with my free hand. "By the way, did you find out anything else about Winfred?"

"I talked to Lori's uncle on the phone," he said.

"Yeah?"

"He was dodgy, I can tell you that."

"What did he say?"

"He wouldn't talk to me. He acted like he didn't even speak English."

"He actually pretended?"

"He actually pretended."

"That's amazing. I mean I've heard him, and his English is as good as mine. Though, oh," I said. "Did you say who you were?"

He snorted. "Yes."

"Did you forget you're one of the two people who witnessed his sister shoot a guy in the neck?"

"Ah," he said. "Right."

"Maybe he just got flustered."

Luckily for us, we'd both declined to testify against Yujin. She was Lori's mom, and we found we didn't have much that was nice to say.

"I was thinking about stopping by the shop, but maybe it would be better if you came with me." He chuckled. "Maybe it'll help you take your mind off things, too."

"Jesus," I said. "Is this my life? All rocks and hard places?"

"It's your call, Song. I can handle him myself if you want."

"When were you going to go?"

"Sometime today."

"I want to call Detective Sanchez, and then I'll meet you at the office."

"Sure," he said. "Break a leg."

* * *

"Juniper Song," she said by way of greeting. "I was hoping you'd call."

"You have my number in your phone? I'm flattered."

"Well I'm a murder detective, and you seem to be involved in every murder in L.A."

"You mean Winfred Park?"

"Joe Tilley and Winfred Park. A movie star and a K-Town thug. I wouldn't think they were connected, except both of their lines seem to run through you. Why?"

"Have you considered it might be coincidence?"

"Coincidence is for lazy detectives," she said. "Not for me, and I'd hope not for you."

"Well I don't know what to tell you. I'm not calling about Winfred. Couldn't care less about him."

"So, what are you calling about?"

"You made an arrest. Congratulations."

"Right, that. Thank you," she said. "And we did it without your help."

"How's he doing, by the way? Wasn't he attacked with a baseball bat, like, five minutes ago?" I asked sharply. "Real nice timing."

"He's fine. Some bruising. Last thing on his mind, I'm sure."

"What happened? You found his DNA at the crime scene?" I asked. "Did you also find the DNA of a hundred other people?"

"Do you have anything to report? Because otherwise you're wasting my time, Juniper Song."

"I'm sorry," I said, lowering my voice. "I'm just pretty upset about this."

"Listen," she said, softening her tone, too. "I don't mean to be a bitch here, but this is *my* case. If you want to help me, then go ahead, but I don't have time to sit here and listen to you question my judgment."

"What if he is innocent? Isn't that something you would want to know?"

"Sure," she said. "What do you know that I don't?"

I ran through the notes in my head and found them all in a jumble. Daphne's rape sat there, partially processed, impossible to clear away. I was haunted by sorrow, but I was also frustrated with her, by her continued insistence on hiding things from me when I was doing my best to help her and Jamie. And then there was the obvious question: What did it mean that Joe Tilley had raped his prime murder suspect's girlfriend and gotten away with it? I'd been committed to Jamie's innocence, and I had a gut feeling that the wrong person was in jail. But even I had to admit that this latest discovery tightened the case against him. Then again, it introduced new possibilities. Detective Sanchez was already interested in Lanya Waters, a person I now knew had motive. Daphne had lied to me so easily and so often that it was satisfying to know I could get her in deep shit if I chose. But I wasn't about to bring her name into the fray, and even if I did, it would only hurt Jamie's case. If I was sick with anger on hearing about the rape, I could only imagine how Jamie might have felt.

I'd been silent a long time when I heard Detective Sanchez tut-tut on the other end of the line.

"Don't be fooled by a pretty face," she said.

For an alarming instant, I thought she was talking about Daphne, until I remembered which face had been under discussion. My annoyance brought me back into the moment.

"Please, Veronica. Don't patronize me."

But as I hung up, Jamie's woeful eyes flashed darkly across my mind. They protested his innocence, but I knew well enough that they had no proof.

* * *

I picked Chaz up from the office at ten thirty after a binge of cigarettes and coffee. My conversation with Detective Sanchez had not gone well, and it left a terrible taste I couldn't expunge. Chaz read my mood as he got in the car and kept his questions brief.

Our office was only a half-mile from T & J Collision Center, across a representative chunk of Koreatown, crammed tall with redolent restaurants and low-rent office space. Signposts advertised in tacky block letters, many of them Korean, another large chunk of them in Spanish. When angry white Americans worried about losing control of their country, Koreatown was the wrecked city of their nightmares. Ancient Koreans lived in sallow, stucco apartments, within short bus rides of their Korean markets, doctors, and video stores. My own grandparents had spent their last years in a one-bedroom on New Hampshire, dying without five words of English between them. The Mexicans working in Koreatown didn't bother with English either, but they could rattle off Korean with the soft round tones of native speakers.

T & J was on Eighth Street, on the south side of Koreatown. We parked on the street and made our way up the slope of the driveway. A dozen cars crowded the concrete, some opened up, some whole and shining, in various stages of surgery. It felt strange to be here. It was my first visit, but Chaz had been once before, tracking the stolen car of his murdered brother-in-law. I surveyed the anonymous cars and wondered what stories they told.

The office was set deep behind the driveway, a hideous white building with molded pillars that must have been left over from another phase of the body shop's life. Maybe it had been a statue garden, selling peeing cherub fountains. We knocked and entered without waiting for a response. A bell rang, two-toned and sonorous.

A Korean boy in his early twenties sat up straight and greeted us in English when we walked in. He had a sweet, bland face about the size of a stop sign.

"Is your boss in?" asked Chaz.

"He'll be back in a few minutes. He just went to get food," said the boy. He indicated a lumpy-looking couch and a coffee table covered in Korean magazines. "You can wait here if you want. Do you want water or anything?"

I felt bad imposing on his hospitality when we weren't paying customers, but Chaz said, "Sure" and made himself comfortable. The boy walked to a water cooler and tapped cold water into two small paper cups. While his back was turned, Chaz and I exchanged a look. He pointed at my chest then changed his hand into a thumbs-up.

When the boy handed me my water, I thanked him and asked, "What's your name?"

"Simon," he said. "Yours?"

"Chaz," said Chaz, extending a thick hand and a big cheese of a smile. "And this here's Juniper. Watch out for her."

"I know your boss, actually," I told Simon.

"Yeah? Mr. Chung?"

"Yeah, I live with his niece."

"Lori?"

"You know her?"

"Oh, yeah," he said. "How could I not?"

There was nothing slimy about his tone, but I gave him a wry side eye just in case. His face went red as a steamed crab.

"She visits a lot, I mean," he said, recovering.

"When was she last here?"

"Actually she hasn't been in for a while. Maybe two or three weeks?" He thought about it, chanting *um, um, um.* "Oh I remember. She ran into Winfred."

I knew from the way he said the name that he didn't know he was talking about a dead man. There was a lilt and an eye roll in his tone that suggested annoyance but no taint of danger. That worked well enough for us. I could almost hear the same wheels turning in Chaz's head, right next to me.

"Is that the guy who's been stalking her?" I asked, more colloquially than truth demanded.

"Has he been? I had a feeling he might try and bother her."

"What's his deal? Should I be worried?"

"I don't know him that well."

"He doesn't work here?"

"No. I know he has some kind of thing with Mr. Chung, but I don't really know what it's about."

"Does he come here a lot?"

"Maybe a couple times a week?"

"Since when?"

He looked at the ceiling and mouthed while he thought. "Two or three months? I don't know. A while."

"And he only ran into Lori two weeks ago?"

"Honestly, I think Mr. Chung must have been trying to keep them separated."

"Because Winfred is . . ." I prompted him.

"Kind of a tough guy asshole?" He wrinkled his face and shrugged.

"Have you interacted with him much?"

"No. I doubt he even knows my name. But I can hear him talking to Mr. Chung. He's loud when he's mad, and he seems mad all the time."

"About anything in particular?"

"Geez, Song, what's with the interrogation, huh?" Chaz interjected with a corny laugh.

He must have thought I was being unsubtle. I knew he was trying to help, but I glared at him. "I'm just curious about this guy because he won't leave my roommate alone. Fair enough?"

He raised his hands, innocent and smug.

"I don't mind," said Simon. "The guy gives me the creeps."

"So, what's he yelling at Taejin for?"

He shrugged. "I'm not supposed to be listening or anything."

"But that's his office right there, isn't it? And you work in here?"

"Yeah, exactly."

"So, anything worth eavesdropping?"

"Well I know Mr. Chung owes him something, because he says that all the time. My Korean isn't amazing or anything, but I know that phrase pretty well by now. He calls himself Mr. Chung's personal savior, and he calls him a little mouse."

"He yells at him in Korean?"

"Both. You know how that goes, I'm sure."

I thought about my rare conversations with my mother, so evenly bilingual I never noticed when I was switching.

"But you don't know what Winfred's role is here?"

"I asked Mr. Chung when Winfred first started coming around, but I could tell it made him uncomfortable. He gave me some vague answer about business, and I didn't ask again." He hesitated, then lowered his voice. "Part of me wonders if it's something illegal. He's a scary guy, and he's all tatted up, too."

"I noticed as much," I said. "Anything concrete?"

He shook his head and smiled. "I just have a paranoid streak."

Chaz shifted his weight and tapped his knee against mine. *If he only knew*, said the knee.

The doorbell sang, and Taejin Chung walked in carrying an open cardboard box loaded with napkins and foam containers. The pungent smell of kimchi cut across the room and I was suddenly aware of my boss as a white man. Taejin looked up, and when he saw me and Chaz, he bowed as deeply as he could with his lunch held in front of him. I bowed back, a short one, and greeted him in Korean.

Taejin was a small man, about five foot four and slight all around—there wasn't much mass in the Chung/Lim family gene pool. He was in his early forties, with a full head of silver hair that clashed pleasantly with his youthful, tanned face. He looked a lot like both Lori and her mother, with fine features that would be called beautiful on any woman. His hairless, bony arms poked out of a rolled-up button-down, open across the front to reveal a ribbed wife beater, already sullied with a splash of peppery orange soup.

He walked past me and Chaz to hand the food off to Simon. "Change," he said in English, passing him a couple old bills.

Chaz cleared his throat and introduced himself. "Mr. Chung, I'm Chaz Lindley. We spoke on the phone yesterday."

Taejin looked up and whitened slightly before going pink. "Oh," he said. "Hello."

"Do you have a minute?"

"Yeah," he said. He was flustered, caught off guard with an armful of hot soup. He set it down on the coffee table and turned to Simon. "Sorry, Simon. Can you take a ten-minute walk? We'll eat after."

Simon looked surprised, then a little hurt, before he turned around to leave us alone. He bowed out and the three of us walked into Taejin's office and shut the door.

The room was small and unorganized, with a wood laminate

desk piled high with loose paper. Weak daylight came in through white plastic blinds, a few of them tangled together like crooked teeth. He sat in his swivel chair behind the desk and opened two folding chairs for me and Chaz. He spoke to me first, saying only, "Juniper, right?"

I nodded. There was no question as to whether he recognized me. We'd only met once, when he helped Lori move, but his sister had all but tried to murder me, before pulling the trigger on someone else.

"How's Lori?" he asked. Small talk, invoking our most neutral common ground.

"Rattled," I said. "She's had a bit of a shock."

"How's that?"

Chaz chimed in. "Your English is pretty damn good, TJ."

Taejin colored again. "I'm sorry," he said. "I'm very embarrassed."

"Why'd you pretend you couldn't speak English?"

"I wasn't thinking, and you made me very nervous."

"And how did I do that?"

"You mentioned Winfred Park."

"And why does the mention of Winfred Park make you nervous?"

Chaz was trying to determine whether Taejin knew Winfred was dead. It hadn't been long since his body was found, and Taejin wasn't exactly his kin. We only knew because we'd been looking. Then again gossip traveled fast in Koreatown, fast as heroin through any bloodstream. And murder was high-value gossip.

"I would rather not talk about that man, okay? He's bad luck."

"He *had* bad luck," said Chaz. "He had the bad luck to get killed yesterday. Did you hear?"

Taejin brought both hands to his face like he was gaging the temperature in his cheeks. If it was a play at surprise, it was a good one, followed almost immediately by a look of sheer relief.

"No," he said. "I didn't hear that. How did it happen?"

"Shot in the head in his own home."

Taejin nodded blankly for a while, then muttered something under his breath.

"What?" Chaz asked.

Taejin looked at him and set his jaw. "He had it coming," he said.

Chaz leaned forward and scratched the side of his mouth with a rough thumbnail. When he spoke, his voice was kind and inviting. "Want to tell us why?"

Taejin shook his head with disgust, his lip raised and his nostrils slightly flared.

"I met him," I told him. "Lori brought him out the other night. She didn't say so directly, but it sounded like it was for your benefit."

His eyes flashed and he shot back, "What's that supposed to mean?"

"Nothing ambiguous," I said, and I knew now that I was angry with him. "It sounded a lot like you made her entertain him."

"I didn't *make* her do—"

"Okay, let's calm down, guys," Chaz said reasonably. "Sorry, TJ, if we're being a little overzealous, but you should know that we're here to help you. We're all family here, got it?"

"Are we?" he scoffed, and looked at me. "Because *my sister* is in jail right now, and I can't help but think you had something to do with that."

"Sure," I said. "I practically forced her to pull the trigger. I mean what the hell are you talking about?"

"Never mind," he said, looking away. He needed someone to

blame who wasn't his sister, and I had apparently filled that role. Whether or not I was at fault had very little to do with it, and it would only anger him further to wave my innocence in his face.

"Fine. Whatever. You can believe what you want. But the fact is that Yujin asked me to take care of Lori, and for the last year, I've been there for her every single day. She *is* family to me, and by extension, you are, too. It doesn't mean we have to like each other, but our interests certainly overlap."

He was silent, though I could see a wave of protest quiver and die before it could leave his mouth.

"Look, I know you wouldn't have pushed that man on Lori without a reason. It must have been a pretty damn compelling one, too. What was it? What did you owe him?"

Taejin's face was tight, and he held my eye with righteous defiance. All at once I imagined getting up from my chair and smacking him. I heard the bright, dry sound of it echo in my head, felt the phantom sting heat up my palm. He had no right to be smug and adversarial, and if he insisted, I was going to break him down.

"Lori told me you asked her to be 'nice' to him. What the hell was that supposed to mean? You knew he was attracted to her. I saw the way he looked at her. Like a fucking wolf." I shook my head with disgust. "He didn't *like* her, either. No more than he might have liked a blow-up doll. He would have had no problem hurting her if she didn't give him what he wanted. And you know what he wanted. Don't even try to tell me you don't."

He was going white, and I could feel Chaz next to me, ready to spring if I took it too far. I didn't want him to stop me.

"And you knew what kind of person he was, didn't you? You were afraid of him. Turns out he was scary. A legitimately dangerous guy. He put Lori's boyfriend in the hospital, and I don't even want to *think* about what he might have done to Lori. I saw him putting his hands all over her, and that was enough to make me sick. Your tolerance must be higher."

Taejin lowered his head into one hand and started emitting a breathy, rhythmic sound like the hydraulic pump of a train engine. His shoulders started to heave in tempo, and after a few seconds he was bawling with naked self-pity. I had touched the right pressure points, and I hoped this meant he'd crumbled.

"I didn't have a choice," he sobbed.

"Bullshit," I said.

He glared at me, and his big eyes were scorched with red.

Chaz cleared his throat. "What she means, I think, is why were your hands tied? We all know you wouldn't put your niece in harm's way if you could help it. But help us understand, and maybe we can avoid this kind of thing in the future, huh?"

I nodded along. That was sort of what I meant.

"It's money, isn't it?" I asked. "You borrowed money from Winfred, or his gang, and you couldn't pay it back."

He shook his head and snorted, inhaling a big glob of snot.

"You needed money for Yujin's defense, didn't you? You couldn't stand to think of her getting some shitty public defender, so you shelled out for a big-ticket attorney."

His head stopped moving for a second and then he nodded miserably.

I felt a pang of pity. How Korean of him, to require quality he couldn't afford.

"But I didn't borrow," he said, trying to swallow the lump in his throat. "I worked for it."

There was a moment of silence as Chaz and I processed the implications.

"Oh, Jesus Christ," Chaz said, slapping his knee. "Are you running a goddamn chop shop?"

Taejin closed his eyes and dropped his chin by ten degrees. Chaz had scored a bull's-eye.

I had only a vague idea of what went into running a chop shop. I knew vehicle theft was common enough, especially in a place like Los Angeles, where cars seemed to outnumber people. I remembered a drunken night soon after college, walking around Hancock Park with my best friend at the time. We made a game of testing car doors as we walked by, the ones parked on the street, big gleaming jewels in a display case the width of the city. It was shocking how many doors clicked open at the laziest tug. Nothing stood between us and those cars but the ordinary scruples and the ordinary fears.

Of course, those were strong enough, and to ignore them would have engendered an irrevocable shift in our everyday lives. Taejin Chung had accepted that shift.

"Have you always run a chop shop?" I asked. Lori's mother, I knew, had had a criminal streak well before I'd met her. She was a scrappy woman, set on prosperity after a painful childhood she'd shared with Taejin. She'd used his garage as a vehicular graveyard, and it seemed likely she wasn't the only one.

But Taejin answered with a solemn "no." "Only these last six months or so," he said. "I didn't need much, just for myself."

"So you worked with Winfred, and through him, with the Rampart Gang."

He nodded, and his swollen eyelids creased over with exhaustion.

"But if you were just working together, stealing cars, breaking them down, having a royal good time," Chaz broke in, "then why were you in such a hole with Winfred?"

"Because I was talking to the police," he whispered. "They tracked a stolen Civic to my shop and brought me in for questioning."

If Winfred was capable of enlisting two other men to beat up an innocent stranger, then there was no real limit on what he might have done to a police informant. The picture came in a lot clearer now, and I started to sympathize, a little, with Taejin's plight.

"And Winfred found out?"

"Yes."

"How?"

"I guess I was acting dodgy. He followed me."

"Are you actually an informant?"

"I don't know," he said. "I don't have that much information. Just what happens in my shop. And I didn't have time to do much damage before Winfred got to me."

"When was this?"

"Not long ago. A couple months."

"And what did he do?"

"He punched me once, hard, right here." He pointed to his solar plexus and I winced for him. Winfred was about twice his size in every direction. "He said he would kill me if I ratted him out to the cops. I believed him."

"It sounds like he was convincing."

"And it wasn't just that. He hinted that he might tell others about my meeting, too."

"Others?"

"Never mentioned anyone by name. But the implication was clear. Others who wouldn't think twice about getting me out of the way."

"Why did he do that?"

"So he'd have me in his pocket. So he could get a bigger bite of my business."

"And that's what Lori walked into?"

He tried to swallow again, but there was no moisture there. "Yes. I had this feeling, ever since I met Winfred, that I should keep him separated from Lori. I'm not the overprotective type, but I just got a bad feeling from him. I know the way men react to Lori, and I didn't want him to catch sight of her."

"Even before he was essentially blackmailing you?"

"Yes. I also didn't want Lori to know I was doing anything illegal. So I tried to discourage her from coming to the shop as much as she might have otherwise."

"But you live here. And in a way, you're the only family she has right now."

The corners of his mouth turned up as he held back another sob.

"She would find reasons to come see me. *'Samchun,* I brought you *kimbab.' 'Samchun,* did you do your laundry this week?'"

I almost smiled. Lori was both spoiled and mothering, a combination that was easy to love.

"When they finally did meet, I thought, Well nothing is going to happen, because I've already imagined the worst. Why couldn't I be wrong, for once?"

Chaz spoke softly, with a tone of deepest respect. "TJ—I have to ask you. Did you kill Winfred Park?"

The accusation chilled me, and I waited for Taejin's roar of wounded anger. It never came.

"I'm not going to sit here and pretend the thought never crossed my mind. Frankly, I'm very relieved—even happy—that he's dead. But I didn't do it, and I don't think I would have, even if I had the chance."

I believed him on instinct. For one thing, I couldn't imagine Taejin overpowering Winfred on his own turf, even with a gun in his hand. But there was a ring of truth to what he said, maybe because I shared in that sigh of relief.

"So, what now?" I asked. "Are all your problems dead and buried with this guy?"

"Ha," he said. "If it were that simple, I might have killed him after all."

Fourteen

Chaz bought me lunch at a *soondubu* restaurant on Wilshire. He commended me on my performance in the interview then talked about his kids for half an hour. It was a nice break in a heavy day, and I was grateful for his company. When we got back to the office, Daphne was waiting for me, legs crossed, eyes bloodshot, looking unhappy.

Chaz saw her first. He stopped moving on his way in through the door. I almost ran into him from behind.

"Hello . . ." he said. "Can I help you?"

She stood up and gave him her hand. "Daphne Freamon. You must be Song's boss. Do you mind if I borrow her for a minute?"

It felt like years since I'd seen her—never mind that I'd only known her, the little I did, for a matter of weeks. She even looked different. She seemed spectral, almost, her skin thin and glowing, poised to molt. I tried to remember the lies she'd told me, to lay them out in order so I could fold them and put them away. It was hard to keep them straight.

I liked to think of myself as an honest person, someone who valued truth above comfort, sometimes even above kindness. It was one of the virtues I allowed myself to admit, that gave me a measure of pride. I'd lost friends and family over festering lies, amputated them like a sinner set on heaven. It might have been this impulse that led me to private detection in the first place—the Marlowe drive, the itchy longing to uncover ugly soil, to dislodge the bad fruit that rooted below.

Daphne had told me some big lies in a short period of time, enough to make me dismiss almost anyone as a pathological liar. But when I saw her, my heart softened against my will.

I turned to Chaz. "We'll just go grab a drink. We won't be gone long."

We walked around the corner to a dive bar with a half-assed pirate theme. Netting hung on a couple of walls, along with banners of Johnny Depp from *Pirates of the Caribbean*, printed off the Internet. The place was empty—it was three in the afternoon. I ordered a Bloody Mary by way of acknowledging the early hour. It was a functional mix of V8 and vodka, on fast-melting ice. Daphne got a glass of chardonnay.

"They arrested Jamie," I said, staring into my drink.

"I heard."

The silence grew long and awkward, and we sat there, sipping in turns to avoid conversation.

"I had to go to the station," she said finally. "Detective Sanchez said to tell you hello."

"When?"

"A few hours ago."

"She questioned you?"

"For a long time."

"What did you tell her?"

She smiled. "Not much. I think she wanted to use me as a sounding board for her own theories. I think she was hoping I'd react to something. Like throwing spaghetti against a wall."

"Did anything stick?"

"I believe I disappointed her."

I nodded. I was far from surprised.

"But she had a theory I'd like you to hear. It's a classic tale of Hollywood. You've heard parts of it before."

I raised my head and took another silent sip of tomato vodka. "I'm listening," I said.

"Once upon a time, there was a girl who wanted to be a star. She grew up in an abusive home, within ten miles of the shining center of the Tinseltown universe. And every night, after her stepfather put her away, she dreamed about the life she'd have when she could finally leave home."

I closed my eyes and nodded with my hand on my face.

"She moved away to the magical land, but she found it was hard to get into the castle. So she set up camp on the periphery, doing stepdaughter things. One day, she got an invitation inside— she would be allowed across the drawbridge, as the lowliest servant. When the crowned prince himself took notice of her over all the other servants, she was powerless to stop him. At first, she didn't want to—but later, she did. It was too late then. He took what he wanted, and he couldn't give it back."

I looked up to see if she was crying. There was a tremor in her voice, but her face was still, like she was in a trance.

"The girl was angry, and ashamed, and heartbroken. Maybe it was childish of her, but she thought that nightmare was locked in her past, that once she escaped she'd be safe in the wider world.

She didn't think princes could be so beastly, and she was so angry. You can't imagine how angry.

"But she saw that what was done couldn't be taken back, so she made the best of a bad situation. Lemons, lemonade. But she never forgot."

I opened my mouth to say something, but I had no words to share.

"So the girl left again. Tried one more time for a good life, a *decent* life. And she succeeded, more or less, in finding some measure of peace and happiness. She found independence, gained stature in the eyes of the world. She even met a boy—a boy who loved her.

"The boy had his own dreams, dreams that looked back to the world she'd fled. She wanted nothing less than to go back to Hollywood, and she almost left him. But she saw how badly he wanted, and she remembered the man who hurt her, and she decided he still owed her. She hadn't seen him in years, since that one night, and as far as she was concerned, she didn't have to see him again. But he was a powerful man, a career maker, as she already knew. So she made a few phone calls, and sent the boy walking toward that shiny old dream.

"She never told him how she did it. He didn't have to know. And so he became friends with the man, who was lonely, and needy, and full of secrets. One night, the man told the boy his greatest secret, the one about the girl. After that, the boy felt a flash of the girl's anger, and he killed the man."

I listened with my mouth clamped so tight I felt an ache in my jaw when she stopped talking.

"That's the working theory, at any rate," she added.

My Bloody Mary was decimated. I ordered another one and thought about lighting a cigarette. This was the kind of bar that would turn a blind eye, and I wanted something else to focus on, even for seconds at a time.

"I talked to Rory Buckner," I said. "After I saw you."

She smirked. "Why?"

"I had a feeling you hadn't told me everything."

"So what if I hadn't?"

"I don't like being lied to, first of all. And second, you're my client. Knowing your story is part of my job."

"You don't have to know everything," she said, enunciating sharply. "What I just told you, the parts that were true, was about as personal as anything gets."

"I'm sorry," I said. "I'm not trying to be nosy. And it's not just my job to know, either. I'd like for you to be able to talk to me."

"I'm talking to you now."

"Can I ask you something?"

She raised her eyebrows and nodded tentatively.

"Don't take this the wrong way, because I can think of a lot of good answers. I just want to know yours."

"Okay," she said.

"Why didn't you report the rape?"

"You're from L.A. You followed the Kobe Bryant rape case, right?"

"Yeah," I said. I'd been in college then, one of the few Angelenos in my dorm. It was a huge story—Kobe was the biggest name in basketball, and Los Angeles worshipped him. People I barely knew would stop me in the halls to talk about it, and I ended up being a sort of authority. I was surprised by the level of controversy surrounding the case. It was as if talent converted to virtue at a hidden rate, as naturally as mass to energy. I remembered one boy in particular, who was incensed by the greed and frivolity of Kobe's accuser—she wanted a koala and a boob job with her settlement money, and those details made this boy angrier than anything else about the entire story.

"So you have some idea of how popular she was with the public?"

I nodded. The question was clearly rhetorical. The woman had refused to testify after her reputation went on trial.

"And where is Kobe now? Who talks about that *incident* now?" She laughed. "Kobe is a black man who raped a white woman, but she was still a woman. How do you think I would've done? What do you think Joe Tilley's team would have said about me?"

I pictured Alex Caldwell in that cold office, spinning and spinning until the truth was shrouded in eight layers of bullshit.

"They would have said you were lying."

"Of course. And I was guilty of a great sin to begin with—I wanted to be famous."

"And what better way . . ."

"There are better ways to get famous, sure. But maybe none so surefire as getting your name in the papers, or even just the tabloids, next to a name the size of Joe Tilley's."

"But he raped you. Wouldn't a doctor have known that?"

"Maybe. Or maybe I'm just a wild girl, one of those kinky jezebels who like it rough. It's not like he cuffed me to his bed and held a knife to my throat. And I couldn't deny that I followed him into that room of my own free will."

"But he got off scot-free. Doesn't that make you sick?"

"He might have gotten off scot-free anyway. What do people say about Kobe these days? And besides—he's dead now. If the police are to be believed, he didn't get away with it at all."

"Are the police to be believed, then?"

She smiled. "You think I know?"

"You have the air of someone who knows all things at all times."

"Is that a compliment?"

"It is, actually."

"That's too bad for me, then. Because it isn't true."

"Did you ever tell Jamie?"

"About the rape? The abuse?" She shook her head. "No on both counts."

"Too personal?"

"I didn't think it was any of his business," she said.

"Did you talk to him about your past at all?"

"Of course. I told him all he needed to know about me, about all the things I did. That night, with Joe Tilley—that's his secret, not mine."

"Do you think he could have found out and killed Joe?"

"I don't know," she said. "He's a sweet man."

"As motives go, his wouldn't have been the meanest," I said. "If he somehow found out, if Tilley told him what he'd done and he lost control . . ."

"It was supposed to look like a suicide, right?" she asked. "It was staged. That sounds premeditated."

"I'll bet the police are asking around about his bathing habits," I said. "If he liked taking baths, then Jamie might have seen an easy opportunity."

She shook her head. "That just doesn't sound like Jamie."

I agreed, but I stopped myself from saying so. What did I know about Jamie, really? I remembered the feeling of his lips on mine, as if that could tell me anything.

"Jamie came over the other night," I told her.

She arched one eyebrow. "That's special," she said.

"He wanted someone to talk to. After you broke up with him."

"What kind of comfort was he after?"

"It wasn't like that," I said. And it hadn't been, I thought. Certainly not at first. "He was really upset. Can I ask why you broke up with him?"

"You can ask, sure. But it's complicated," she said. "Do you need another drink?"

I nodded and flagged down a waiter for another chardonnay and bloody mary.

"I told him about Lanya Waters, and about how I started my art career. I left out some of the details—the ones the police think he might have known. Still, it was a weight off my chest."

"He said he forgave you. That that wasn't the problem."

"He did. He did forgive me. And maybe that was it—the presumption that he could forgive me for something I never did to him."

"You did lie to him."

She shrugged. "I just didn't tell him everything. And anyway, I didn't ask to be forgiven."

"You broke up with him over that?"

"No. I broke up with him because after all that, after the clutter was cleared away, I saw that I didn't love him. And once I saw that, I couldn't stand to pretend, not even for a minute."

I winced. "That's not complicated. It's harsh, but it's not complicated. Did you tell him that?"

"No," she said. "And maybe it would be best if you didn't either."

I nodded and sipped at my drink. "Did you think about waiting until this all blew over?"

"Of course I thought about it. But I couldn't do it. I couldn't stand by him and hold his hand and pretend like I'd always be there. It felt perverse. It made my stomach turn."

"Have you talked to him since? Today, for instance?"

She shook her head. "I will."

"He's had a rough run of it."

"I know," she said. "But it's been a long day for me, too."

We had one more round, then she paid the whole check and said she had to go. I suspected she wanted to be alone.

"Thank you," she said as soon as we left the bar. "For listening, understanding, everything. I know I haven't been the easiest person to work for."

"No." I laughed, a little tipsily. "You haven't."

"We'll talk soon."

She gave me a long, squeezing hug then turned and walked away.

I was less than sober when I got back to the office, and Chaz noticed as soon as I walked in his door.

"Is it wet outside?" he asked, shaking his head.

I slinked into a chair, feeling pretty fluid. "Kind of a rough conversation."

I gave him the latest and he nodded along.

"I wonder," he said. "If someone told me he'd raped Molly . . ."

"What, you might kill him?"

He shrugged. "Probably not, but how would I know?"

"I'm getting paid to prove his innocence."

"Sure," he said. "Didn't OJ vow to find the real killer, too?"

I sighed. "I don't know, man. My brain's all cooked."

"Take it easy, girl detective. I'd send you home, but you should probably dry out first."

* * *

I sat long enough to metabolize the vodka in my system. I still had a couple hours to kill before my meeting with Donnie, and I decided to visit Jackie and baby Cristina. They were both home when I called and Jackie told me to come on over as long as I didn't mind a mess.

She gave me a strange look when she opened the door.

"What?" I asked.

She sniffed conspicuously.

"Oh," I said. "I had a few Bloody Marys. Stressful day."

She wrinkled her nose and I remembered how she used to annoy me sometimes, when Diego was still alive. "It's a Tuesday. The sun's still out."

"Ah, yeah, I know. But Bloody Marys are always respectable."

She smiled and I realized she was actually uncomfortable.

"I can come back if you're worried I'll get the baby drunk," I said.

"No, come in. Honestly, I envy you. I haven't had a Bloody Mary in over a year."

We sat down on the couch and Jackie asked me, a little pointedly, if I wanted anything to drink. I declined.

"Did you get in touch with a lawyer?" she asked.

"I passed along the contact info you gave me, but I don't know what was decided." I sighed. "I imagine he's lawyered up by now, though."

"Why, did something happen?"

"Ha," I said. "Yeah. A whole lot of shit."

"Are you okay?"

"Basically. Just stressed out. Client was arrested today."

She blinked meaningfully. "Song, your client—he isn't the guy they say killed Joe Tilley, is he?"

I stiffened at the name of the dead man. It wasn't generally acceptable for a private eye to go around advertising her client list. I shouldn't have said anything about Jamie getting arrested—it was too much of a giveaway. But now that she'd caught on, I realized I'd put out the bait on purpose. I wanted her to ask, because I wanted an excuse to tell her.

When Diego was around, I had his ear whenever I wanted it. I could tell him anything, and I'd know with absolute certainty that I could trust him to keep my confidence. But Diego was dead, and Jackie was, by default, my oldest friend. I was aching to talk to her.

"This stays between you and me," I said, and I started to recount my bloody adventure.

She listened, slumped back against the couch, with a look of worry and horror taking shape on her face.

"Wait," she said. "Wait, wait, wait. This Winfred guy, he was murdered, too?"

"Yeah, can you believe it?"

She was silent for a while, but a tightness in her features told me to wait for her to talk.

"It's happening again," she said finally.

"What do you mean?" I asked, as if I didn't know.

"People are getting killed, lives are being ruined, and you're standing there, in the middle of it, dragging the whole mess around."

"It isn't like that," I said. "This is my job."

"Then don't bring it to me. You shouldn't have told me these things."

All at once I saw myself as she saw me, and the vision left me mortified and stinging. I missed Diego with fiercer longing than I'd felt for anything in a long time. "I'm sorry," I said. "It's just that if Diego were here I'd be telling him, and you—"

"Well guess what, Song," she said icily. "Diego's not here. He died during your last rampage across the city."

She softened when she saw the tears forming, and though we made up, I left shortly after. Neither of us mentioned Cristina. I didn't get to see her at all.

Fifteen

I was supposed to meet Donnie at El Cholo on Western, in the heart of Koreatown. It was an old stately Mexican joint that pre-dated the big influx of Korean immigrants in the sixties and seventies. It was a survivor from another phase of the neighborhood, a jellyfish swimming among dolphins.

I had more time on my hands than I'd thought I would, and decided to settle in early. I chose a booth in the back corner of the restaurant. A waitress in a full flamenco skirt came by, and I asked her for a margarita. I wondered if I was wasting my time meeting Donnie. He'd insinuated that he might know something about the Tilley murder, but now that I was waiting for him, I started to doubt he had any solid information. I hoped I was wrong. I felt the screws tighten with Jamie's arrest, and any lead was worth chasing down. Besides, I had to eat dinner sometime.

Donnie arrived looking more put together than he had before. He wore pants and real shoes, and a short-sleeved button-down with a tank top underneath. His hat was gone, and I saw that his hair line was prematurely receding.

"Sorry," he said brightly. "Traffic, am I right? I'm starving."

He sat down and opened a menu. We ordered dinner, tamales and fajitas, and I gathered, more or less, that I was on a date.

"You like Mexican food?" he asked.

"Sure."

"How about Mexican dudes?"

"Some of them. Are you Mexican?"

"Yeah, girl, I'm a Cholo." He laughed.

I saw a dubious opportunity and took it. "What's your last name?" I asked.

"Perez," he said.

I remembered the same last name on his car's registration. A mom, maybe, or an aunt.

"And you're like, Korean or what?"

Donnie was talkative, and I spent most of the meal nodding and letting him expound on dogs and soccer and Batman. He struck me as sweet and harmless for a member of a criminal organization, maybe a Bobby Bacala sort of guy. He wasn't too smart, which was okay by me.

"So," I said, when there was a lull in his conversation. "Do you really know anything about Joe Tilley's murder, or were you just trying to lure me out to dinner?"

"You caught me." He smiled. "Honestly, I have no idea how that worked."

I smirked. "So Tilley wasn't scamming Young King somehow?"

"Doubt it. And neither was Jamie, as far as I saw."

"They think he did it," I said. "They arrested him. Did you see that happen?"

"Nah," he said. "I got taken off him the minute he got mixed up in that murder. Ain't nobody—"

"You what?"

My tone froze him and he looked at me with shifting eyes.

"Then what were you doing outside my house the other morning?"

"Shit." He smiled guiltily and rubbed at his forehead.

I remembered him sleeping while Jamie drove away. "You didn't even know he was there, did you?"

He shook his head.

"So who were you looking for?" I swallowed a thick glob of saliva. "Me?"

"Alright, just between you and me, okay?" He motioned for me to bring my face closer. "It was this other guy. Same kind of deal. Boss thought he was misbehaving."

"What other guy? Why my house?"

"I guess he was supposed to show up there. And he did. About an hour after you left."

I felt a tingle at the back of my head, a premonition that started to make me dizzy.

"What was his name?"

"Something funny. Like a dog's name." He tapped at his chin with one finger. I took a long sip from my margarita, letting him know he should keep on thinking. "Got it," he said with a high laugh. "It was Winfred Bark."

"No," I said reflexively.

"What? You know the name?" Donnie looked at me with concern, then started waving his hand in my face. "Earth to Song, is anyone home?"

I batted the hand away. "You know that's a dead man, don't you?"

"Who? Winfred Bark?"

"He got shot in the face, sometime yesterday."

His jaw dropped and he brought a hand up as if to put it back in place.

"You're that surprised?" I asked. "I mean what did you think Young King wanted with him?"

"I didn't think anything. I just did what I was told, you know?"

"Which was what?"

"See if he showed up at that address, and if so, follow him and see where he went."

"And where did he go?"

"He stood outside that apartment for a while, I guess trying to get let in. Then he went to another apartment in K-Town, maybe just home. I don't know."

I didn't ask him what he did next. I could fill in the blanks as well as he could, and I didn't want to alienate him. I regretted telling him Winfred had died at all.

"You look kind of shaken," I said. "I mean, you hang around with some scary people. Dead bodies aren't so unheard of, I wouldn't think."

"I'm new to this crew. I was just doing, like, small-time drug stuff before. Stupid street stuff."

"For the Rampart Gang?"

He shook his head. "Nah. The San Fernando Cobras."

"Sounds like a shitty baseball team. Is that Tin Tin's outfit?"

"Yeah."

"But not Young King's? How'd you get involved with him?"

"I met him at a party and tried to sell him shit. He kind of clowned on me but we hit it off and he ended up recruiting me."

"And what, there were no consequences from the Cobras?"

"People respect the Young King. And now I'm like the go-between."

"How long's it been?"

"Just a few months."

"Better benefits?"

"What?"

"How do you like the new job?"

"It's been good. I just work for Young King now. It's like, simple. But I haven't seen any shit yet, you know?" He shook his head. "Young King, he keeps things clean."

"What's that supposed to mean? Obviously, he isn't avoiding criminal activity."

"You don't understand. Young King is special."

"How so?"

"He has presence, you know? He doesn't come off like some thug. He's smart, and that's why people respect him."

"For his brain."

"He didn't go to college or nothing but he knows people, like it's a gift. He can just tell who's going to prosper, who's going to fold, what he can do to them, what they'll let him get away with. And that's why he's the Young King."

He was talking fast now, and I felt sorry for him, this naïve little gangster in awe of his master.

"Maybe," I said gently. "But maybe he kills people, too."

When we stepped out of the restaurant, there was a man leaning against the building, watching the doorway. He was short and muscular with a ruddy tinge to his skin. He looked young, maybe twenty-four or twenty-five, and he was dressed like a high school student, in a big white T-shirt and cargo pants. But there was something dead serious about his demeanor, his graceful femi-nine features turned stony through the set of his jaw, the hard glint in his deep brown eyes. There was a cold intelligence in his expression. He turned these on Donnie, who stopped moving. "Hey man," Donnie said. "What're you doing here?"

The man shoved off the wall and walked toward us with large, confident steps. "Come with me, Donnie. I need to talk to you." Then he looked at me, and his gaze was both distant and pene-trating. "You come, too."

"Sorry," I said. "Who are you?"

He pressed his hand to his stomach, and the T-shirt moved around the outline of something hard in his waistband—something hard and mechanical. "Just come," he said. He flicked toward a black Corolla with his head, and we followed.

He got in the driver's seat, and Donnie sat up front. I climbed into the back, feeling my heartbeat in my ears. I'd only seen a gun up close once, and that one, sure as Chekhov's, had fired away.

The man turned to me and, handing me a black handkerchief, ordered, "Give me your stuff and put this on." I obeyed, taking care to show him the empty inside of every pocket before tying the blind tight around my head.

"What's going on, man?" Donnie asked, and by the mixture of chumminess and suppressed fear in his tone, I gathered we were riding with the Young King.

I tried to recall everything I knew about this man, and found that the list of facts was frightfully short. He'd been responsible for recruiting Jamie into the drug business; he'd sent little goon Donnie after two men who ended up on different sides of two different murders. And now, he had kidnapped me from the side of the road, with nothing to lure me but the threat of death.

Young King was silent, and Donnie persisted. "King? Yo, King? What's going on?"

When he piped up for a third time, I heard a clapping sound—Young King had silenced Donnie, I guessed by putting a hand on his mouth.

I kept quiet, and the three of us drove in bumpy silence for a distended, indeterminable period of time. I could see nothing through the black cloth of the handkerchief save for variations in texture when I blinked. Instead, I felt the road beneath us like I was an animal, running on treacherous ground. Each turn sent my inner compass spinning, and each bump reached up and grabbed at my stomach. When we finally stopped, it was after a series of short turns that suggested we were prowling along residential streets. Young King pulled in and got out of the car with the engine still running.

I felt Donnie turn to me, and without seeing him at all I read my worst fears reflected in him.

"You'll be okay," he said in a tight whisper, addressed, ostensibly, to me.

"The key." I looked down and moved my mouth as little as possible. "Is it still in the ignition?"

"Yeah. But he's right there."

We were considering the same mode of escape, weighing its improbability, its possible necessity.

"Where are we?" I asked. "Where did he go?"

There was a heavy sound like the fall of a ladder, and Donnie said, "Shh, he's coming back."

Young King returned to the car and drove it forward some fifteen feet. I wondered if he could sense our impulse and failure to run. I wondered if he left the key in the ignition on purpose.

He killed the engine and the car filled with light.

"You can take that off now," he said.

I pushed the tight handkerchief up on my forehead and rubbed my eyes. We were sitting in a small garage—a residential one, not like Taejin's. I stopped myself from looking around too frantically. I wanted most of all to catch a glimpse of Young King's face in the rearview mirror, but I found I couldn't bring myself to look. I remembered standing in the bathroom as a child, chanting Bloody Mary twice before giving up and finding my mother. As if something irrevocable would happen if I dared myself to stare into the glass.

The light faded out again, and we sat in the dark listening to a close din of crickets. My face was warm and getting damp with the creeping perspiration of imminent illness. The handkerchief felt like a blanket on a hot night, and I pulled it off my head.

After several minutes, Young King spoke again, for the second time all night. "Donnie," he said. "Come help."

Donnie unbuckled his seat belt like he was on a timed trial, and the two of them exited the car. As I hadn't been given instructions, I stayed put in the backseat, my eyes still adjusting to the unlit space.

I watched them through the screen of the rear window as they walked to the open garage door. They stood silhouetted against the jumbled dark of the Los Angeles night. I tried to make out any landmarks, to see if I could guess at our location. There were no clues on that backdrop, no stars or skyline I could even try to navigate.

Donnie stood half a head taller than his boss, and his head leaned in with a submissive tilt. I could tell they were talking, but couldn't make out a word with the doors and windows closed. After a few minutes, Young King pointed to the open garage door, and Donnie reached up and grabbed the hanging bottom edge. He pulled down and it rolled shut with a loud wooden rumble.

As Donnie worked, I saw Young King's hand go into his waistband. It was too quick for me to shout, but no warning would have saved him.

It happened in seconds. The gunshot was quiet, much quieter than the garage door. The door crashed against the concrete, there was a muffled whistling sound, then faster than I could process, Donnie went tumbling down.

I couldn't see him anymore, and after a minute, Young King crouched out of my field of view to join him. My heartbeat seemed to fill the whole car like a subwoofer, and I feared that it might remind the murderous King of my presence.

He stood up without looking at me and let himself into the house. False relief flooded my nerves, relaxing every tensed extremity. It didn't last.

The key was still in the ignition, but it was clear enough there was no garage door opener in the car. I thought of what I'd need to do to drive it out: get out of the backseat, step over Donnie, get back in the front seat, start the engine, and back over the dead or dying body. It was like a rigged version of some terrible children's game. I would never make it out without alerting Young King to the time-consuming effort. The idea of running over a human body, even a corpse, didn't appeal to me, either.

I wondered if Donnie could be alive. There was only one gunshot, and I didn't see where it got him. If he could talk, I might want to talk to him, if only to receive the last words of a dying man. I was already as fucked as I was going to be. If Young King hadn't been bothered by my presence five minutes ago, I was willing to bet leaving the car wouldn't change my situation.

I opened the door and stepped out into the garage, staying light on my feet. There was, after all, no need to draw attention to myself. The air smelled of sweat and blood, though the power of suggestion might have accounted for both. Donnie was on the floor, slumped into a pile of flesh and clothing that didn't inspire confidence. He wasn't moving.

I walked over, and I didn't have to check his pulse to determine his state. He'd landed with his head in profile, and there was a hole in it right at the temple. I closed my eyes and made a mask of my palm, breathing into it like it held all the oxygen in the room.

The light turned on and I jumped. Young King was at the entrance to the house, his hand on the switch. I hadn't heard him come back. He was either quiet as a ninja, or the blood pumping in my ears was loud enough to drown out all external sound. Both possibilities seemed equally likely.

I took in a sharp breath and felt my eyes twitch. Young King stood still, regarding me with a neutral expression that sent chills running down the length of me. Then he lowered his head and shook it, emitting a husky chuckle devoid of humor.

I couldn't see him clearly. I'd had no time to evaluate him before he became a murderer right before my eyes. My fear of him crowded out all other thought, until it was all I could do to remember his name—the false one, the code, the only one I knew.

When he finally spoke, it took me a long time to hear him, like we were separated by a well as deep as Earth, with me looking up from the bottom. "Did you want to help?" The words reached me at last like dropped stones.

I looked back at the body without meaning to. The garage was light now, and I wished I could pretend to explore its walls, catalog the various objects it held in storage. But there were only two points that summoned any amount of attention, and as my eyes fled from Young King they found poor dead Donnie on the ground.

The gore was new and bright, and a greasy splatter of head now decorated the old wood of the garage door. I felt a surge of bile but caught myself and managed not to vomit, my mouth filling with bitter air instead. I shook my head. I did not want to help.

"Then sit tight," he said, and indicated the Corolla.

I climbed into the backseat and listened as Young King dragged Donnie's body across the floor and carried him into the house. It seemed like he was gone for a long time, but I didn't even think about the garage door, or the key in the ignition. I let myself scan the garage for a concealable weapon, but there was nothing there I could see, not a single sharp object I could bring into play.

I wondered if I was set to die in this anonymous place, surrounded by no one and nothing. Yielding to the self-indulgence, I started to imagine my funeral. I found the proceedings and crowd pretty lacking, but I saw the faces of the people who mattered. My mother, Lori, Chaz. Jackie and Cristina. For a moment, Jamie and Daphne. I'd spent the last year in a funk of self-pity, but I felt, for now anyway, that I had more than I needed to live for. It was a pretty realization, and I hoped it would prove useful in the future. I set my teeth and prayed to God I wouldn't die.

Young King came back in, and this time I heard him. He was wearing a new T-shirt and shorts, and his hands were clean. He reopened the garage door, then entered the car.

He sat next to me in the backseat and pulled out a cell phone. It was a bulky flip phone with a plastic body—it looked disposable. I heard the ring tone and a soft click on the other line.

"Clean up on aisle 13," he said. And then he hung up.

He fished the handkerchief out of his shorts and tied it back around my head, knotting it with a forceful yank. As the black cotton took over my view, it occurred to me that Young King was likely to let me live. He'd bothered to blindfold me on my way into and out of the garage. He didn't want me knowing where it was, and that meant there'd be a time when I might try to disclose the location.

But he'd also specifically told me to remove the blind in time to witness the murder. He'd set me up in the theater box of his backseat, and put on a show I could never forget in a location I'd never visit again. His plan had an almost artistic design, but the intention must have been much more practical.

"I wouldn't bother calling the police," he said, derailing my train of thought. "No one will even look for him."

"Why did you do it?"

"Loose lips," he said. "I've got a big ship."

"Why did you bring me into it?"

"I wanted to show you what I can do. What I can get away with," he said, without emotion. "I'd do the same to woman or child—and I know the ones you'd miss."

I recalled Cristina's pudgy face resting on Jackie's shoulder and felt a physical protest inside my body.

"What is it you want from me?" I asked.

"Only peace of mind," he said, and I felt his eyes on my face as my lips trembled. "And I've got that now."

He dropped me off at my apartment, where he took back his handkerchief, gave me my purse, and wished me good night. He didn't need directions, and I never assumed he did.

* * *

I stumbled into the apartment in a haze of fear and trauma. It was a relief to be home, out of the direct company of a murderer, but the immediate release uncorked my bottled up panic, and I felt anything but safe.

Lori was home, and she called to me when I went in. I barely heard her as I stomped into my bedroom and submerged myself under the covers. She appeared in my doorway, and I looked up at her from my bed, with my hand over my chest, measuring the beat of my heart.

"*Unni,*" she said. "What's going on? Are you okay?"

She sat next to me and the bed creaked to accommodate her. "Feel," I said, and guided her hand to my neck.

Her eyes went wide. "How long has it been like this? Do we need to call an ambulance?"

I shook my head. "Just stay here a minute."

She stayed for much longer, and at some point, I fell into something like sleep.

Sixteen

❦

The next morning, I went into work with no idea what I'd say to Chaz. I was on edge the whole drive to Koreatown. The cigarettes didn't smooth me out at all.

When I got to Lindley & Flores, Chaz was sitting in his office looking downright placid. He was sorting through this or that on his computer, like any family man working a nine-to-five.

"Doesn't it ever get to you?" I asked.

"Well, good morning to you. You look like shit."

"I feel like shit."

"What were you saying?"

"I asked, doesn't it ever get to you?"

He cocked an eyebrow. "What? This job?"

I nodded.

"Well, most of the time, this job isn't that stressful. You have a knack for picking the hard ones, I guess."

"It's not like you haven't been in it," I said. "I mean we witnessed a fucking murder together."

"Yeah," he said, with a cringe. "And I guess I never want to be in a place where something like that doesn't affect me. But I know that life goes on, and I like to think that I do some good to help it along."

"Do I do anyone any good?" I asked.

"Why do you like Marlowe, Song? Is it 'cause he's a hero who swoops in and saves everyone?"

I shook my head.

"You should talk to Art sometime, about his time on the force. You think that was a pleasant job?" He chuckled. "But he stuck with it through the bad stuff, and it had its rewards, and he was fighting a good fight."

"But what if I can't help anyone?"

"That's nonsense, girl. Our job is to help people, and you're damn good at it."

I closed the door and sat down across from him. "It keeps piling up, Chaz. There's another fucking body."

I told him what happened to Donnie, and he listened to my story with a sympathetic scowl. It was a relief to get it out, and I was confident telling Chaz was as good as telling no one as far as Young King was concerned. There were few people I trusted unconditionally, but Chaz I trusted with my life at least.

"What do I do?" I asked him.

"What do you want to do? You want to go to the police?"

"Maybe," I said. "I don't know. Maybe I can just talk to Detective Sanchez. Find out if she knows anything about this guy."

"You think he'd kill you for it?"

"Yes. I'm sure he would if he found out. 'Loose lips.' That's what did Donnie in, or so he said." I leaned forward and held my head in my hands. "And that isn't even all of it, Chaz. I think Young King killed Winfred Park."

His eyes bulged. "What?"

"He had Donnie following him around maybe hours before he got shot."

"But why? That doesn't make any sense."

"I have no idea why, but I'll bet it makes perfect sense. Everything's converging, Chaz. All the evil in the city's closing in on us, and there's not one damn thing we can do to make it stop."

I took time to regulate my breathing, then dialed Detective Sanchez's number.

"Did you want to waste my time again, Juniper Song?"

"I hope not," I said. "That's never been my intention."

"How goddamn polite. What do you want?"

"I wanted to ask about a person of interest in the Tilley murder."

"You're upset your boyfriend's in the clink, huh?"

I pressed on, "What can you tell me about a Donaldo Perez?"

"You mean the one Donaldo Perez in all of Los Angeles?"

I ignored her sarcasm. "Doesn't ring a bell? He might have a record."

"Juniper Song," she said. "Do you have any idea how big my brain would have to be to know every name attached to a 'record'?"

"Bigger than it is, I guess." I hesitated. "How about someone who goes by the name 'Young King'?"

"Young King . . ." she said, drifting into thoughtful silence. "Well, something's sticking. That alias sounds familiar."

"Maybe a higher-up drug dealer, somehow involved in organized crime. Maybe Jamie mentioned him."

"Ah," she said. "I know who you're talking about."

"Really?"

"If I give you this gemstone, will you stop calling me with
nonsense?"

"I can try," I said, committing to nothing.

"Alright, it's not much anyway. One of my colleagues in Nar-
cotics is real curious about this guy, but no one knows a thing
about him. He's like Kaiser Soze—his name just comes up once
in a while, then disappears before you can attach anything to it."
She paused. "There's a little ditty about him, and honest to God
it's the biggest piece of info we have."

"What, a song? That's festive."

"Young King Cole was a scary old soul, and a scary old soul was he . . ."

The tune gave me an eerie, tickled feeling. It looped in my
head like a noxious jingle, in Detective Sanchez's stoic tones.

I spent the day in the office, happy to be in a familiar place with
Chaz and Arturo nearby. Arturo was in and out as usual, but
Chaz stayed at his desk, with occasional trips to my part of the
office to talk about his kids, or show me funny videos on You-
Tube. It might have been a light day for him, but it was just as
likely he was looking out for me. I accepted the kindness without
pointing it out.

My big accomplishment for the day was a jag of Internet research on organized crime in Greater L.A. I scanned Wikipedia
articles on the Rampart Boulevard Gang and the San Fernando
Cobras, scrolled through lengthy department of justice reports.
It was fascinating material, with details that seemed borrowed

from the province of fiction: secret tunnels and child assassins, gangsters greased with lotion to slip away from police. But while the reading was educational, I had a hard time seeing the big picture. I'd brushed with crime in very real ways, but its structures seemed almost impossibly inscrutable. I could visualize the layer running beneath the skin of the city, flickering faint blue like ill-defined veins.

I caught Arturo in the late afternoon. He kept his door closed, but he bade me come in when I knocked. I hadn't spent much time in his office. It was a handsome, orderly place without a single wall hanging or picture frame to make it feel homey. Arturo was a bachelor, a sort of classic lone-wolf private detective. I couldn't imagine Spade or Marlowe putting up posters in their offices.

"How's everything going?" he asked.

"Terrible," I said.

"I'm sorry to hear that."

"Chaz hasn't been filling you in?"

He shrugged. "I've had plenty to worry about on my end."

"In that case, I'll spare you. It's a long story."

He looked at me with a bland smile on his face, waiting for me to state my purpose.

"I need a sort of history lesson," I said.

"Oh?"

"What can you tell me about gangs in L.A.?"

He ran a hand across his hair. "They exist. We're the gang capital of the U.S. Do you want to be more specific?"

"Like, what's the structure?"

"Of organized crime in L.A.?"

"Sure."

He smiled. "You're asking about the structure of a tangled web of societies. I can't exactly give you a flow chart."

I tried again. "You know the Rampart Boulevard Gang?"

"Of course," he said. "They're one of the biggest and most troublesome."

"Are they mainly drug dealers or what?"

"They aren't mainly anything. They started as a Mexican gang, but now they've got everybody. They started in L.A. but now they're all over the world. There are tens of thousands of them and they do every criminal activity you can think of on every single level."

"In other words, they're a whole society."

"Look, Song. You're a smart girl, but you're asking questions on the wrong scale. Every crew is different, and every gangster is his own problem."

"Are there a lot of them getting away with murder these days?"

"Every day," he said, wearily. "Every damn day."

I got home close to seven, and Lori was waiting in a sweater dress and tights, with full makeup and a smile on her face.

"Date?" I asked.

She blushed. "Yeah."

"You worked things out with Isaac?"

"Yeah. I called him today. We're going to dinner."

"Good for you."

"I'm really happy about it," she said. "I feel kind of guilty."

"Don't. Have fun."

She nodded and heated up my dinner. She sat with me while I ate and we talked idly about safe topics. I didn't want her to go—I was tired and sad, hitting up against a wall, and all I wanted to do was have a peaceful night without any need for thought—but

I didn't say so. When Isaac called, she went down to meet him, and I faced the silence of evening alone.

I was mixing myself a drink when I heard a sound like pebbles hitting my window. It didn't register for a few minutes—it was just background noise, until I heard the pattern, a slow rhythm like a patient man, knocking. I got up to investigate and opened the curtains that shielded my kitchen from the street. I squinted into the dark and saw a man in silhouette, and behind him, a silver car.

My heart jumped and I hurried downstairs to the front door. Jamie was already walking up the driveway when I swung it open.

"What are you doing here?" I asked. "I thought you were . . ."

"In jail?" He smiled. There was no sharpness to his tone. He was worn down and wasted, like a dollar bill put through the wash. "Can I come in?"

I hesitated. It was stupid of me to bound down to greet him, like he wasn't a murder suspect who had showed up unannounced at my house in the dead of night. It had been less than forty-eight hours since his arrest—how was he even here?

I had my phone in my pocket. I would need a half second to speed dial Chaz, thirty seconds tops to get to Veronica Sanchez. I had heavy objects and knives in my apartment. I looked at Jamie, and calculated my risk—his blank, tired face made me feel paranoid.

His shoulders fell forward and his jaw went slack. "You don't trust me, do you?"

I waved a hand to dismiss him. The seed of suspicion lost out to the thought that I might hurt this boy while he was writhing on the ground. "I'm just surprised to see you. That's all. Come in."

I led the way upstairs and he followed dutifully, his footsteps unassertive. The light was out in Lori's room, but I decided it was late enough that she could be in there, sleeping. It felt strange to volunteer that we were alone, and I didn't think he would ask.

We sat on the couch in silence for a while. He laid his head back against the cushion and stared at the motionless ceiling fan. I glanced in his direction every now and then to see if he'd budged. I sat still until I got restless, and then I walked to the fridge for a beer.

"Can I get one, too?" he asked.

I uncapped both beers and carried them back to the couch, where Jamie had lifted his head and hunched forward. He took the bottle with a quiet thanks.

"So why are you here, Jamie? Or I guess I should ask how. I'm not harboring a fugitive, am I?"

He shook his head. "Daphne posted bail for me."

"When?"

"Earlier today."

"What have you been doing since then?"

He shrugged, slugged a long gulp of the beer. "Trying my best to keep a low profile," he said. "I've had people on me all day. Press, I guess. Just on my ass every goddamn minute."

I remembered the crowd around Tilley's house. Vultures in news vans and baseball caps, salivating at the gory remains of a fresh death.

"I went home, but my roommates were acting pretty weird. I could tell they were trying to be cheerful, avoiding the topic and acting like normal. And that, of course, meant they thought it was possible I did it." He smiled, a pointy, garish smile that betrayed no mirth. "I apologized for not being able to walk the dog, and Neal actually stood up and waved his hands around to say, 'No problem! No problem at all!' Might as well have added, 'Don't hurt my dog, man.' Fucking asshole. You know his dad died in March, and I drove him to the hospital every day so he wouldn't have to sit in traffic alone. You'd think that would count for something."

I didn't say anything. I was happy to see him, happier than I thought I could be, but I couldn't pretend I was completely comfortable with him sitting inside my house.

"Do you think I'm a killer, too?" he asked.

I couldn't contain the whole flinch. The question unnerved me, as did the apparent fact that he could read my mind.

"No," I said. "I don't."

He stared at me, his mouth an inch open, looking grave and disappointed.

"I *don't*," I said. "You asked if I thought you were a killer. You didn't ask if I thought it was impossible."

"Do you think I could be a killer?"

"I don't think it's impossible."

He drained his beer with a gleam of hurt in his eyes. I didn't backtrack. I had nothing to feel guilty about.

"Are you scared of me?"

"Not really. Even if you did kill Joe Tilley, you wouldn't have much of a reason to hurt me."

"And you really think I could've done it."

"Look, Jamie. I like you. I think, fundamentally, you're a good guy. Would I be surprised if you were the murderer? Sure, I might be pretty damn surprised. But I've been surprised before."

"Well thanks, I guess. For at least being straight with me."

I finished my beer and went to the fridge for another round. Then I looked at the handle of rye on the counter and thought that was a better idea. I poured out two glasses and brought them back to the couch.

"Are you trying to get me drunk?" he asked. His tone was slightly playful, to my relief.

I shrugged and sat back down. The silence was a little more comfortable, and I lit up a Lucky Strike.

"So why are you here?" I asked.

"I couldn't stand being at home."

"But why *here*? You have a lot of friends in L.A., and I know this specifically because I was hired to spy on you all around town."

"Do I really have a lot of friends? I mean, sure, I know a lot of people. If I just wanted company for a beer, there are a couple dozen people I could call—there were, anyway, until last week." He shook his head. "And you know what, I think most of those people even like me, casually. They'd definitely party with me, and they might even get my back in a Facebook argument. But damn it if I can't think of one person in this whole fucking city I could *lean* on. I haven't built a single strong foundation. I'm learning that all too fast."

"Have you tried? Leaning?"

"You don't lean on sand castles, Song."

"I take it you haven't gotten a ton of supportive e-mails?"

"Not one," he said, enunciating bitterly. "The thing is, most people here know me as Joe Tilley's friend. That made me someone worth knowing. Being just a nice guy or whatever wouldn't have gotten me anywhere. And now I'm not even that, apparently."

"And who am I supposed to be? Your friend?"

He reached out a hand so that it arced toward my face. I felt a rush of blood anticipating the touch, but he only plucked the lit cigarette from my fingers. I watched him take a long draw, and he held my eyes and smiled.

"I needed to go somewhere, and when I ran through my options, I just got fucking depressed. Then I thought about you, and the other night, how fun that was in spite of the bullshit around it. And I thought, well, maybe you'd save me again. Maybe you'd help me ignore rock bottom."

"All I did was pump you full of whiskey, man. Cheers."

As we clinked glasses, he brought his face close to mine, and I responded to its pull in a way that seemed almost involuntary. The kiss was inevitable. Our nerves were high and the room pulsed with a chaotic energy that demanded release. He kissed me with a zeal that edged on desperation, and the sirens in my head sounded like music for that minute. When we separated, I excused myself to use the bathroom.

I stood at the sink and took a long look in the mirror. I hadn't seen my face since much earlier in the day, but as suspected, I wasn't looking my best. My morning swipes of eyeliner were day-old and smudgy. I looked as tired as I felt, maybe more so. I wet my thumb and cleaned the skin under my eyes, but I knew that no matter what I did, I wasn't about to rival Daphne.

The thought of her made me feel guilty, and I resented Jamie for his cavalier intrusions, for all but assuming I'd be game for his advances. Despite his boyishness and self-effacing manners, Jamie was a good-looking, confident man with a bounty of natural charisma. I, on the other hand, was gloomy and scornful, and most of the few fierce connections I'd made in my life had dissolved, leaving sadness, barrenness, waste. My romantic life had never been lush, but in the last year it had become almost nunnishly celibate, with brief flare-ups of lust unaccompanied by affection. The truth was Jamie had picked the loneliest girl at the dance, and I was this close to surrendering my heart into his hands.

I flushed the toilet and walked out feeling firm, in control of my body and emotions. I rejoined him on the couch and he handed me back my drink with a brilliant, loving smile. The world strobed black after that.

I remembered the next few hours in snatches of light, in pictures snipped from fevered, color-rich dreams. We were laughing, drinking and smoking, snuggling and kissing on the couch. Some time later, minutes or hours, we were in my room, and this, I retained— the fumbling struggle at the catch of my jeans, my hand swatting his, ineffectual as the paper wings of a moth. There was my heart racing, faster and more alert than the rest of my body, paralyzed in the brief moments when I felt awake. And then Jamie, shirt open, briefs tented, hovering over me with a dazed grin on his face, one hand pinning my shoulder to the bed.

Lori's voice, calling *unni, I'm home*, then *unni?* and louder, *unni?* punctuated now with a door hinge and a scream.

I woke up with a gasp and sat up in my bed. Lori was next to me, and when she felt me move, she snapped awake with me.

My head throbbed and I felt soaked through with sleep. Lori was looking at me with wide-awake eyes, ringed red and stinging with a watchful panic.

"*Unni?*" she asked. "Are you okay?"

I ventured a nod, but I felt terrible. I'd had a lot of hangovers in my life, but this one felt different, like a recovery from hibernation. I'd been sleeping, it seemed, for a long, long time.

"*Unni?*"

I imagined myself talking, moved my tongue in my mouth. It felt enlarged and chalky, and it took me seconds to make a sound. "The fuck happened?" I finally managed. "I feel like I traveled through time."

Lori's eyes filled, and she fell across me like a puppy climbing her owner. "Do you remember me coming home?"

I tried, and I retrieved the sound of her voice, calling after me from another dimension. "Vaguely," I said. "What time was that?"

"Around two," she said. "I'm so sorry. I was out with Isaac and he dropped me off. He's here now, too."

"Isaac slept over?"

She nodded. "In my room. I mean somebody—" she hesitated, looking to my closed door. "Somebody had to keep an eye on *him.*"

All the heat in my body disappeared at once when I heard her pronounce that word. The fragments of the night came forward and arranged themselves to tell one inevitable story, like single points that defined a line. It took me a minute to speak.

"He's still here?" Rage displaced some of the drowsiness vying for my body. "Where?"

"What do you remember?" she asked, hesitant and gentle.

"Enough. Where is he?"

"He's in my room," she said. "We didn't know what to do with him. He passed out almost as soon as we got home, but we didn't want him to slip away in the morning. Isaac was an eagle scout. He tied him up with some of your shirts."

I laughed at that, but I was feeling pretty grave. "I guess we should go relieve Isaac."

Isaac was asleep in Lori's desk chair, but the second we touched her door his posture bolted to that of a soldier's. His hair was messy and there was a sweaty sheen to his complexion. I hadn't seen him since his run-in with Winfred, and I was pleased to see that his face was recognizable, handsome still, the patches of puffed and healing skin lending it a roughed edge he couldn't have dreamed of a week ago.

Cautiously, I followed Lori into the room, where Jamie was lying on the floor, naked, it looked like, with a throw blanket over his hips. He was tethered to a corner of her bed in a way that was anything but erotic. There was a big bruise sprawled across one side of his face.

"Waste of a bed," I said.

"I didn't want to get too relaxed," Isaac said. "We figured we shouldn't let him leave."

"And I wasn't going to let him sleep in *my* bed," Lori said sharply. She was almost shuddering with anger.

"When you came in . . ." I thought about how to phrase the question, and I hesitated, aware of Isaac listening from his perch five feet away. "I remember what he was trying to do. I don't re-member if he was successful."

"He wasn't," she said firmly. "We walked in on him trying to put on a condom. He was sitting on your bed, completely naked, trying to tear open the wrapper."

"Ace timing," I said.

"It looked like it might have taken him a long time. He was really out of it. I watched him for, like, ten seconds without say-ing anything. I was standing there looking at him, then looking at you, making sure I wasn't just intruding, and the whole time he was trying to open the condom like it was really hard or some-thing."

"What was I doing?"

"You weren't doing anything," she said. "You looked dead. It was really freaky."

"Did I have anything on?"

She turned red, though she looked more angry than embarrassed. "Just on top, and your shirt was unbuttoned all the way down."

My stomach clamped like a fist and I sat down on the edge of Lori's bed. "I'm sorry you guys had to see that," I said, trying for a feeble laugh. "So, what did you do then?"

"It took me a minute to figure out what was going on, but then I screamed."

Isaac jumped in. "I was right behind her and at first I thought we just walked in on you. But when she started yelling I thought, 'Oh Jesus,' and was getting ready to whale on him when Lori just attacked."

"Attacked? What did you do?"

"I hit him in the face with my purse. Isaac has a nice camera I was carrying for him. It's maybe broken now."

"Did he fight you?"

"No. He just kind of looked confused, and he didn't talk. It almost seemed like he didn't notice me. He was really out of it. At one point he just kind of keeled over, so Isaac dragged him out of the room and we decided I'd stay with you while he watched him."

"Thank you," I said. Then I pulled her to me and hugged her, tightly, pressing my head into the inward curve of her stomach. She softened in my arms, and stroked my head, combing my hair with her gentle fingers. "Thank you, Lori," I said again.

I thought I might cry then, felt the motion of hurt and disgust roil deep inside of me, ancient, permanent, and profound. But I didn't. I willed myself to stay calm, to yield my emotions to the balm of shock, and to take stock of the scene instead. Jamie had tried to make me a victim, but all he did was give me deeper access to the truth of things than I'd ever had before. I stood up and walked back to my room.

I was aware of Lori trailing behind me as I stooped down and picked up his jeans off the floor. He hadn't had a bag, or even a sweater, so I went straight for his pockets and turned them inside out.

Various dude detritus—a leather wallet, loose coins, car keys, cell phone, ChapStick. Then there was an extra condom, and in the same pocket, two small Baggies, one with powder, the other with tablets, both the same chalky white. This was the fun pocket, then, his own little rape kit.

I wanted a shower, but decided it would have to wait. I washed my face and changed out of my pajamas instead, the T-shirt and shorts Lori had wrangled onto me while I slept. I put on a clean shirt and jeans, and even a thin layer of makeup. I wanted to look like a woman in control.

I filled a glass with water and went back into Lori's room to stand over his knocked-out body. He looked dead, and that made me feel good. My feelings toward him were suddenly and wholly uncomplicated—I wanted him gone to hell.

"Guys," I said, not taking my eyes off of Jamie. "Can you leave us alone for a minute?"

I felt Lori and Isaac hesitate, but a few seconds later, they got up quietly and left the room. They left the door a crack open, and I pushed it all the way shut.

I yanked the blanket off of Jamie, and I took some pleasure in my physical dominance over the scene. He was still asleep, his penis limp, flopped over his balls like a garden slug. I sat down in

Lori's desk chair and lit a cigarette to keep me steady. Then I dumped the glass of water on his head.

He coughed and snorted, shaking his head like a wet dog. It took him awhile to notice me, longer still to notice he was bound. When he finally caught my eye, he laughed. "What the hell, Song?" he asked, but his tone was playful. "Did you tie me up?"

I shifted in my chair and tilted my head at him, disbelieving. Then I leaned back and sucked at my cigarette. "You don't remember?" I asked.

"I mean I remember *some* stuff," he said.

I pulled the Baggie of white tablets out of my pocket. It was too much to pretend we were waking up from a romantic encounter. It was just too far from anything.

"Do you remember taking these?"

He squinted at my hand, and his eyes widened. "Let me see those," he said.

I set them down on Lori's desk and shook my head. "Roofies? You came to my house begging for my sympathy, and you brought fucking roofies?"

"Hey, don't call them that, Song. Give me a break. I was feeling bad and I wanted to get wasted."

"What do you mean don't call them that?"

"You're making me sound like a rapist or something," he said.

He spoke with a straight face, solemn and sober, despite the pull of a groggy hangover. His tone was admonishing; hurt, even. Like he thought I knew him better than that.

I laughed. "What, are you kidding me? Like you weren't one prick hair from raping me less than seven hours ago?"

His whole face turned an ugly shade of red. I waited for him to defend himself.

"I don't remember much of last night," he said. "But if you

think I tried to rape you, there must be a massive misunderstanding here. I am not that kind of guy."

"What kind of guy—a rapist?"

"Goddamnit, Song. Stop saying that word."

"You may not think you're 'that kind of guy,'" I said. "But the only thing you need to do to be 'that kind of guy' is to try and rape someone."

"I didn't try to rape you," he said.

I picked up the Rohypnol again, and shook the bag like I was ringing a dinner bell.

"I don't remember using those, okay?" he said. "But if I did, then it would have been pretty late in the game, and it would've been for both of us, just to loosen us up. And come on, Song. You knew we were going to bed together the minute you let me in the house."

"Maybe *you* knew that. *I* didn't. When I let you in last night, I was helping a friend in need."

"Are we 'friends'? Is that what we are? That wasn't exactly the vibe I was getting."

"Jamie, if you don't know the difference between flirting and consent to sexual intercourse, I don't know what to fucking tell you."

"I know the difference." He was pouting, indignant. "You must have consented."

It took longer than it should have to sink in, but it was a hard thing to understand. Jamie, in his heart of hearts, fully believed in his own innocence. He was the kind of man who despised the seedy predators snatching at joggers in the park, who heard the word "rape" and pictured women dragged by their ankles, kicking and clawing until their nails tore off.

And then I heard Daphne, explaining in her calm way why

she didn't report Joe Tilley. How she didn't trust that anyone would believe her, under the circumstances.

"You didn't kill Tilley," I said.

His eyes brightened, and he flashed me an optimistic smile. "Of course not."

I stood up and left without another word.

Seventeen

I told Lori and Isaac I had to leave for a while, and ran out to my car with weak sounds of protest trailing after me. I was already rolling down Santa Ynez when I realized I had no idea where to find Daphne.

She had no fixed address, and she sure as hell wasn't staying with Jamie. She knew where I lived, where I worked, and she could tap my shoulder and have me at attention any second she liked. Our bicoastal friendship had felt even-footed, despite its contractual nature. In the same city, I saw the slope of things, and wondered that I'd ever ignored it.

Then again, I'd taken the larger view with Daphne all along. I'd listened to all of her lies, and even when I'd found them out, I'd let her have the highest available remainder of my trust each time. That quantity had melted with the inevitability of a snowman, until I was left with a puddle that never looked quite human after all.

I knew she was a liar. Now I was starting to see, with mounting, awful clarity, how and why she'd lied. Jamie's visit had filled in a lot of the blanks; my mind flooded with screaming conjectures that demanded reply.

I was relieved when she picked up the phone.

"Jamie came to see me," I said. "Where are you? We need to talk."

"I'm nowhere in particular. Tell me where to meet you."

My place was out, and I didn't want to bring her back to the office. I was driving down Sunset now, riding west without a destination.

"You know the Silver Lake Reservoir? There's a dog park. Meet me there on the big-dog side."

It was the first place I thought of that might work for a private conversation in a public place. It took me a second to remember I only knew it because I'd followed Jamie there when he took his roommate's dog. I recalled the day with instinctual fondness, until the more relevant revulsion took over.

I found street parking within a block of the park and walked to the chain-link fence. It was a warm day, and the park was busier than I'd imagined. I forgot, on occasion, how many people worked nontraditional jobs in L.A. Until I started with Chaz, I'd been one of them, though more aimless, I supposed, than even the average model or screenwriter. I wondered if I were less aimless now, if I even wanted a career in private detection. I knew I'd see this case through—the moment Daphne hired me I was shot out of a cannon and had no choice but to free fall in that predestined parabola. But I didn't know how much more I could take.

Dogs prowled around the park, rolling in dirt and slobbering on each other while their owners watched in various stages of attention. I walked around the perimeter and kept one eye at the gate.

Ten minutes later, Daphne walked in, wearing tight jeans and a red silk blouse, with big sunglasses obscuring half her face. I stopped my rotation around the park, and she walked toward me, ignoring the dogs that leapt at her knees.

She was so smooth and assured, every movement in control: she smoldered evenly, like blue flame that looked cool until you melted skin to touch it. I would never meet anyone like her again.

She stopped within a few feet of me and took off her sunglasses. She looked me in the eye and nodded.

"Jamie came over last night," I told her.

"You guys are thick as thieves, huh?"

I fished the Baggie of Rohypnol out of my pocket and let it hang like a tea bag from my fingers. "Recognize these?"

She stared at the round white tablets, her lip drooping and her tongue poised for speech. "Are those Jamie's?" she asked.

I nodded.

"Where did you . . ." She trailed off, and I was sure she knew the answer.

"He tried to do it to me, too."

We sat in silence, staring at the roofies. Her hard eyes glimmered under a film of nascent tears.

"I'm so sorry," she said. "I didn't think . . ."

"I got lucky," I added. "Lori came home at a critical moment and basically knocked him out. He took some for himself, too."

She nodded, absent, remembering. I lit a cigarette and let her wade through her thoughts.

"I don't know how you pretended so long," I said.

"It wasn't all pretend."

"Tell me what happened."

"We met at a gallery," she said. "And he pursued me pretty persistently. I thought it was annoying, but also romantic. He seemed like a nice, thoughtful, smitten kind of guy, like in the movies."

Jamie had told me this part of the story himself, and I wondered now how I'd missed the red flags. Then I remembered: I'd seen them, even commented on them, and then I'd let him explain them away. I was attracted to him, and more simply, I liked him. I didn't know him well enough to decide anything with certainty, but on a structural level built on a series of general impressions, my mind had placed limits on the kind of person I thought he could be. It took a lot more than a concerning anecdote to uproot those fences. I wondered if Daphne had been caught off guard the same way.

"So we went out, finally," she continued. "He took me to a nice restaurant he could barely afford, and we had a bottle of wine and went back to his apartment after. The next thing I actually remember is waking up. Jamie lived in this shoe box East Village apartment, with a bed and a dresser and a tiny stovetop. I got to know it well enough, but that was the first time I ever saw it. He was at the stove, cooking breakfast, and the whole room smelled like bacon. I could hear it sizzling in the pan, and he was whistling along, some cheerful good-morning tune. I panicked. He was naked except for an apron, and when I looked at myself, I saw that I was naked, too. I almost screamed."

I cringed. It was a blessing that I'd woken up with Lori in my bed.

"But he must have heard me waking up, because he turned around and gave me the most radiant smile. A few minutes later I was wearing one of his T-shirts and we were eating breakfast in bed. After breakfast, we slept together, and I told myself there was nothing wrong."

"How long did you believe that?"

"Months," she said. "Six months."

"Wow."

"It wasn't hard, honestly. Jamie can be so sweet, and I truly believe that he loved me."

"Were you happy with him?"

She shrugged. "In retrospect, I think there was something off the whole time. But I don't really know. It's possible I was happy. I can hardly remember."

"Were you in love with him?"

"I think so," she said. "But it must have been complicated. It's hard to bring back what it felt like to be with him then."

"When did you figure it out?"

"We went out to the same restaurant for our six-month anniversary. We drank another bottle of wine, and we went back to his apartment to drink some more. We were on the couch pouring out whiskey when I saw him put those white tablets in our drinks, one each. And I asked what they were."

"And he told you?"

"He didn't think he'd done anything wrong."

"Did you blow up at him?"

She shook her head. "I got mad at him, but I let it sit. Then I got angrier and angrier every day. The thing is, it still took me a while to call it what it was. I'd been raped before, by two different men, and this was not the same thing."

"Jesus," I said. "What is that they say about lightning?"

"The thing about lightning, it strikes one in maybe ten thousand people. Rape is about as common as disaster can get. And here's something else fucked up: Once you get raped, you're more likely to get raped again. It's like biting your tongue."

"Why?"

She shrugged. "I guess something like that just leaves a mark. Sometimes it breaks you altogether."

We stood in silence, and I thought about the horrors condensed into Daphne's life. We were the same age and, for a moment, that seemed remarkable. But twenty-seven years had been a lifetime enough for my own sorrows—maybe that's why we'd found each other. I felt, at last, like I understood her.

"So, how'd you do it?" I asked quietly, dropping my cigarette to the ground.

She didn't insult me by playing dumb. She didn't say anything at all.

"I didn't ask you why you stayed with Jamie," I said. "You realized he'd raped you six months into your relationship. I know you were together a lot longer than that."

"Are you asking why?"

"No," I said. "I know why. You knew he'd get away with it, like your stepdad and Tilley before him. Especially after you dated him for that long, and all your friends saw you all happy together. No prosecutor would have gone after him, and before that, you wouldn't even have tried. But three times was enough. You decided to get justice."

Her face remained impassive, not a flicker of indignation, not a flinch of denial.

"So you set Jamie up for Tilley's murder. Two birds, one stone." I kept my eyes on her as I lit another cigarette. "Of course that means you killed Tilley. And I understand why, but the how looks pretty complicated. You must have planned it a long time."

"I didn't kill him," she said. "I couldn't have killed him. I was in New York."

"I know. You weren't the one who slit his wrists, but you gave the order. Colson did the rest."

Her eyes betrayed the slightest surprise at hearing the name.

"It didn't occur to me when I met him," I said. "I guess I assumed your brothers were black."

When I looked back up at her, the shade of surprise was already gone. Her expression was calm and yielding.

"You know what they say about assuming," she said.

"So your dad's black and your mom's white."

"My mom is Mexican, but both my brothers can pass as white. I'm the one little black sheep of the family."

I knew her childhood hadn't been happy, and I couldn't help but imagine that her color came into play. She might have had her mother's exact set of features, but her blackness would have aligned her with her departed, anonymous, detested father. I wondered if it made it easier for Rudy to dehumanize her, and as a result, to rape her.

"I used to pretend I was adopted. I hoped for it. I looked into it after I left home. No such luck. That feckless woman really is my mother."

My mind raced, spurred by sympathy, and I felt a keen desire to sit down and ask her about her childhood—not just the abuse, but the smaller alienations, her experience as a black girl in a white household, her relationship with her mother. But I willed myself to focus on the things I needed to know.

"You told me you weren't in touch with your family. But maybe you and Colson have a stronger bond." I hesitated, but it was too late to be delicate. "Did Rudy abuse him, too?"

The question hung between us, and I grew keenly aware of an aggressive dog in the corner of my vision, mounting its playfellows to the scolding dismay of his owner.

She shook her head slowly, parting her lips. "Not in the way you're thinking," she said. "Rudy wasn't into boys."

She didn't mention that Rudy and Colson were blood related, and I wondered if she thought that mattered.

"I was five when Cole was born, and I didn't like him one bit. My mom loved him and I knew even at that age that I was the interloper. There's normal sibling jealousy, and there's the kind that lasts because it's based on something hurtful and real. But Cole loved me. He'd follow me around, and he'd cry when I'd tell him to go away.

"And because he loved me, and couldn't leave me alone, he was the only one who noticed when Rudy started abusing me. He couldn't have been seven years old when he started knocking on the door, hollering for us to let him in. He didn't know what was going on, just that it was evil. One day, he hid in a closet for hours, so he was there when Rudy dragged me in and took off my clothes. When I started crying, Cole jumped out and screamed, 'Daddy! Leave Lani alone!'

"I was only twelve, you know, but I felt so old, like a sphinx or an oracle. So when I saw him burst out of that closet, I swear to God, Song, I saw exactly what would happen. I knew Rudy wouldn't stop, and what could a little boy do to make him? After that, Cole was part of Rudy's entertainment. For the five years until I left home, Rudy took every chance he could to get me and Cole in a room together, and treat us however he liked."

I wanted to plug my ears but I needed her to keep talking. "Until you left home? It stopped then?"

"He still beat him, but like I said, Rudy never touched him in that way. Not directly."

She gave me a look full of dire meaning, and I nodded to let her know that she didn't have to explain.

"So when I told you I wasn't in touch with my family, that was mostly true. Cole and I, we didn't keep in touch much after I left. It was better that way, for both of us."

"Daphne," I said in a near whisper. "How did Rudy Roberts die?"

She smiled. "Car accident. You can look into it if you'd like, but Cole and I had nothing to do with it."

"Did you go to the funeral?"

"I did. To make sure he was dead. I shouldn't have." She chuckled. "I thought it was karma, you know? Him getting cut down like that. But hundreds of people came to his funeral, cried for him, talked about how much he loved his family. Only Cole and I knew, and we didn't say a word to each other."

"That was eight years ago, right? When did you see each other again?"

"I heard he was getting in trouble through Sam, my other brother. I'd hear updates now and then—Cole was skipping school, Cole joined a gang, Mom found a gun and ran him out of the house. And then after the thing with Joe, I wanted to talk to him more than anyone else. So I saw him before I left for New York. I haven't seen him since."

"I don't believe you."

"I don't blame you, Song, but for what it's worth, I'm not going to lie to you anymore. You know more about me than anyone else in the world. It hasn't been easy letting that happen, but it's all there now. If you have no faith in my character, at least believe that my store of secrets is all but exhausted. You can have at whatever's left."

There was something persuasive about this argument, maybe its total lack of dependence on any sort of virtue. She was cornered now, and I had enough clarity to see through her at last. I picked up the thread. "So you haven't seen him, then. But you've talked to him. You've been talking to him ever since you found out about Jamie."

She nodded.

"And that's when you hatched the plan. You got Jamie the job, convinced him to move out here." I paused. "You said Colson got Jamie into dealing. How?"

"It's weird, hearing you talk this out. Like I made this intricate clock and you want to rebuild it cog by cog." She sighed. "I don't like to think of myself as calculating, but I guess I am. I had to think hard to make every piece of it."

"You said you'd tell me whatever I want to know."

"I am telling you," she said. "Cole kept an eye on Jamie from the day he came in."

"He trailed him. Or he had Donnie or someone else do it."

She was quiet.

"I don't know if Colson told you, but I saw him the day before yesterday. He shot a man in the head not ten feet away from me."

She closed her eyes. "I'm sorry."

"You knew, I guess." I peered at her with new wonder. "Shit. Of course. You told him not to hurt me, didn't you?"

"He didn't hurt you, did he?"

"Not physically, no. But I gather psychological hurt wasn't off limits. Or rather traumatizing me was the explicit goal."

"I don't expect you to thank me."

"I wasn't about to," I said. "Anyway, he was watching Jamie

and saw one of his benders. And what, Jamie happened to be buying from one of his underlings?"

"Not exactly," she said. "Cole isn't really a drug dealer. From what I understand, he isn't part of anything that organized."

"What is he, then?"

"He's a man on the fringes of things. The fringes of fringes. He has ties with every shadowy group in town, but he isn't part of any one of them." She squinted, thinking. "But he has everyone scared of him. He surfaces once in a while, gets whatever he needs, and disappears again. And he always gets what he needs. No one in his right mind will disobey a phantom."

"So he got Jamie an in. But why?"

She shrugged. "For one, it was easy. For another, I guess—" She paused and a harsh smile played on her lips. "To get him dirty. Drug dealers are as hated as whores."

"Well, something worked. The world thinks Jamie's a murderer," I said. "How did the Young King pull it off?"

She hesitated, and for a moment, I thought she'd go back to denial, faced now with the moment of irrevocable confession.

"You want details? Ask, and I'll tell you whatever you want to know."

"How'd he get in?"

"During the party. He got in like all the other guests. No one knew everyone who was there."

"Didn't people see him?"

"Sure, people saw him. He was a handsome white boy dressed for a party in Hollywood. He wasn't famous or weird, so he was practically invisible. He has a knack for blending in, apparently. He told me no one would mention him, and no one has. Probably none of the other guests could pick him out of a lineup."

"But Tilley wasn't murdered when the party was in full swing. Did he just hang out at the party like any normal guest?"

"He milled around for a while, smiling with a drink in one hand. He didn't talk to anyone, but he didn't avoid interaction, either. After enough time to be plausible, he started stumbling and pretended to pass out on a couch away from the heart of the traffic. He wasn't the only one collapsed like that, and no one paid him any attention. Later, when the crowd was thinning out, he stole upstairs and did the same thing on Joe's bed."

"Lucky he didn't bring a girl up, I guess."

"Sure, that could've pushed us to a plan B, and that would've been inconvenient. But I waited a long time to get even with Joe. There was no reason it had to be that night."

"Then what? He just waited for Joe to get naked and pass out in the tub?"

"He stayed there until Joe came in to go to bed. Joe saw him right away—he wasn't hiding, just acting drunkenly invasive. So Joe woke him up and said the party was over, and that he should probably figure out how to leave."

"Who else was there at that point?"

"Just Jamie. It was late, around five in the morning. Everyone else had left a while earlier."

"So how did Colson play it? Did he try to befriend him or did he get right to it?"

"He didn't have to befriend him," she said. "He had a gun."

I pictured the scene: the transformation of the drunk, slovenly idiot to Young King Cole, with those steely eyes in his head and a gun in his hand. It was hard to pity Joe Tilley, but I could feel his fear in my heart right then. It was a particular fear that I'd never forget, one I'd shared with no known persons still among the living.

"So he did whatever was necessary to set the scene. Like a director. How appropriate."

It was easy enough to picture—Colson with his gun, a neat dose of roofies in his pocket. The bathtub was in the center of the room, so colossal and picturesque that it demanded a part in the drama. I heard the water running. I heard the halting, heavy breathing.

"I take it Tilley didn't shout. Jamie didn't hear anything." I paused. "Or did Colson manage to drug him, too?"

She shook her head. "For one thing, it would have been hard to slip him something without attracting attention. But mainly, Jamie needed to be able to wake up, even if he was asleep."

"So what was the contingency plan?"

"For what?"

"For if Jamie woke up. Walked in. Found his friend and employer getting naked with a gun pointed at his head."

She locked her eyes onto mine and bobbed her head at a tilt. Her expression was easy enough to read: The answer, it said, should be obvious enough.

"Ah," I said. "There were at least two bullets in that gun, I take it."

She nodded. "It was much better that he didn't wake up, but we didn't think it unlikely that he would. Things could have gone either way."

"Christ. And then, what? You were going to send me in there? Have me stumble on a murder suicide?"

"Things could have gone either way," she said, talking over me. "But Cole made it go the way it did. He kept Joe quiet, and Jamie didn't hear a thing."

"Sure," I said. "Fine. Okay, next question. Why slash his wrists? Why not just make him overdose? It's not like he couldn't have stood over him until his heart stopped."

"It had to be bloody. It had to look intentional."

"For Jamie?"

She nodded. "I wanted Joe dead, and I didn't want it to come back to me. But this was the shot I was taking. It had to catch Jamie, too."

"What if it was ruled a suicide?"

"It was supposed to look like a suicide," she said.

"Jesus. Blinds on blinds on blinds."

"Not that complicated, if you think about it."

"Right," I said. "Staged suicide means premeditated murder and nothing else. But what if they didn't make it that far?"

"Then I guess that would've been my luck," she said. "There was a chance they'd rule it a suicide and call it a day, but it was a pretty slim chance."

"You left a lot to chance, considering."

"Nothing important, in the scheme of things. The plan had to be flexible, but it was always going to work. Tilley wasn't surviving the night, and neither was Jamie's life of carefree taking."

Her voice was so calm and neutral it was almost hard to believe we were talking about murder. She sounded more like a white-coated doctor, recounting the finer points of a successful surgery to a fascinated family.

"Why wouldn't the cops have ruled it a suicide? Just because he was so high?"

"That, yes. But more because there was no blade within reach of the body."

I remembered the blood-darkened bathwater. I'd assumed the blade was in its depths, sunk somewhere between the cold tub and the cold body.

"What did he do with it?"

"He cleaned it and took it with him. It was a little razor blade, this big." She indicated a tight interval between her thumb and forefinger.

"The kind you might keep on hand if you're planning to snort a few lines."

"Right."

"Nice detail, that." I shook my head. "So you and Colson, you created this whole set piece for the cops to discover, one part at a time. But I'm trying to think, what possible reason could Jamie have had to get rid of the blade when he could have just dropped it in the water? I mean, it was fishy enough that he'd slit his wrists when an OD would've done just fine."

"You're thinking about this all wrong. Not every little thing needs an explanation. I mean it's a good question, sure. If you were trying to make a murder look like a suicide, of course it would make sense to leave the weapon at the scene. But I doubt any murder makes sense on every level. There are details that can and will be explained, even if the solutions are clumsy. Then there are facts that point to necessary conclusions. Those are the ones that demand attention."

It was true enough. The absence of that blade was damning, no matter how you cut it.

"How is it that no one saw him leave?" I asked without particular interest.

"He was staying at The Roosevelt, on another floor. He was there for three days."

We were silent for a while, and I could feel Daphne waiting patiently for the interview to be over.

"Did Tilley know what was happening to him?" I asked.

"Yes."

"Did he know why?"

"Yes."

I saw him in that bathtub, losing consciousness and waiting for the axe to fall. My pity for the man had narrow limits, but the violence of his end made me shiver. "I've seen so much death in the last week, I feel like I'm in a fucking Greek tragedy," I said. "Did you have to do Winfred, too?"

She paused and spoke with a shake of her head. "Is Lori upset about his death?"

"Very."

"She shouldn't be," she said. "The world is a better place because he's dead."

"So that was you and Cole, too?" I asked. "Are you just a couple of vigilante serial killers?"

She cast me a stern look, like she was my teacher and I'd talked out of turn. "What would have happened if I hadn't intervened?"

"I don't know," I answered softly. "I don't even want to think about it."

"I do know," she said. "He would have shown her hell, and she would never have recovered. So, you tell me what his life was worth."

We both knew I liked him better dead, and I found I couldn't reproach her further. I tried to visualize the divide between us, to zoom in and determine what it was really made of. Maybe I wasn't better than her at all. I thought I'd had the high ground, but maybe all I had was a dimmer imagination.

I shook my head against the thought as if a fly had buzzed in my ear.

We stood there without speech or motion, dog sounds filling the still air between us. It felt like hours had passed when I sensed Daphne shifting her weight, getting ready to leave the scene. "I want to talk to Jamie," she said. "Can you take me to him?"

* * *

I called Lori and she let me know she and Isaac had Jamie tied up and ready to face whatever was coming. She sounded triumphant, and I loved her for it.

Daphne, I realized, didn't have a car, and she drove back with me. I wondered how she'd arrived, but I didn't ask. We drove in silence. There was a tacit agreement that our talk was on hold until she got Jamie in a room.

Jamie was as I'd left him, with Isaac and Lori waiting in a frenzied quiet for me to come home.

"Hi, Lori," said Daphne. "Good to see you again."

Lori looked at her with an arch, suspicious expression, and I realized she thought of her as of a pair with Jamie. My impulse was to say something to defend her, to dispel the cloud of evil by association. I couldn't decide if that was correct.

"I'd like to talk to him alone," she said. "Would you mind if I went in?"

I gestured toward the door with an upturned palm, and she opened and closed it behind her.

I lingered outside while Lori gaped at me, and I listened until I felt dirty, for about a minute, maybe less. I heard Jamie say her name with joy, a joy that crumbled when he remembered the totality of his situation. Daphne was silent, and without seeing her face, I knew her look was destructive. Jamie started pleading before she said a word.

"*Unni* do you want coffee or something?" Lori asked.

"Sure." I abandoned the door and followed her and Isaac into the kitchen.

She made coffee with one eye on me, as if I might vanish if she looked away. We sat down at our table, Isaac mute and uncomfortable, Lori staring at me openly. I widened my eyes to acknowledge her.

"What's going on?" she whispered.

Her question sent me tumbling through the chaos that started the day Daphne Freamon came into my life.

"I don't know," I said, and that, at least, was truthful.

"Are you okay?" she asked.

I took a bitter gulp of my coffee and let the question sink into me, tried to measure the waves it made.

"Less okay than usual, I guess."

She scooted her chair next to mine and rested her head against my shoulder. I tilted my head to stack onto hers. It was an unnatural pose that strained my neck, but the contact was warm and welcome.

Winfred had been killed on Lori's behalf. This knowledge swirled through my head like a whisper that might pass from my ear into hers. I closed my eyes and imagined telling her. I even mouthed it, a silent sentence that moved my jaw and caused her head to stir beneath mine. I couldn't bring myself to say it out loud.

I must have fallen asleep because when Daphne emerged, my head snapped to and there was a dull, knotted pain in my neck. Lori woke up, too, and as she removed her head from my shoulder I saw a nickel spot of drool darkening my shirt. Even Isaac looked surprised out of slumber, and it occurred to me that all of us must be incredibly tired.

Daphne closed the door behind her, and we were still for a minute, watching and listening. Jamie was still quarantined in Lori's room, and I wondered if he was bound by physical restraint or if fear and shame were enough to imprison him for a while. I could hear him crying as quietly as he could manage, with gasping, breathy sobs that seemed to leak out against his will.

Daphne was the only one standing, and she stood so straight and tall that all three of us looked up at her in stuporous awe.

"Can I talk to you alone?" Her question had the quality of a command.

"Lori," I said. "Maybe you and Isaac can go for a walk or something."

The two of them scrambled, mumbling something about lunch. They were out the door within a minute.

"I gather you told Jamie a thing or two," I said when they were gone.

She smirked. "You could say that."

He was calmer now, but the apartment was so still that I could hear his smallest simper. I had no doubt he could hear every word of our conversation.

"What now?" I asked. "We all know he didn't kill Tilley, even if he is guilty of a"—I paused—"well, another crime."

"Were you about to say 'lesser'?"

She'd caught me. I nodded, somewhat sheepishly. "I mean, it is a lesser crime."

"Legally, sure. But morally?" She puffed her cheeks and blew out the air in a pouting stream. "Look at it this way: Who's more sympathetic—the man who drugs and rapes women, or the man who kills his girlfriend's rapist?"

The question thickened the air like a storm cloud, sopping and horrible with the weight of practical importance. It took me a minute to find my voice.

"You put that question to Jamie, didn't you? You gave him that choice."

She nodded.

"What did he say?"

"I think he figured it out. He's a writer, after all. He knows only one of those stories lets him play a hero."

"But only one of the stories is true."

She shrugged. "I know Jamie. He thinks they're both false."

"But you think he'll cop to a murder he didn't commit?"

"He won't buy his exoneration by painting himself as a rapist. Even if he won't accept that he is one, he knows that the truth depends on my belief that he raped me."

"You think he'll go to jail for you just to save face?"

"I think he'll go to trial if he has to. Honestly, he'll never be convicted. There can't be enough evidence, and he'll do well with any jury."

"Even when the murder victim is an internationally known celebrity?"

"Who will be outed as the rapist of the defendant's girlfriend."

"Girlfriend, huh?"

"If he goes to trial, I play that role again. I'll take my story to TMZ. I'll call him my white knight. And when the time comes, I'll stand in the courtroom and look somber for the cameras."

"Is that what you worked out in there?"

She didn't say anything, but that was enough. I had to admire the elegance of her plan. Rarely in the history of fall guys had there been a better fall guy. The only way he could be better was if he were dead.

"There's something I still don't understand," I said.

"What?" she asked. Her dark eyes were unnervingly calm, almost generous.

I thought about the last few months, about the dim, long hours spent watching, trailing, only to come to this end. I thought about

Paul Auster's poor private investigator, Blue, trapped in a circular case by a chess-master client, pushed along like some pawn in his own story. Daphne had lied, and manipulated, and molded this outcome. She'd had its shape in mind before she made her first move, knew who to sacrifice, and when, and how, to topple the offending king.

I tried not to sound petulant, or hurt, though I was very much both. "Why?" I asked. "Why did you need me?"

I thought back on the time she'd put into this farce, the hours we'd spent together, working toward what should have been a common goal. In that time, I'd felt as close to her in some ways as I'd ever been to anyone. And then it hit me with the force of a physical blow: She'd seduced me, sure as any femme fatale.

"I know this will sound like a lie," she said. "But I want you to know that I consider you a friend, Song."

"You're right," I said bitterly. "It does sound like a lie."

"I needed you on my side. From the beginning, that was important to me, to my plan, if you want to call it that."

"What else am I supposed to call it?"

"I needed a sympathetic ear, an eye that would see things my way. You weren't the first one I tried. You were the one I wanted."

My eyes stung. "Why? I didn't help you. You didn't need me to get everything to fall in place."

She looked down and spoke slowly, with care but without apology. "I needed someone to keep me posted." She paused, then added, "I needed you to tell me when to run."

"What's that supposed to mean?" I asked, already knowing.

"I'm in your hands, Song. You decide what happens to me. If you tell everything to the police, I just want you to give me a head start."

"And you'd do what?"

"I'm not going to jail for this. My life is all mine now, and it's just beginning. I'll start over if I have to. I'll disappear, shed my history, build a new one from scratch."

"From scratch? Oh, Daph. You think you can shed a murder? You couldn't even shed Lanya."

"I was close enough," she said. "I can do it again if I have to."

"And what about me? Do you expect me to help you?"

"No," she said. "I don't need your help."

"If you don't need my help, why are you still here? Why stick around until you're in a position to get caught?"

"It's a fair question," she said coolly. "I could have taken off days ago. I made all the arrangements before I left New York. I came here knowing I might never go back."

"So why didn't you leave?"

"Because I knew I might not have to." She said this so breezily that I almost wanted to shake her.

"Oh? And why not?"

"There was always a chance, a pretty good one, that I'd get caught. In that case, I had you to let me know when that might happen. But there was a chance, too, that no one would ever find out."

"Was?"

"There's still a chance, I think. A good one."

I stared at her, trying to determine whether there was a threat between the lines. "Didn't you tell me the other day, how freeing it was to become someone new? Why not take off, have that clean start?"

"I wasn't lying," she said. "It was incredibly freeing. But back then, I hated who I was. I was a nobody from nowhere, nothing at all but a victim. It's not like that anymore. I'm twenty-seven now. Still young, maybe, but an adult, with a place in the world that I've earned for myself, that it'd be pretty damn hard to re-create. I'm not asking you to feel sorry for me, Song, but you know what I've been through. I deserve to keep what I've earned."

"You deserve to get away with murder?"

"I deserved revenge."

"So, what, you think I'll let you walk out of love for you?"

She winced, and I almost felt bad for the bite in my tone. "In part, I would hope. But no."

"What then?"

"Taejin Chung. Lori's uncle. He's something to you, isn't he?"

It took me a second to process what she was saying—I hadn't expected to hear that name from her lips, and the non sequitur threw me. When I did I blinked hard at her, then made my gaze cold. "Are you threatening him?"

She shook her head quickly, almost laughing, like we'd had the most benign misunderstanding. "No, I would never do that."

I wondered about the sort of thing Daphne Freamon would never do. She'd crossed the bridge on deceit, betrayal, and mur-der. She'd thrown away every decent notion of sex and love in the name of revenge. She was angry, burning and dangerous.

And yet as soon as she said it, I knew she would never hurt Taejin, who had never hurt her. I knew, and had known all along, that she would never hurt me. She scared me, but it was her im-mensity that did it. I feared her like an insomniac fears the death of the sun.

I softened my tone. "What about him, then?"

"He's in trouble, isn't he?"

I gave her a tentative nod. I wanted to see where she was going.

"If you let me be, and—listen, because this is more impor-tant—if you let Cole be, then no one will go near Taejin ever again. Cole can guarantee that." She bit her lip and added, "And that goes for Lori, too."

It wasn't a threat, but an offer of protection, a provision of something I hadn't had before. Until recently I'd thought I could be Lori's whole shelter. But I knew now that I had no power—that if Daphne hadn't removed Winfred, he would have done all he could to coerce her into being his possession.

"You're asking me to cover up murder."

"Joe Tilley, Winfred Park—these guys didn't deserve anything better."

"You forgot about Donnie. He was an idiot, but he didn't deserve to be executed."

She shifted her eyes. "No," she said. "I didn't know about him. Cole killed him for his own reasons. Those reasons have nothing to do with me, or you."

The logic was flimsy and self-serving, and I realized my moral core was still too weakened to fight it. I was picturing a life without shadows approaching just beyond the horizon, of a lasting, comfortable peace for me and mine.

"Never mind," I said. "Cole is a killer, and there's no sense pretending he's some vigilante bringing evil men to justice. You're offering me something I can't buy anywhere else. The price is a piece of my good character, low as all hell in the scheme of things. No need to sugarcoat that."

I walked to the sink, feeling Daphne's eyes on my back. I drank water out of the dirty cup of my hand. I splashed my face and stood in silence, squeezing hard at my temples.

I opened the refrigerator on an idle impulse. It was a full fridge, the first I'd lived with since reaching adulthood. I stared at the stacked containers of kimchi fried rice; Lori's cooking, my nourishment. I paced around the apartment, taking in the shared totality of the place where I lived. My home.

It was the first home I'd had in almost ten years that amounted to more than a few plain walls and a roof over my head. I hadn't lived with family or anyone else since my sister committed suicide. My mom was good for a phone call now and then, for occasional spoonfuls of love ladled with guilt she couldn't handle. I knew better than to demand any more than that. Lori was my family now. She was the sister who remained among the living, the only one I could count on, and who continued to count on me.

I sat back down and Daphne waited for me to speak.

"It's a deal, okay? No one goes near Taejin, no one even breathes in Lori's direction, and I won't say a true word about you or Colson from this moment on."

She pushed forward out of her seat and threw her arms around me. Her lips grazed my cheek. "Thank you, Song. You're a good friend."

"Just promise me I'll never see you again."

I accepted the embrace, and it filled me with shame and remorse.

She went back to Lori's bedroom and emerged with Jamie a minute later. He was fully dressed and had a rumpled, mournful look, his back curved and his head hung low. I stared at him as he walked across the room. He couldn't meet my eyes. None of us said a word, and when they left I walked to the door and locked it decisively behind them.

Eighteen

✦

I spent the rest of the day in a funk of misery, self-loathing, rage, and denial. Lori came home at some point, having dismissed Isaac to speed to my side. She trailed me around the apartment like an obsequious dog, refusing to let me alone. To be fair, I never asked her to leave, and I didn't much want her to, either.

She sat with me while I drank myself stupid, and she fed me when she thought I should eat. It was obvious enough that she was waiting for me to talk to her, but I found I couldn't trust myself to say anything at all.

I didn't like having secrets: They festered, gangrenous, and diminished my relationships with the people I valued. Lori had a right to know what had happened to Winfred, and about the dubious agreement I'd struck with Daphne. She would have had an opinion, might have urged me to do the right thing. But as she ran circles around me, attending to my every need with such tenderness I thought, many times, I might cry, I came to an easy decision. Lori didn't need to know any of it, and I would never tell her.

I'd lived twenty-seven years as an honest person, but that phase of my life was over. I was part of the nastiness now, another cheap asshole willing to shoulder her share of corruption. I had no illusions of martyrdom, but I'd gone to a place where I couldn't take anyone without transmitting the taint of my sin. Lori's uninfected innocence was worth more than my peace of mind. I would bear this criminal's cross alone.

I was asleep by nine o'clock, and I stayed that way for over twelve hours. When I woke up, I felt for a long moment that I had only the vaguest idea of where, or who, I was.

The phone was ringing, a sound I remembered from the other side of consciousness. I picked it up almost on reflex, mumbled a sleep-drenched greeting.

"It's Veronica Sanchez," she said. "I'm sorry to say this, but Jamie Landon is dead."

The news woke me up like a bucket of water. I sat up and gripped my forehead, willed my mouth to shape itself around a word. "What?" I asked after a long silence. "When? Where? How?"

"Last night, it looks like. Roommates found him in his room this morning. Looks like an overdose, but that's about all the detail I've got so far."

"Accidental?"

"Unclear," she said.

"No note?" I asked.

"No," she said. "Written confession would've been nice. We don't really get that lucky."

"Do you think it was suicide?"

"Could've been, sure. He was in a tight spot, and he had the means." She sighed. "It's too bad. It's not like he would've gotten the death penalty, even if he were convicted."

I found myself nodding to the rhythm of her voice.

"Are you there?"

"I'm here."

"I'm sorry. I know you liked him."

"I did, yeah," I said. "Thanks for getting in touch. Very decent of you."

"You're taking it okay, huh?"

The shock had dispersed into a detached appreciation of loss that must have come through in my voice. I recognized that I would have been much more distraught just the day before. "I'm just stunned, I guess. Were you hoping to comfort me?"

"You're too butch for my tastes, Juniper Song." She let out a loose laugh, somber enough for the occasion.

I lay back down with my free arm flung across my forehead. "So, what happens now?"

There was a long pause followed by a quick exhale. "Well," she said. "I guess we all go home."

I stayed in bed for another hour, examining the texture of the ceiling. I had a lot to process.

Jamie Landon was dead. Suicide was plausible, as was a fatal disregard for the act of staying alive. I found I didn't care much, one way or another. I was even a little surprised at the extent of my callousness.

But one train of thought kept passing through my head: Jamie's death was almost too perfect to have been unplotted.

Daphne's plan had been a good one, but Jamie's death gave it a lasting, imperturbable elegance. His shame had been her insurance, but his death was clearly stronger. She was free, free, free. He could never speak against her now.

There was neatness and symmetry, too, that didn't exist with Jamie alive. The facts supported a universal rule: Daphne's rapists didn't live long.

I wondered if she and Young King could have pulled it off. Found Jamie home alone, forced him to snort enough coke to make sure his heart stopped. I wondered if it were possible, and whether she would have cared to try. My brain tied itself into knots, wondering and wondering.

So I stopped. Jamie was dead, and Daphne, after branding me, was out of my life for good. I would never know all the answers, and what would I do with them anyway? I got out of bed and went to work.

I practiced lying to Chaz on my way to the office. I kept the radio off and sounded out my sentences, crafting them around crutches of truth, listening for telltale notes of hollowness. I had never lied to him before. I had never even been tempted.

He was in his office and he seemed to be waiting for me when I came in.

"Sit down," he said.

"Have you heard?" I asked. "Jamie's dead."

"What? Jesus H. Christ."

"I guess the news isn't out yet. Detective Sanchez called me this morning."

"How did it happen?"

"Cocaine overdose. No call on whether it was accidental or not. Either way seems plausible, given his position."

He nodded and rubbed at his chin. "How're you holding up? I know you had some affection for the guy."

"Thanks. I'm okay," I said. "I guess I might be in shock or something."

"What happens with the Tilley investigation?"

"I don't know," I said. "But it sounds probable that this is the end of it. The prime suspect is dead. There aren't any others on the table."

"What do you think? Do you think Jamie Landon murdered Joe Tilley after all?"

My heart grew unruly, and I tried my best to ignore it. "Yeah, I do," I said.

"Really? What changed your mind?"

I shrugged. "He looks guilty, doesn't he? He's out of jail for five minutes and he ODs? That doesn't seem like the righteous action of a wrongfully accused man."

"So, why would he have wanted to hire you?"

"I asked you that same question two days ago and you said something about OJ. Are you suddenly set on his innocence?"

"I found something interesting," he said.

"What is it?" I spoke too eagerly, overcompensating for my sense of dread.

"Do you remember he had a little notch on his college record?"

"Vaguely," I said. "I think it was just some kind of reprimand."

"Well, I did some digging. Found out what it was about."

My mouth went dry. His school record had come up on InvestiGate, but I hadn't thought to explore it. I would have followed up on a suspension, maybe, but the reprimand had seemed too trivial.

"And?"

"He got busted for sexual assault. If you can call that slap on the wrist getting busted."

"Sexual assault? How?"

"I tracked down the girl. She was happy to talk to me. She says he raped her at a party. He either slipped her something or picked her up when she was black-out drunk."

"And she went to the administration?"

"Yeah, for all the good it did her."

I closed my eyes. Jamie was twenty-nine. He got hit with that disciplinary action at nineteen. How many women had he violated in his long career?

And then my attention shifted. Chaz was getting at something. He was pointing toward the truth.

"What does this have to do with anything, though, Chaz?"

"I have this theory. It's kind of out there, but hear me out."

I nodded for him to go on.

"Maybe Jamie didn't kill Tilley. What was his motive, after all? If he was a frat-house rapist, I wonder if he would even have called what happened between Daphne and Tilley rape." He cleared his throat and continued. "Maybe Jamie raped Daphne, and she killed Tilley and framed Jamie to get rid of both of them."

I was so stunned by his unerring aim that I laughed more or less naturally. "What? That's quite a theory. She wasn't even in town until after Tilley was killed."

"Contract killers must be easy enough to find. Once you set your mind to something like that, anyway."

"No," I said. I chose my words carefully, and followed this lie with something like truth. "I know Daphne, Chaz, and she's no cold-blooded killer."

He sighed. "Ultimately, it's up to the police. This is just a theory, and like I said, it's kind of out there. She'd have to be a crazy bitch for it to work."

"And trust me," I said with conviction. "Daphne is not a crazy bitch."

"This is your case, Song. If you're satisfied, I'm satisfied and we'll leave it at that. Are you satisfied?"

He folded his hands in front of him and gave me such a loving, compassionate look that I knew at once I didn't fool him. This was my chance to come clean, to affirm that I was the person he expected me to be.

"I'm satisfied," I said, forcing a smile. I looked at the wall just past his eyes.

Epilogue

The L.A.P.D. dropped the case of the movie star's murder, content, apparently, with the explanation in hand. The media took a little longer to lose interest. Joe Tilley's murder, the grand theory of rape and revenge, capped, in the end, by the antihero's death, was the most scandalous feast of gossip that had hit Hollywood in years. Both Willow Hemingway and Abby Hart had their time in the spotlight, and after running the TV circuit, they inked competing books. Thor Tilla had his fifteen minutes, with high YouTube traffic and murmurs of a record deal. Anyone who'd ever met with Tilley or Jamie had a snippet of memoir, posted and reposted all over the Internet. The tabloids ran anything that could pass as a story. Nothing new spilled out, but the words still managed to multiply.

Daphne's career was in a good place before the murder, but it took off when she went back to New York. She was a tragic media sweetheart, and she had enough beauty and talent to hold on to the spotlight without much effort. Even her hidden identity didn't hurt her—it only added to her air of living myth. Some blogger called her "Lady Lazarus," and the nickname stuck. I kept tabs on her over the Internet. I couldn't help myself. A part of me despised her, and another wanted the world for her, but there was no part that was indifferent. I thought about her every day.

Three months passed in a monotone of guilt and depression. I did the bare minimum at work, and I skulked around the apartment when I wasn't in the office. Chaz and Lori were supportive, but there was water between us now. Chaz knew I was hiding something and while he never brought it up, I could tell that he held me at a subtly greater distance than he'd allowed before. Even Lori acted different. No one else would even come near me.

I tried seeing a therapist, but I was so much a sinner I couldn't even tell her what ailed me. I started taking long solitary walks, often with a book in hand. This became my primary hobby, my main mollifying source of comfort. I walked to Los Feliz, and I walked downtown, but most days I just looped Echo Park Lake, treading the cracked strip of pavement around the tarp-hooded fence.

Then, one Saturday in June, I left the apartment and saw a fountain spraying white against the skyline. The chain-link fence, the black tarp, the everyday ugliness of my view had vanished. The park was there, shining like brand-new skin with the gauze stripped away.

I went back in the apartment and told Lori to come out. She put on shoes and scurried out behind me.

"Look," I said. "We live by a lake."

"Wow, *unni*. It's beautiful."

We walked down Santa Ynez and crossed the bare pavement that had been my footpath these past months. The park beyond the old covered perimeter was a dazzling revelation. A stone walkway curved around the lake, flanked on both sides by fresh plots of greenery. Black ducks swam among lotuses and lily pads, and a row of honking geese waddled onto a playground. There were people everywhere, old couples, teenagers, families with dogs.

"This is wonderful," Lori said. "I almost forgot there was a lake here. How long was it closed?"

"Two years, I think."

"Was it like this before?"

"No, I don't think it was this nice."

"Didn't Jack Nicholson come here in that *Chinatown* movie?"

I smiled. I'd made Lori watch *Chinatown* with me when we'd moved in together. I'd forgotten about the scene in Echo Park, and she'd been excited about it. "Yeah, he rode on a rowboat."

"What is that?" Lori pointed at a sign posted in the ground. It prohibited swimming and diving in the lake, and on the white space, someone had scribbled the letters RBG.

I shook my head. "It's a gang tag. Jesus Christ, that was fast."

"It's a territory thing?"

"Yeah. Like dogs with urine."

"But look at this place," she said. "It isn't gangster territory, *unni*. Who cares if they Sharpied a No-Diving sign?"

She smiled at me and the smile was brilliant. In the sky and the water and the flash of her teeth, I saw the dim light of my future calling me forward.